Visible Lives

MAY 2010

Visible Lives

Three Stories in Tribute to E. LYNN HARRIS

Terrance Dean

James Earl Hardy

Stanley Bennett Clay

KENSINGTON BOOKS

www.kensingtonbooks.com

DAFINA BOOKS are published by

Kensington Publishing Corp.
119 West 40th Street
New York, NY 10018

Compilation copyright © 2010 by Kensington Publishing Corp.
Foreword copyright © 2010 by Victoria Christopher Murray
"The Intern" copyright © 2010 by Terrance Dean
"Is It Still Jood to Ya?" copyright © 2010 by James Earl Hardy
"House of John" copyright © 2010 by Stanley Bennett Clay

All Kensington titles, imprints, and distributed lines are available at special quantity discounts for bulk purchases for sales promotion, premiums, fund-raising, educational, or institutional use.

Special book excerpts or customized printings can also be created to fit specific needs. For details, write or phone the office of the Kensington Special Sales Manager: Kensington Publishing Corp., 119 West 40th Street, New York, NY 10018. Attn. Special Sales Department. Phone: 1-800-221-2647.

Dafina and the Dafina logo Reg. U.S. Pat. & TM Off.

ISBN-13: 978-0-7582-5575-4
ISBN-10: 0-7582-5575-6

First Printing: June 2010
10 9 8 7 6 5 4 3 2 1

Printed in the United States of America

Contents

Foreword

Victoria Christopher Murray

When I was first asked to write the foreword to this tribute anthology, I thought it was such an honor and would be an effortless task. After all, I counted E. Lynn among my dear friends and I'd spent quite a bit of time talking to him, working with him, laughing with him. Surely this was going to be one of the easiest pieces I'd ever had to write.

Then, I sat down. And for days, I just couldn't find the words. How do you sum up the life of a man who did so much for so many? How could I do justice to the man who meant so much to me?

It took hours—days, really—to come up with three words: faith, family, and friends. Simple words, but ones that truly describe the essence of E. Lynn Harris.

I don't think many knew of E. Lynn's love for the Lord as he expressed it in the acknowledgments of his last novel. But E. Lynn's spirituality was at his center—it was his faith that made him such a gentle, caring soul who wanted to live right and live for others. It was his faith that helped him to be steadfast in his beliefs and to accept and love the many who did not accept or love him.

Then, there was E. Lynn—the family man. As quiet as it was kept, E. Lynn really could have been called a mama's boy who expressed his love for his mother and his aunt openly and honestly. And the love he had for his son, Brandon, and his godson, Sean, who both brought years of joy to E. Lynn's life. He couldn't do enough for either of his sons—working hard to give them what he didn't have growing up: the best of everything. Even as E. Lynn's celebrity grew, his familial roots remained strong. Nothing was ever going to come before those he loved.

And finally, there were E. Lynn's friends, although none of us ever felt that we were in the backseat in any part of his life. One of his greatest strengths was his ability to make you feel as if you were the most important person at any particular moment. Not only did his friends feel this way, but so did the thousands of readers who received personal e-mails, Christmas cards, or birthday notes from him. E. Lynn's desire was always to stay connected—he was determined to let readers know how grateful he was for them, how aware he was that so much of his success was because of them.

It was his faith, his family, and his friends that made E. Lynn give so much of himself. I cannot count the number of authors who have E. Lynn Harris quotes on their novels, or the number of aspiring writers who have an E. Lynn Harris e-mail with a heartening word, or the number of author friends who achieved new levels of publishing success because E. Lynn passed on a good (stern) word of advice.

Just sitting and pondering all that E. Lynn has done lets me know that there are not enough words, not enough accolades that can be given to the man who arguably had the greatest professional and personal impact on the literary world in the last twenty years. He opened the eyes of an entire generation of women (and men) with his page-turning, hard-hitting novels about men on the down-low. He paved the path for many self-published authors. He helped to open publishing houses' doors to many African American writers who would have never been given a chance before Terry McMillan and E. Lynn Harris.

But with all that I've said, there is one thing that I know for sure. If E. Lynn were reading this tribute right now, he would say that none of the above really matters. I can almost hear him. . . .

"The only thing that counts, Vicki, is that people knew that I was a good son, a good father, a good friend. Did I accomplish that?"

And, I would answer him with a resounding "Yes!"

E. Lynn was an amazing son, father, and friend, and so I was not surprised when these authors—Terrance Dean, Stanley Bennett Clay, and James Earl Hardy—decided to come together to do their own E. Lynn tribute to honor the man who impacted their lives . . . to step forward and pay their respect in the manner that E. Lynn loved so much: through the written word, through three captivating stories.

It makes me so sad to think that I will never again hear, in this life, the calming voice of my friend, passing on to me an encouraging word, or a silly story, or even a thought-provoking discussion about the challenges in this industry. But then, in the next moment, my sadness is replaced by happiness when I think of the positive impact that Lynn had on me and countless others. It makes me smile to know that I will one day get the chance to see him again.

What a joy it is to be part of this tribute to a man who cared and loved beyond limits. Rest in peace, my dear friend. You have left a legacy of literature and love that few will ever be able to match.

A Tribute

By Terrance Dean

**Originally published in *The Advocate* magazine,
September 2009 issue**

In the summer of 1992, I'd just graduated from Fisk University in Nashville and broken up with my girlfriend. I went to Atlanta with some of my down-low friends to hang out and explore the burgeoning gay scene in the rising black metropolis. While at our host's apartment I saw a tattered book on the coffee table. The title, *Invisible Life*, immediately leapt to my attention. For the next six hours, as I sat engrossed in this novel, the sounds of talk and laughter all around me receded.

I hung on every word. Page after page, I consumed the intricate life of the protagonist, Raymond. His life was so much like mine. He was confused, angry, sad, forever asking, "Why was I this way?" I couldn't help but wonder who had taken a peek into my own secret life and put it in a book.

I frequently turned the book over to read the title and author's name, *E. Lynn Harris*. How did he understand how it felt to be caught like this, between two worlds, heterosexual and homosexual? Like Raymond, and like thousands of men, I later discovered, I felt like an anomaly. There were so many of us, and we all felt uniquely burdened and isolated. But, that summer, after reading Harris's breakthrough novel, I felt I was not alone.

Seventeen years later, while driving from Detroit back home to New York City on July 24th, I received a message on my Black-Berry from my publisher stating, "E. Lynn Harris died." Shocked, I immediately called. My fingers trembled as I pushed the num-bers on my cell phone. What was this nonsense about E. Lynn dying? He couldn't be. I had just heard from him earlier that week. He was in good spirits. My publisher confirmed the mes-sage, "Yes, sweetie, E. Lynn is dead." I burst into tears. I screamed. I couldn't focus on the road. I pulled off in a rest area and wept. I cried for my friend and mentor.

I met E. Lynn in 1999, when I invited him to be a featured guest at an event I was organizing at the Harlem YMCA. "Of course I will come," he said at the time. "It would be my honor." Gracious, humble, accommodating—three attributes I would come to know as integral parts of his character.

I was unprepared for Harris's fan base. Women lined up, out the door, and around the corner of our small room at the Harlem Y, to meet him. He smiled, shook hands, took pictures, and signed many, many copies of his books without complaint. Black women loved E. Lynn. For the first time he gave them a glance into a hidden world of intricate and compelling love stories between athletes and professionals, gays and men on the down-low. Black men loved E. Lynn, too. His novels told our stories, in our words. He was a trailblazer, a pioneer. And, whether he recognized it or not, he carved out a unique literary niche that made publishers take notice.

He embodied the Harlem Renaissance, the spirit of the so-cial activism of James Baldwin, the cunning and wit of Langston Hughes, the romance of Countee Cullen, and the in-genious storytelling of Zora Neale Hurston. He became the voice of the black gay community, and because of his books we were all talking about the new phenomenon to which he had introduced us. His writing about the down-low sparked a national dialogue.

In August 2003 the *New York Times Magazine* wrote on the topic and the floodgates opened. Magazines, newspapers, even Oprah, all dove in. E. Lynn had created a sensation but he never took credit. He merely said, "I just want to write books and tell stories that are personal to me."

His courageousness helped to open the doors to other black gay writers such as Keith Boykin, James Earl Hardy, Stanley Bennett Clay, Fred Smith, J.L. King, Lee Hayes, Rodney Lofton, and me. Harris also influenced female writers—Zane, Karen E. Quinones Miller, and Victoria Christopher Murray—to include gay and down-low characters in their works.

E. Lynn was a movement. Before he died from a heart attack in his hotel room in Los Angeles, he was gearing up for the promotion of his newest book, *Mama Dearest,* and had just met with a television producer. I'm told he signed over the rights to his books to be developed for TV.

My introduction to E. Lynn, *Invisible Life,* was the book he had self-published and sold from the trunk of his car to salons and beauty parlors in Atlanta. Since then, ten of his books became *New York Times* best sellers. The publishing world was once nearly void of contemporary black gay literature. Now it's filled with over four million copies in print by Harris alone.

Over the years he often encouraged me to not be afraid to share my voice. "Boy, you got a story to tell," he would often say. "Don't be afraid to share it. There are many men just like you who would benefit from your words." Like few others who've walked this earth, E. Lynn knew the power that comes from telling our stories. He will be missed more than he could have known.

I miss you dearly!

THE INTERN

Based on a semi-true story . . .

Terrance Dean

Chapter One

I really want the noise to stop.

I mean, must the construction workers start so early in the morning?

Sheesh!

New York, love it or hate it, they don't give a fuck about your space and your sleep. This is the city that never sleeps.

And, they refuse to let me get any while I enjoy getting my dick sucked.

Slurp.

Slurp.

Lick.

Eric's head is slowly moving up and down the shaft, swallowing every inch of my dick.

There is a steady stream of pounding on the thick hard walls.

BAM!

BAM!

BAM!

Wait a minute.

Those sounds are really close.

Nearby.

As if someone is actually drumming on the door, doing an African tribal war call.

It grows louder.

Louder.

Rat-a-tat-tat.

Rat-a-tat-tat.

A brief pause.

Then BOOM!

BOOM!

BOOM!

"I know your ass is in there! Your car is outside. Open up this motherfucking door!" a woman yells.

I push Eric's moist lips off my dick.

I sit up in shock.

We stare at one another.

BOOM!

BOOM!

BOOM!

I jump out of the bed naked.

Crust in my eyes.

My semi-erect dick swinging in the air.

I frantically rush around the bed scooping up my shirt and pants.

Shit!

I can't find my underwear.

I toss the comforter off the bed.

Damn!

Where are my drawers!?!

Fuck it!

I struggle and wrestle putting on my Antik jeans.

Come on.

Come on.

One leg at a time.

I swing my arms into my white linen oxford button-down shirt.

I skip buttons.

No time for perfection.

I drop to the floor and hunt for my underwear under the bed.

I do a quick scan and sweep with my hand.

There they are.

Next to my Nike Air Jordans.

I snatch my Sean John boxer briefs and stuff them into my back pocket.

"Chase! Shush! Be quiet," Eric says, bug-eyed, with his finger to his mouth. "Just calm down, she doesn't know I'm really here and she can't get in."

"Calm down! Calm down!" I'm jamming my feet into my sneakers. "There is a woman banging on the door and you're telling me to calm down." I grab my Apple iPhone off the nightstand.

Eric pushes me and I fall back onto the bed.

"Just stay here in the bedroom. If we keep quiet she will go away," Eric says. He's in his blue and gray plaid boxers. His six-foot-four, two-hundred-thirty-five-pound, pure muscle body is standing sheepishly hunched over, peering out the doorway.

His olive brown skin is rich and silky.

His thighs are massive and muscular.

His enormous biceps are like ripe cantaloupes.

Chest broad and solid.

His body has me going.

Okay, focus.

Regroup.

"What!?! Man, you're bugging." I push past Eric and storm toward the living room.

"Please, don't go out there." Eric rushes after me and tries to grab my arm, but I slip out of his reach.

As soon as I get to the door there is a loud BANG!

It sounds like a gunshot.

Frightened, I dive to the floor.

Eric runs and cowers next to me. "Come on!" He grabs me by the arm.

We both run back to the bedroom with our arms over our heads.

"Yo, get in the closet," Eric says.

"What?" I look at him like he is crazy. "What the hell I look like, cowering in a closet?"

"Chase, please, get in the closet," Eric says, his hazel eyes pleading as they always do when he wants to suck my dick.

Eat my ass.

Fuck.

And, I give in.

"Man, this is some fucked-up shit," I say and hurry into the closet.

"I'll handle it."

"You better handle this shit."

I crouch in the closet and crack the door open.

I see Eric easing out the bedroom on his tiptoes.

"I'm calling the police!" he yells with his phone in his hands. I see him pushing the buttons.

"I don't give a fuck! Call the motherfucking police," the woman screams.

BANG!

BANG!

"Hello! Hello! Yes, this is Eric Sanderfield. I play for the New York Giants. There is a woman trying to break down my door. Please get the cops here fast!"

There is a pause.

"I am at Twenty-seven East Seventy-seventh Street. The penthouse apartment."

Another pause.

A long pause.

Then BAM!

BAM!

"Please hurry!" he yells.

"I know you got another woman in there. Does she know you got a wife and three kids?"

I know she didn't say wife and three kids. He told me he was divorced, I say to myself.

I crack the door wider and peek around Eric's massive bedroom for any signs or pictures of a family.

There is nothing.

No pictures on the maroon-colored walls.

The nightstand.

The long cherry oak wood dresser.

The windowsill of the ten-foot windows.

No pictures anywhere.

The only thing prominently displayed is the team autographed brown pigskin football in the center of the dresser.

Encased.

When I met Eric four months ago he presented himself as a recent divorcé trying to get custody of his three kids from an angry and drug-addicted baby momma.

"It's been a long battle in the courts. The system doesn't look out for men. I just want to take care of my children," Eric told me with sadness in his eyes.

Commendable.

Upstanding.

He had his shit together.

I fell for it.

Why would he lie? He had nothing to prove to me.

Besides, he was a tight end for the New York Giants.

Whatever that is.

I am not a football fan.

I only know the basics about the sport, and if given the choice I'd rather watch the Cartoon Network on Monday nights.

Family Guy.

American Dad.

Hell, even *King of the Hill.*

But, it was his dazzling smile.

Thick succulent lips.

Beautiful perfect white teeth.

And charming personality that won me over.

We were at the New York Urban League's annual dinner. He asked one of his down-low friends, Omar, to introduce him to someone.

Someone nice.

Cool.

Easy-going.

Omar called me.

Me and Omar have been friends for a little over three years. I met him when I used to date the reality television star Dexter Holmur. He was a contestant on the show *Survivor.* He almost won, too, but in the end it came down to him and the beautiful blonde from Oklahoma. America, and the other *Survivor* contestants, decided to give the bubbly, breast-enhanced blonde the million dollars.

"Okay, Omar. I trust you. I hope this is not some favor you're doing for a lonely, depressed, and bitter gay man. I can't do it anymore. I am not at that place in my life."

"No, trust me, you will like him."

Omar refused to give me any details about Eric.

I begged.

Pleaded.

"Just show up. I guarantee you'll thank me," Omar said.

Yes, oh yes, oh yes.

When Eric walked in.

No, he strolled.

That black man confident walk.

Slight pep in his step with a pimp.

Hands controlled.

Dipping slightly behind his back.

I felt my body shiver.

Every reactive hormonal cell in my body cheered.

Standing ovation.

Eric was everything I'd been praying for in a man ever since I knew I was gay.

Fine.

Fine.

Fine.

His tailored black Armani suit hugged his body.

Clinging to each of his muscles.

His eyes pierced me from across the room.

Calling my name, "Chase, Chase, Chase."

Omar had done well.

Very well.

I knew Eric was the one for me.

I could tell.

It's like you know what you know that you know.

And, I knowed.

Eric made his way over and introduced himself.

"Hello. Eric Sanderfield. Nice to meet you." His thick burly hands gripped mine.

"Chase Kennedy," I replied. "It's nice to meet you as well." My insides flipped outside.

Oozing with lust.

I smiled cordially. Trying to conceal my sexual thoughts.

Eric smiled with his eyes.

I noticed the glint as he winked.

The entire night we talked.

In his car.

On the way to his penthouse apartment.

In his living room.

In his bed.

In my ear.

His hard rough voice reverberated inside me just as I pumped inside him.

Slowly.

Tenderly.

Easily.

I took my time.

"I just want you to stay in me," Eric whispered.

And I wanted to.

I was caught up in Eric. So fucking caught up I am now crawling on top of a pile of football cleats and running shoes.

Hiding in a closet hoping this ordeal will be over soon.

I can't believe this shit! What the fuck am I doing? This has nothing to do with me. He fucked up. She is mad at him, not me.

I then quickly assess the situation over my loud, rapidly beating heart.

Okay, so maybe I'd rather be in the closet than going toe-to-toe with an angry, neglected, dejected and hostile black woman.

With my back against the wall I pull out my Apple iPhone.

Palms sweaty.

Fingers shaking.

I push the speed dial button of the only person I can call in a crisis like this.

My best friend, Ashley Colby.

"Come on, Ashley, pick up, pick up."

"Hey boy," Ashley sings in the phone.

"Ashley, you're not going to believe this. I'm trapped in the closet," I whisper.

"What!?! What's going on?"

"I'm at Eric's and his wife is trying to break down the door to get in."

"Oh no, Chase. You are R. Kelly right now!" she laughs.

"Ha, ha, very funny. What should I do?"

"Boy, get out of there."

"I can't. She is screaming at the top of her lungs and won't leave. She thinks he's in here with another woman. I doubt very seriously things are going to go well if she sees me."

"Wait a minute. Did you say his wife? I thought he was divorced."

"I know. That's what he told me."

"Hold up. Let me turn off *The View*. This is much better than the drama between these bitches."

"Shit. I need to come up with something quick."

"Well, I suggest you get out of the closet, introduce yourself, and tell her the beef she has is not with you, but with him. And then you get the hell out of there."

"I don't think she is the reasoning type."

"Where's Eric?" Ashley asks.

"I don't know," I say and peek my head out of the door. "I can't see him. I am so sick of this shit."

"You need to pull yourself together."

"Why do I keep getting the fucked-up types? Just when I think everything is going well it all goes downhill. What did I do to piss off God?"

"Well, right now is not the time to . . ."

"Shhh," I cut Ashley off. "I hear someone coming into the room." I inch further into the closet.

Cleats in my ass.

Pants and shirts blocking my view.

The door flings open. I scream and drop my phone.

"Chase! Chase! What's going on?" I hear Ashley yelling.

A black shiny shoe steps inside.

I notice a navy blue pant leg.

I hear some voices coming from a walkie.

I sigh as the policeman reaches out his hand and pulls me to my feet.

I reach down and pick up my Apple iPhone. "Ashley, I'll call you back. The police are here."

Chapter Two

I spend a grueling hour in Eric's apartment with the police. They want us to recount the story of what happened. I know this is it. We are about to be exposed.

Revealed.

Our secret splashed across the newspapers.

Newsday.

The *Daily News.*

The New York Times.

News broadcasts will feature us on the five o'clock news.

I will be the joke of every comedian's late-night rant.

Conan O'Brien.

Jimmy Fallon.

Jay Leno.

David Letterman.

I keep wringing my hands. Wiping them on my jeans.

I nervously bite my bottom lip.

I am not going down for him, I say to myself.

I glance over at Eric. He is calm.

Cool.

Collected.

"We had a late night with some girls," Eric tells the police officer. "I am in the middle of a divorce. Me and my boy just wanted to party and have some fun. You know what I mean?" he joked and smiled at the officer.

The tall dark policeman grinned. "Where are the girls?" He asks, staring at me. I look over at Eric. My heart is attempting to leap out of my chest. I can feel the perspiration dripping from under my arm.

"The girls . . ." I say. I start biting my bottom lip again.

"They left early this morning," Eric jumps in, stammering. "I put them in a cab for the airport because they had to get back to Atlanta."

"Yeah, Atlanta," I mumble. *Damn, he is good,* I think. The policeman grins at me and winks.

My head drops. I won't allow myself to look in his eyes. I know he knows the truth.

It's obvious.

There are no signs of women being here.

It's just two men.

Alone in an apartment.

And me, hiding in the closet.

Yeah, we had some girls last night.

Bullshit.

I take a few deep breaths and lift my head. For the first time I get a look at Eric's wife. She is stunning. Her freshly curled hair, manicured nails, and fabulously done make-up does not give the impression of a drug-addicted woman.

The police have her in handcuffs. She's jumping up and down, stomping her feet, and spewing curses toward everyone, especially Eric. "With your no-good trifling ass. This ain't over," she screams repeatedly as the police lead her into the elevator.

"Can I leave now?" I ask the policeman.

"Uhm, yeah. I think we have everything we need." He smiles wider at me. His dark lips reveal his dark gums. I stand and make my way toward the door, walking past him. He flips through his small black notepad. "If we need anything further we have your contact information."

Chapter Three

I hop into a yellow cab in front of Eric's building.

"I need to get uptown to One-hundred Thirty-ninth Street and Adam Clayton Powell!" I bark at the cab driver. "And make it fast." I slam the door as Eric is speaking to me. He is relentless.

Begging for forgiveness.

"Chase, I'm sorry about this. I'll call you later."

I can't believe this big-ass football player is in the middle of the street pleading with me.

The cab squeals off and I sink into the seat. The driver is dodging and weaving through traffic.

I am flustered.

My head is starting to ache.

My stomach is flipping with bile that needs to be released.

I rest my head against the window.

I am dog-tired of men. As much as I want to believe in love and finding the right man, I never seem to be lucky in getting either.

Before I started dating Eric I had my fair share of men. Terrell was a man I met while I was in Stew Leonard's grocery store in Yonkers. We kept giving one another the eye before he brushed up against me.

I knew this game.

I was a willing participant.

You see me.

I see you.

You make a move.

I do too.

We were in the produce aisle and he asked if I could help him pick out a ripe watermelon. "I've been trying for twenty minutes to get the right one," he said. His muscular arms were protruding through his T-shirt.

Horny, I obliged.

Ten minutes into our "selecting" watermelons, Terrell was rapping his game.

"Listen, I just moved to New York from Atlanta." His southern twang danced in my ears. "It would be great to have some company for dinner tonight."

I thought about it for a second. His pick-up line wasn't original, but he was. "Sure, I can make it."

I was smitten.

The Georgia Peach was looking to mingle with a BIG New York Apple.

After Terrell made a wonderful dinner of sautéed chicken with pasta and asparagus, he topped it off with a strip tease show for dessert. I love a man who can move his body, especially in bed.

After a few in-home dates I asked Terrell why we never went out for an official date. "I like to entertain at home," Terrell responded. "I'm not much of a social person." True indeed, he wasn't. After enough pestering, Terrell relented and we went to the movies. While we were watching the upcoming previews a couple in front of us was engaged in a conversation. "I hope these motherfuckers don't talk during the movie," Terrell said, agitated. I jerked my head toward Terrell in shock. "They heard me." He stood and balled his fists. His large knuckles were darker than his light brown skin and looked like they had met many faces in a fight. "They better shut the fuck up. I'm trying to enjoy the movie." I sunk in my seat and put my head down. *Lord, just let me make it through this night. This is over,* I said in a prayer to myself.

Then of course there was Carlton.

A flashy dresser.

Drove a black Lexus.

And lived on the top floor in Lenox Terrace Towers on One-hundred Thirty-fifth Street. He was a practicing attorney and loved to look good. All he talked about was his new Armani suits.

Ferragamo shoes.

Silk handmade ties.

And extravagant trips he took around the world.

I thought Carlton would be different. He was educated.

Well-traveled.

Cultured.

And, he took care of himself.

Carlton was perfect for me.

On our first date we went to Houston's Restaurant.

The entire evening he showered me with compliments. "Damn, you are sexy. You are a catch. I want to be your man. I want to take care of you."

When the bill arrived for the meal Carlton patted his pockets. He searched frantically in his pants and suit jacket. "I think I left my wallet at home," he said.

No problem.

I picked up the ninety-seven-dollar dinner tab. But then it became a trend. Every time we went out Carlton seemed to have misplaced his wallet, or didn't have his credit cards on him. After the fourth outing I left him sitting at the dinner table. I excused myself. "I'll be right back. I have to go to the restroom." I made a beeline straight for the exit and never saw Carlton again.

Yet, here I am again in a situation with a man who presented himself to be wonderful. But, like my best friend Ashley always says, "Just because it look good, don't make it so."

As I sit in the backseat of the cab I make a vow that this is it. I am not going to be anyone's fool anymore. No more lies.

Games.

Or, bullshit.

I am going to take care of me. It is high time I become first in somebody's life. I look out the window into the sunny blue sky. I point my index finger upward and mumble, "I am finally going to look out for number one—me."

My cell phone rings. I reluctantly pull it out. I hope this is not Eric calling to beg some more. I am not in the mood. I glance at the screen. It's Ashley. "Hello."

"Chase, are you okay?" Ashley asks.

"I really can't believe this. I am in the cab on my way home."

"So what happened?"

"Ashley, I really don't want to go over it again."

"I keep telling you, you got that Good-Looking-Gay-Man-Successful-Disease. You're attractive, wealthy, and with a wardrobe to die for, but just like us women, you keep picking the wrong guys."

"Dante was a good man," I whine in the phone defending myself. I don't want to believe what Ashley is saying about me. "And so was Braxton."

"Dante was a functioning weed head and Braxton had a little dick," Ashley says. We both laugh.

"I guess you're right," I say. "Ashley, he had the smallest dick I'd ever seen."

"There you go," Ashley says. "You got to laugh at yourself."

"I am tired of meeting broke-down men who are living paycheck-to-paycheck, baby daddys, married men, and wannabe rap stars," I sigh as the taxi whips past other cars.

"I keep trying to tell you I know the perfect thing for you," Ashley says.

"Please, don't tell me about dating some young boy. You and I are both thirty-eight years old. I can't date any man under thirty. I am too old for that. And so are you."

"Chase, I'm telling you," Ashley sang in the phone, "you get a young man between twenty-one and twenty-five and they will be loyal to you. All you got to do is get them some new sneakers, some jeans, and pay their cell phone bill. They will not put you through all this drama and they know how to put it down."

I envy Ashley's sexual inhibitions. She isn't afraid to explore her womanly needs and desires. It's nothing for her to pick up a young boy and turn him out. At times I want to live life on the edge, and of course seek out my own sexual pleasures. I don't want to continue to live vicariously through Ashley. It is time for me to open my mind to new experiences.

"You realize you are paying for sex. That's not something I am into," I say as the cab zips up Adam Clayton Powell Boulevard. "Besides, it seems desp . . ." I catch myself.

"It's all right," Ashley laughs. "At least I know what I'm getting and I'm being satisfied at the same time. It's my money, my life, and my pussy. I can't sit around hoping and waiting for Mr. Right to show up. I tell you, Chase, if I meet another brother who after four or five humps tells me he's done, I'll scream." I laugh out loud because I am quite familiar with Ashley's sentiments. Men are eager to brag to me how they are ample lovers and can go the distance. With the anticipation and hopes of being satisfied, I am often met with disappointment.

"I tell you what," Ashley says, "turn around and go back to Eric's apartment. Call up little-dick Braxton, or better yet, invite drug-addicted Dante over to your place and then you tell me if you won't at least consider a younger man."

There is a cold silence on the phone. Ashley has summed up my dating life. For the first time in a long time I am at a loss for words. "Do it for you," Ashley pleads. "You deserve to have love, and a good life."

Chapter Four

For the next six months Ashley's words play over and over in my head.

"*Get a younger man. It will be good for you. Give it a try.*"

But, I refuse to date.

Have sex.

Be with another human.

Physically.

Emotionally.

Mentally.

I need a break.

Rather, I am forced to take a break because I am thirty-eight years old. In gay years that is ancient. I am too old to be in the club, bopping around trying to keep up with the latest dances, and Hip Hop sounds. I'm still trying to memorize the lyrics of Lil' Kim, Foxy Brown, Jay-Z, and Biggie.

I won't even dare consider online dating. All the guys seem to have too many stipulations listed on their profiles:

No fats.

No fems.

Everyone is a thug, or on the down-low looking for the same.

And the words in blaring bold caps in a forty-eight point font stating: **NO GUYS OVER THIRTY.**

Men in my age range are outsiders.

Kicked to the curb.

Discarded.

Then nearly every profile displays pictures of their abs.

Chest.

Dick.

And asses with no qualms.

Is everyone an amateur porn star?

It feels like an audition for America's Next Top Porn Actor.

NOT!

I cannot and will not participate in that. Granted, I do have a nice body, and I maintain my one-hundred-eighty-pound frame, but I am not putting it all out there for the world to gawk at.

What do I look like, having my dick and nuts dangling on some pervert's screen to enjoy?

And, I simply cannot see myself getting involved with a young tender. That is not my style. It's Ashley's. Her world of boy toys and playing sugah momma. Not mines.

I still think about Eric every now and then. But I am slowly, and surely, working him out of my system. Yes, I miss him.

His smell.

Deep baritone voice whispering in my ear.

His big strong arms holding me.

His stocky muscular body under mines.

Then on top.

I can't even watch his football games on television.

I refuse.

I have a new focus.

It's all about work.

All about me.

Then summer arrives. Now it's all about . . .

Chapter Five

"Uhm, excuse me, Ashley, he is only twenty-two years old," I practically yell into the phone. "Besides, I am through with men. Done. Finished. Work is my new love. My new man." I begin biting my bottom lip.

"Chase, you think just because you're the Vice President of Production for GBS Television that you don't have needs?" Ashley says facetiously. "Vice presidents have sex, too."

"I am not thinking about him. He is just a boy," I say, but I am lying through my teeth. I swivel in my black executive chair and stare out into the New York skyline. My corner office has the perfect view overlooking Times Square.

"Whatever. And stop biting your bottom lip," Ashley says.

"What are you talking about?" I put my hand over my mouth and look around my office.

"I know you are biting your bottom lip. You do it every time you are nervous or excited. And I know that intern is working you over."

"Nobody is working anything. He is too young. And the operative word is INTERN!"

"Who cares?" Ashley snickers. "You're both adults. What does age have to do with anything?"

"I am a professional, and I am sixteen years his senior. How would that look? Me fraternizing with an intern in my department. I have no interest or desire in sleeping with a young man. This is ridiculous. I am not in high school, or college," I bark.

"All I'm saying is that you got needs and no man is meeting yours. I am sure you could use a good man to lay hands on your third leg and bless your boy coochie, amen," Ashley laughs. "How long has it been anyway?"

I hesitate before I answer. It's been six months since I've been touched, licked, or held in some strong man's arms. Besides, three months ago I was promoted to Vice President. I don't have time to think about a man, especially not at a time like this. Our department is very busy with the upcoming Reality TV Awards.

"Look, I don't think about it and neither should you," I respond sarcastically. "Even though you are my best friend, Ashley, I am not in your business and asking who you're sexing."

"Yeah, Chase, but I am not afraid to explore and have my sexual needs met, either. I am certain yours need to be tended to," she snaps.

"My only need is a man who is single, with no baby-momma drama, or girlfriends lurking somewhere, and who has a good relationship with his mother, making a good living for himself, and not dependent on me. It's really becoming difficult to find a successful black man with his own house, car, and money."

Ashley sucks her teeth.

She is right. I do have needs, but I have been burned so many times I simply block out any desire to have sex. I mean, it's normal for a thirty-eight-year-old man, right? I'm trying to remain abstinent.

Be faithful in prayer.

But, dear Lord, I know one thing, my hormones are racing.

My loins are hungry.
My body is thirsty.
As much as I try to deny it, I need a man bad.
Very bad.
And, the new intern *is* working me over.

Chapter Six

My assistant had the daunting task of locating the summer intern for our department. I entrusted her with locating someone who would be perfect for us.

I needed someone with a desire and interest in television production. I wanted someone who knew and understood they would be working hard and it wouldn't be a cake walk.

I also needed someone who was smart.

Quick.

A fast thinker.

And definitely black.

I am about helping young black brothers and sisters make it in this business. It's a beast in the entertainment industry and there are definitely not too many of us at the top. We are few and far between. The entertainment business is ninety percent who you know and ten percent what you know.

I made it to the top because I have three things:

The first two are tenacity and drive.

The third is I attended Vanderbilt University with Charles Goldstein, the son of the President of GBS Television.

Charles Goldstein and I were roommates the first two years of college and became good friends. We are both from New York City. But, Charles is from the Upper East Side and I am from Brooklyn.

Two very vastly different worlds.

He is rich.

I was not.

However, we shared the bond of having the world's epicenter of fashion and culture as our home.

Charles knew I wanted to work in television and he convinced his father to give me an internship with GBS Television my junior year. By the time I graduated I was offered a full-time position as the department assistant in production events. I worked hard, but having the president of the company as a friend, well, let's just say it has helped a hell of a lot.

When my assistant informed me she found the perfect candidate, I let her know it was her decision to hire them.

I had no idea it would be Quincy Thornberry.

Quincy's credentials are impressive.

Well, no, that's an understatement.

They are stellar.

I have never seen a young person so eager and passionate about pursuing a career in television as Quincy.

He knows what he wants and where he wants to go. Something that's very hard to find in young people today.

A native New Yorker, from Bedford-Stuyvesant, Brooklyn, Quincy is entering his senior year at Stanford University. He is a film and television major. He earned a full academic scholarship and is on the dean's list with a three-point-eight grade point average.

He plays basketball and is quite impressive on the court. He brought in his portfolio with all his accomplishments. There were several *Los Angeles Times* newspaper clippings about his impressive basketball skills.

When he strolls into my office on the first day of his internship I lose my breath.

Literally, I gasp.

He is the most beautiful creature I have ever seen. He stands six-feet-four—pure muscle. Quincy has the face sculpted to perfection like that of model/actor Boris Kodjoe. He is the deep rich chocolate color of actor Morris Chestnut, and exudes the sexiness of Blair Underwood. His voice is like that of Barry White, but with a heavy Brooklyn accent.

"Hello, Mr. Kennedy. My name is Quincy Thornberry," he says as he extends his massive right hand to shake mine. His voice sinks into my head. It moves and shakes everything in me when he speaks my name.

My.

My.

My.

It feels good to touch a man.

A fine-ass black man.

"Hello, Mr. Quincy Thornberry," I reply. My knees buckle. My heart races as I glide from behind my desk. "Welcome to GBS Television and to production events."

"I am looking forward to learning a lot from you. I am very excited to be in your department. I Googled everything about you." He smiles enthusiastically.

He took the time to Google me. Wow, I am impressed.

"Good, good, Quincy. There is a lot to learn and you only have a few months." I smile. I need to remain professional. I keep reminding myself he is a college student. A young man here for the summer as an intern. There is to be no attraction.

None whatsoever.

No matter how fine he is.

"I am sure my assistant Alicia has shown you around the office." I stare into his dark brown eyes. They smile when he smiles. They are inviting and enticing.

I am sure he has a girlfriend or three, I think. *He's definitely a player. He's on the basketball team.*

"Yes. I have met everyone in the department. You were the last person I had to meet."

"Well, we are glad to have you here with us," I say, tearing my gaze away. I feel his eyes are piercing into my soul. Or, maybe it's my imagination.

I begin walking toward my office door. There is a brief silence. That uncomfortable silence when two people are on a date and neither can think of anything to say. I start biting my bottom lip.

"We still on for lunch?" He smiles, revealing his big white teeth. *Damn, even his teeth are perfect. Does he have any imperfections?*

I surely don't remember making lunch plans with an intern, especially not with Quincy. I must look confused because he quickly speaks, interrupting my thoughts.

"The schedule that your assistant Alicia gave me says that I am to have lunch with you." He points at the itinerary in his hands.

"Oh, is that today?" I ask. Forgetting everything. Losing all train of thought.

"I know you are very busy, Mr. Kennedy. If you can't make it . . ." A disappointed look sweeps across his face.

"No, no, it's no problem at all. I just completely forgot about it," I interject. I am, yet again, lost in his gaze. I reach over and delicately touch him on his left arm. His huge muscular bicep flexes at my touch. A shiver shoots through my spine and into my groin.

"Cool, I can't wait to have lunch with you. I have so many questions." He grins with those succulent kissable thick lips.

"Great," I say. "I'll meet you in the elevator bank at one-thirty." My entire body smiles and I feel my dick becoming erect. *Just give me the strength, Jesus. Just give me the strength,* I silently say to myself.

Chapter Seven

I hate Ashley, sometimes.

She is always right.

Especially when it comes to sex.

She has no problem discussing it.

She loves it, and lives for it.

You see, Ashley is a sassy certified diva who can just walk out of her house and meet a man with no problem. She will call me up after her sexual conquests and give me the complete rundown—where they did it, what they did, how long they did it for, and the size of his dick. I keep telling her I am going to pray for her.

She needs Jesus.

Ashley is good at seducing men. She is beautiful and very attractive. I always tell her that she reminds me of Kim Fields, less the dreads. But just like Kim Fields's character, Regine, on *Living Single,* Ashley has a new hairstyle every time I turn around.

One week it's in a short bob cut.

Three weeks later it's bone-straight and down her back.

Two weeks later it's feathered like Farrah Fawcett.

I just can't keep up with Ashley and her coif.

However, one consistent thing about Ashley is that she barely wears any clothing. She doesn't need to exploit her body, but everything she puts on is provocative and tight. She leaves very little to the imagination. Her life thrives around what's hot and popular to wear, especially from video vixens.

That's actually how we met.

Six years ago she came to one of the auditions we were holding for a new television reality show with our network. She blew us away. Ashley is a standout actress. She's been in several Broadway shows. The girl can sing, dance, and act.

But it was her massive cleavage spilling out of her leopard silk blouse that got her through for a second audition. The director wanted to "see" more of her.

There was no denying Ashley was perfect and had the look. She is thick in all the right places. Standing five-feet-seven-inches, Ashley weighs one-hundred-forty-five pounds and has thirty-four double D breasts, with a huge ass. It's curvaceously round, and as we men say, *"You can sit a beer can on top of it."* She has a body to kill for.

Right before the call-backs for the project, I pulled Ashley to the side. "May I make a suggestion?" I asked. She raised her eyebrows. "It would be nice if you could cover your girls." I pointed to the spillage from her top. "You can present yourself more demure and ladylike. You have some real talent and by far the best we have seen all day. Besides, I don't want to see a sis-tah get played and then not get the job."

Ashley sized me up as she looked me over and smiled politely. "Look, Mr. Men's-Warehouse-business-suit-wearing-sweetness. I thank you for your concern about my appearance, and the like, however, I am not interviewing with you. I am here to see the director and to land this job. So if you will ex-cuse me, I have an appointment to keep." And like that, she turned on her red three-inch come-fuck-me stilettos and sashayed her way down the hall to meet with her fate.

I saw her again later that day as the audition process was narrowed down to three girls. She was one of them.

"I guess the director was impressed with your skills." I smirked at her.

"I blew him away." She smiled, tracing her fingers around her mouth smoothing out her lipstick. "I literally blew him away."

I liked her fiery sassiness.

She was bold.

Snappy.

Quick.

Just like a gay man.

"I like your style," I said, handing her my business card. "I'm Chase Kennedy, the Director of Production here. I have some other projects I would love to talk with you about."

"Thank you, Mr. Kennedy," she said, looking at the card. "I have a host of skills I am sure the network would love to see."

"I'm sure they would," I laughed.

She laughed along with me. I saw something in her, and she saw something hidden deep down inside of me.

I was trying to conceal it.

She unhinged me.

"Boy, I am a fag-hag. I know my gays," she told me after we hung out, traversing through the city, a week after she landed the gig with our network.

Although I call Ashley a sex-fiend, I am the one who desires to be sexed like she is. It's been six months and I haven't been touched by a man. At least one of us was getting some good loving on the regular. I just wish it was me.

Chapter Eight

Quincy and I have lunch at my favorite Italian restaurant, Tony's DiNapoli, on Forty-third Street between Broadway and Sixth Avenue.

I watch Quincy's body react to the food each time he takes a bite. His eyes close and he seems to be savoring every morsel in his mouth. I imagine his luscious lips tasting me. Exploring parts of my body and devouring me.

"This food is really good," he says. His words break my trance. I shift in my seat. I feel an erection coming.

Quincy scoops up another piece of his breaded salmon. "I am definitely going to come back here."

I smile and say a silent prayer, *Lord, please keep my mind off this beautiful man. I am weak right now. Just let me make it through this lunch.*

"I got to bring my mother here." He smiles, taking a sip of his iced tea. "We are very close. She's my best friend."

Hmm, he has a good relationship with his mother. "That would be great," I say. "Your parents are from Brooklyn, right?" I ask.

"Yeah, Fort Greene."

"Oh, really. I am from that area."

"I didn't know you were from Brooklyn. I thought you were from Mt. Vernon or Westchester."

I laugh. "No. I grew up not too far from the Fort Greene Projects on Adelphi Street."

Quincy's head jerks back. "My parents grew up in that area. My mom lived on Vanderbilt Street and my dad grew up in the Fort Greene Projects. He is much older—I am sure you wouldn't know him. He was in his early thirties and my mom was only eighteen when she got pregnant with me."

Oh, great. I am old enough to be his dad, I think.

"After I was born my parents split. Well, basically because my mother's parents pressured my dad to marry her, but he wouldn't. So, they never married, but my dad came around a lot." Quincy takes a sip of his iced tea. "Me and my mother moved to Bed-Stuy when I was around three or four. She went back to school and got her degree and then her master's. She is the head of human resources for Macy's." Quincy smiles.

"That is wonderful," I say. "Your mom sounds great. Are you and your dad close?"

Quincy lets out a heavy sigh. "Not as close as I would like. When I became a teenager my dad stopped coming around. I rarely saw him. I don't know what happened. My mother doesn't say much, and when I do talk with him he's always busy."

"I'm sorry to hear that," I say. Not sure if I should hug him or change the subject.

"It's all good, though. I mean, he's come out to California to see me play before. He played ball at the University of North Carolina and then went overseas for a few years. When he returned he went out for the major leagues, but never got picked up. He moved around a lot and finally got a job as a sanitation worker. I don't think that was his dream. I wish we were closer.

I love him, but only because he is my father." Quincy picks up his fork and stabs a piece of salmon.

I shift in my seat nervously. I don't want to make him appear uncomfortable or uneasy, so I change the subject.

"How is it living in California?" I say.

"I love it. The weather. The beaches. It is beautiful. It's a complete contrast from Brooklyn and the New York winters."

"Yeah, I know," I laugh.

I glance around the restaurant trying not to appear nervous and suspicious. Sitting across from Quincy, a beautiful specimen of a man, I feel guilty. I don't know why. I am not doing anything and it is only an innocent lunch meeting with my department's intern.

But Quincy's presence makes me uncomfortable. His politeness, cute gestures, and warm innocence make me yearn for him. I want to leap across the table and rip off his clothes. But that is my body talking. My rational, thinking, self quickly reminds me that I am a vice president. I am a professional. I am clearly much older than he and I have no time to be involved with young boys.

"You went to Vanderbilt, in Nashville?" he asks.

"Yes. I did."

"Vanderbilt was on my list of top ten schools. I chose Stanford because they have a great business program as well as a great film curriculum. I also wanted to be in a hot, sunny place with beaches."

"You chose a great school." I smile. "Stanford has one of the best film programs. You should feel proud of yourself."

I do not want to have idle chit-chat with him. I just want to do this lunch.

Get it over with.

"I do have a question that I hope won't be offensive." He looks into my eyes.

"Shoot," I say, laying my fork into the salad.

"I noticed there are no other black men in your department. As a matter of fact, I noticed there are very few black men at the company. I also noticed I am the only black male intern. What are the hiring practices of the company? Is it really hard to get into the company or into your department?"

It is a question that catches me off-guard. I know there are not too many people of color in the company. There definitely are not many of us in executive decision-making roles. There is myself, George Irving in Creative, and Tammy Altmore in Ad Sales.

We are the Three Musketeers. We often laugh and joke about being the token Negroes. I, of course, am the house Negro since I am friends with the president of the company, Richard Goldstein.

"Well, that is a good question, Quincy." I smile. I take my napkin from my lap and wipe my mouth. I proceed to tell him what I have told so many other interns and prospective employees. "We are always looking for qualified candidates. We do our best to bring in those who can contribute to the company. We are growing and looking for ways to become more diverse."

"I see." He picks up a piece of bread and butters it. "What are you looking for in a potential candidate?" He grins and pops the bread into his luscious mouth.

Is he being slick? I think to myself. *I know there is a double meaning in that question. Is he sizing me up? Wait a minute; I am out to lunch with Quincy. My intern. This is not a date!* I have to remind myself.

"I need someone who has tenacity and insight into what the company needs." I lean forward and look him intently in his eyes. "I need someone who can help us maintain our number-one spot in homes across the country. More importantly, I need someone who can get the job done without having to be to told what to do and how to do it."

Quincy moves forward, inches away from my face, clasps his huge hands on the table, and with a big smile on his face he says, in his sultry voice, "I've been working since high school. I am very independent. I also follow direction well. I am a fast learner. And, I have no problem in performing well."

He then leans back with a perplexed look on his face. I follow his eyes. They are staring slightly above me. I whip around to see what he is glaring at, and, lo and behold, Ashley is behind me adjusting her breasts in her red leather corset.

"Hey, Chase." She smiles and wiggles her body.

"Ashley!" I stumble out of my chair, fumbling with my napkin. It falls onto the floor as I rise. Quincy quickly reaches for it.

"What are you doing here?" My eyes grow wide.

"I just stopped in to pick up my lunch. I have to rush over to the theater before the afternoon show." She squeezes past me and sashays up to Quincy. "I'm in the production of *The Lion King*. I am playing Simba's mother," she growls at Quincy.

I quickly step between Ashley and Quincy. "This is my new intern, Quincy Thornberry." I gently nudge her in her side because I don't want her to give away that she and I have been discussing him.

"Hi, I'm Ashley, a friend of your boss." She smiles and leans around me, revealing more of her cleavage, and extends her hand.

"Nice to meet you." He flashes his beautiful smile toward her and shakes her hand.

"So you're Quincy." She smirks at me. "I've heard some good things about you. I am sure that I will be seeing more of you this summer."

I squint my eyes and give her an evil glare. If only I had some daggers in my hand she would feel every last one of them.

"I don't know. I am sure that I will be busy with Mr. Kennedy and helping to keep the office running smoothly."

"I'm sure you will." Ashley takes a deep breath and further pokes out her chest. "Well, if you would like to *come* by and see me in *The Lion King* I would love to have you as my personal guest," she purrs and strokes his hand.

"That would be great."

"Here's my number." She reaches into her black purse and

pulls out a pen and small slip of paper. "Just call me when you are ready to *come.*" She coyly smiles. She pushes the piece of paper into his hand.

The maitre d' walks over and hands Ashley her food.

I gently grab her by her arm and usher her toward the front door. "I hate to rush you, Ashley, but I have very little time and I need to finish my lunch meeting with Quincy." I turn and smile at Quincy. "He needs to get back to the office for his next appointment." I try to hold my composure. I do not want Quincy's first impression of me to be Ashley and her sexually flirtatious antics. The quicker I get rid of Ashley, I can save face.

"It's truly a pleasure meeting you," he practically yells to her as I pick up the pace.

She waves her fingers toward him and blows a kiss. When she does this, I lose it. I keep pushing her toward the door.

"Damn, he is fine!" Ashley peers over her shoulder at Quincy. "He is finer than you said."

"What are you doing?" I look at her like she is crazy.

"I was only introducing myself since you didn't seem like you were going to do it."

"He is too young to be played and toyed with." I step into her face.

"Too young for me or you?" She rolls her neck.

"Don't you dare put me in this."

"You were the one who called me and told me how fine he was, remember?"

I just look at her and laugh. That's all I can do. She has me. I did call her when Quincy first sauntered into my office. What was I thinking? I should have known better than to call Ashley and tell her about a new man in town. I definitely should not have told her I was having lunch with him at my favorite place. It would have been unlike her *not* to show up unannounced.

"Like I told you before, he is only twenty-two. And, he is my intern . . ."

"Chase, please." She waves her hand dismissively at me. "Age has nothing to do with it. Besides, he looks like he has a big dick. You sure know how to pick them." She laughs.

"Ashley, I've told you, I am not interested in that boy."

"So, why were you biting your lip?" She delicately places her finger on my mouth.

I push her hand away.

"And you brought him to your favorite restaurant?"

"Because it's close to the office." I tilt my head.

"You only bring men you are interested in to this place," she quips.

"Bitch!"

"A damn good one." She adjusts her breasts. "And, welcome to the family."

"What are you talking about?"

"The cougar family."

"Cougar family?"

"Yeah, but you are a cougay."

"A what?"

"A cougay. An older gay man who dates younger men," Ashley laughs.

"We are not dating, and I am not a cougay." I try to prevent my voice from escalating. "Besides, he's not gay."

"Whatever." Ashley begins to push her way through the door and out into the Manhattan streets. "Did you notice he never once looked at my girls?" Ashley adjusts her large breasts spilling out of her corset. "I'll call you later," she yells as she struts toward Broadway.

I go back to the table where Quincy is finishing the last of his salmon.

"Sorry about the interruption," I say, taking my seat.

"No problem." He flashes his award-winning smile at me. "She sure is a feisty woman. But I'm sure that you know lots of celebrities."

"It comes with the territory. Besides, Ashley is a good friend of mine."

"Well, for the record, and so you'll know, she's not my type at all. I am not into people who throw themselves at me. I get that all the time at school."

I nod my head and smile at him.

"I like a smart and mature person." Quincy grins. "I also like to be the chaser."

"Well, I am sure there are plenty of young women back at Stanford waiting for you."

"Naw. I think the person for me is here at home in New York," he smirks.

With that said he motions for the waiter and asks for the check.

I am impressed.

No, I am floored.

And, did he just say what I think he said?

Are my ears deceiving me?

Quincy is not impressed with Ashley's overflowing titties or gestures of affection and the stroking of his ego.

This twenty-two-year-old sounds more mature than some thirty-year-old men I know.

"Thank you for the lunch," he says. "I don't want to waste too much more of your time. You're a busy man. Besides, I have the entire summer with you. And, I plan on making the most of it."

I smile on the inside. My body temperature rises and my heart races. Something in the way he says those soothing words eases into my ears and soul. *God, are you trying to tell me something?* I whisper.

As we leave the table I notice out the corner of my eye that Quincy has left the piece of paper with Ashley's number sitting in the remnants of the salmon oil on his plate. I feel the exhilaration of joy rush throughout my body as we walk out of the restaurant and back to the office.

Chapter Nine

I wasn't in a rush to get home that evening. Entering my condo alone every night is frustrating and aggravating. I really want a man of my own.

A love.

Someone happy to greet me.

Showering me with affection.

Feeling me up and making me feel needed.

Desired.

Wanted.

I walk into my living room and push the remote for the automatic drapes to close. I kick off my Gucci loafers near my brown suede sofa. I toss my leather black briefcase on the coffee table.

I pull out my Apple iPhone and call the local Thai restaurant for delivery.

The Vietnamese woman who answers recognizes my voice.

"Hello, Mr. Kennedy. How you?" she says in her broken English.

"I am good. I want my regular. Thai noodles with extra sauce."

"No problem," she says. "Twenty minutes."

I enter my bedroom and remove my Tag Heuer watch. I place it on the night stand next to my alarm clock.

I sit on the edge of my king-sized bed. Why did I get this huge ass bed? It's perfect when there is someone in it, but no one has been lying next to me except my goose-down-filled pillows.

I slowly take off my pants and shirt. I sigh as I sit wondering when my life will change. I keep wondering when my good life will begin.

My life in a happy and fun-filled relationship.

I refuse to grow another day.

Another year.

Before the gray hairs start sprouting.

Without someone.

And, I definitely am not interested in a dog.

A cat.

Or, anything non-human replacing my loneliness.

I go inside my walk-in closet and over to my oak dresser. I pull out a pair of gray sweat pants and a wife-beater. As I turn to walk out I catch a glimpse of my nude body in the full-length mirror. I stare at my reflection.

Not too bad.

For a thirty-eight-year-old.

I flex my chest.

Biceps.

I can give any twenty-something a run for his money.

Quincy.

Well, that's another matter.

I saw his hard muscular body beneath his fitted khaki slacks and his yellow polo shirt.

He wore his clothes.

They didn't wear him.

Every muscle protruding.

Big here.

Firm there.

Tight everywhere.

I even hear some of the younger girls gasp when he walks by their desks.

Then I hear Ashley's voice. *He's gay. He didn't even notice my girls.*

Was he flirting when he said he performs well, he is a fast learner, he takes direction?

I know I became aroused when he said it. As I am now just thinking about him.

My mind floods with thoughts of Quincy.

His tall, toned body.

Bass-filled voice.

Hearty laugh.

Huge hands.

He seems to have all the perfect qualities I like and need in a man. I would love to be with him.

Right now.

I imagine him touching me.

My dick grows heavier.

Longer.

Harder.

I walk over and climb onto the bed.

I run my hands over my chest.

Pinching my nipples.

I caress my stomach.

I can feel Quincy lying next to me. I fit perfectly inside his strong arms. I find myself touching my erection wishing they were Quincy's strong hands gripping and pulling my dick.

I gyrate, wanting to experience his body on top of mines.

I slowly stroke myself.

From shaft to head.

Winding my right hand.

Round and round.

Then up and down.

I'm eager to explode and let the warm juices splash on my hot, intense body.

Quincy's face is close to mine.

His lips.

Thick.

Wet.

Nibble on my chest and stomach.

Then finally resting on my dick.

Tongue gliding.

Slurping.

Tickling my balls.

My legs flex.

Toes curl.

My breathing intensifies.

YES!

YES!

I want you! I need you!

My ears ring.

Louder.

Louder.

I'm ready to let go.

Release.

I stroke faster.

Faster.

Harder.

Faster.

The ringing continues.

It's my cell phone.

Do I stop mid-stroke? Do I prevent the warm liquid in my nut sack from shooting out?

"FUCK!!!"

I rush to the phone because maybe it's a man who wants to come over. Someone I can be naked with.

Not be alone.

Again.

Maybe it's Eric.

Dante.

Braxton.

Hell, it can be any man.

"Mr. Kennedy," the voice says.

"Yes. This is Mr. Kennedy." I am excited to hear a man's voice, but unable to recall it.

"Hey, baby," the man says.

Who is this? I'm struggling to recognize the faint deep voice.

"It's me, Trent."

Chapter Ten

Dr. Trent Campbell.

Of the Park Avenue Campbells.

Trent, his two brothers, and father are all graduates of Harvard Medical School. They are part of an elite group of doctors in New York City.

The Campbells are members of the Masons, Alpha Phi Alpha Fraternity, Inc., and 100 Black Men of New York. They are celebrated in the black community because they serve on many philanthropic boards, raising money to help educate the poor young children of Harlem, Queens, Brooklyn, and the Bronx.

I met Trent five years ago, purely innocently. I happened to be working out at the exclusive Harlem Sports Club.

Membership is selective.

Joining is not an option.

You are invited and no one dares turn down an invitation to the Harlem Sports Club.

While waiting on a friend, I saw Trent. He was so handsome in his basketball shorts, tank top, and brand-new sneakers. His muscles were bulging from underneath his wet T-shirt. His six-foot physique was lean, yet toned. His light skin was glowing from the sweat glistening on his body. His curly locks were scattered on top of his head.

I watched him shoot hoops on the basketball court. He turned and saw me staring at him. He caught me just before I could turn away.

He smiled.

I smiled.

He casually made his way over to me, standing next to the juice bar.

"Do I know you?" he asked.

"Uhm, no. I don't think so," I said.

"Are you sure?"

"Yeah, I am pretty sure."

"You look awfully familiar."

"I see," I said as the attendant handed me my smoothie.

"You sure we never met?" he asked.

"I'm pretty sure. I think I would remember if I had met you before."

"Are you a new member?"

"No, I am not."

"Hmph. So, how long have you been coming here?"

"I really must be going." I turned and walked toward the locker room.

"Wait, I didn't get your name."

"Chase Kennedy."

"I'm Dr. Trent Campbell." He extended his hand. "It's nice to meet you."

"Nice to meet you, too, Doctor." I gripped his sweaty hand.

He laughed. "You can call me Trent."

Trent and I talked in the sauna for another twenty minutes before we exchanged numbers. It would take another month before we actually went out on a date. His schedule at Columbia Presbyterian Hospital was very demanding. As head of neurology

Trent rarely had time for a social life. When he did it was because his brothers, and parents, were being honored or asked to speak at an event.

After three months we began dating seriously. In the beginning I didn't mind Trent's busy schedule because I was on the go as well. I had several television productions happening and was traveling extensively.

After a year I wanted something more stable.

Something serious.

I grew tired of our routine.

The cancellation of plans.

Trips.

Broadway shows.

Lunches.

Dinners.

We even had to schedule our sporadic sex.

Trent reluctantly moved in.

I reluctantly let him.

Nothing changed.

Except we lived together.

We still rarely saw one another.

Trent wasn't comfortable living with a man, nor had he ever committed to one. I was his first.

After our second year of living together I came home one day to find Trent gone.

Along with his clothes.

Nothing but a note on the dining room table.

Dear Chase,

You are my first love. I never thought I would meet and fall in love with someone as special as you. You've given me more than I ever gave to you. I don't feel I am able to do this right now. I need some time alone. I've been wanting to tell you this for a while now, but I just didn't know

how to say it. I'm headed to Namibia with Doctors With-
out Borders. I'll call you soon.
    Love always,
    Trent

The world was snatched from under me.

I couldn't move.

My heart fell into the pit of my stomach.

I felt dizzy.

Nauseous.

The man I loved. Who I allowed into my world. Who told me I was his first. The only man he loved and could love.

He left for motherfucking Africa!

For an entire week I stayed in bed.

I cried a year's worth of pain. A year's worth of hurt.

Ashley helped me regain my life. I don't think I would have made it without her.

I didn't hear from Trent until a year later.

I had moved on.

Forgiven him.

But never forgot.

Now he calls about every six months.

And this was that sixth month.

"Did I get you a bad time?" Trent asks.

I do a fake yawn. "Just sleeping."

"Dreaming about me?"

I smirk.

"I miss you," he says.

"How is Namibia?" I ask.

"It's a little depressing, seeing so many young women coming through the clinic. It makes me think about the young girls at home in Harlem, Brooklyn, and the Bronx who can't afford medical care."

"Well, they have one of our best doctors there," I say. "So I am sure that they are getting the best attention."

"Thanks, Chase, but I am only one of many doctors here."

There is a brief silence.

"How's work?" he asks.

"Everything is going well," I say. "I got the GBS Reality Television Awards happening in a few months, so we are busy with figuring out the nominees, presenters, and host of the show."

"Sounds exciting."

"It is."

"I'll be home soon."

My heart starts to race.

My breathing is faster.

It's been over three years since I last saw Trent.

There was no closure.

No ending.

No face-to-face.

"I would love to see you when I return," Trent says.

"Be careful out there," I say. I'm not sure if I want to see him.

"Well, listen, I just wanted to hear your voice," Trent says. I hear the dejection in his.

"All right, talk with you later," I say, and push the OFF button while he is saying something.

I roll over on the bed and stare at the ceiling.

Am I ready to see Trent?

Has my heart really healed?

I let out a deep sigh and shake my head. I remember the nights of Trent lying next to me. The intimate moments we shared.

Curled on the sofa those rainy and snowy nights.

Reading the Sunday paper to each other.

Sharing our dreams of life together.

Our worlds orbiting, never becoming one, yet somehow in sync.

Now, we are in two different atmospheres.

Two different time zones.

I toss my Apple iPhone across the bed. I reach into the drawer of the nightstand and grab the bottle of Wet Platinum Lube.

I pour a handful.

Close my eyes.

And, I finish what Quincy had already started, before my food arrives.

Chapter Eleven

I barely make it in the office and my phone is ringing off the hook. Before I can put the phone to my ear I hear Ashley's voice squealing about Quincy. "Boy, he is fine! You better get him before someone else at GBS gets hold of him. Oh my gosh, the things I would do to him. How much longer is he working for you?"

"Three months." I hate the thought of it. I even hate saying it.

"And you're not at least going to try to get him in the bed?"

"That is not my mission. I told you my policy on this."

"But, Chase, you can't let him get away. I'm telling you he will go there with you if you stop being such a prude. I saw it in his eyes."

I pull the phone away from my ear. I don't want to hear any more.

Yes, he is fine.

Yes, I want him, but I can't cross that line.

It will be utterly unprofessional.

"Ashley, I'll call you back later."

I lean back in my leather chair and look out onto Times

Square. Droves of people are rushing through the streets. Cars, taxis, and trucks weave through the concrete maze. I sip my Starbucks caramel latte.

I start biting my bottom lip.

Just as life seems to be leveling for me I get the curve ball.

Correction.

I get the slider, the knuckleball.

First, Quincy, in all his beautiful-glorious-milk-chocolate-studness shows up to torture me for the summer.

Then, Trent calls and says he's coming home soon and wants to see me.

I take a big gulp of my latte and decide I'll handle Trent when he gets home. And for the next three months of Quincy's internship I will stay away from him.

I will have very little contact with Quincy.

I will have my assistant Alicia deal directly with him. She is his supervisor and it is her job to keep him busy.

It's time to put into effect the covert operation: AVOID QUINCY AT ALL COSTS!

Evade.

Remain busy.

Preoccupied.

Focused.

But that damn Quincy is persistent.

Over the next three weeks he has managed to consistently set up five-, ten-, and fifteen-minute meetings to update me on his learning experience. Each time he sits across from me I notice a gleam in his eyes.

Maybe Ashley is right.

Or, I am seeing what I want to see.

On one occasion while we were talking outside of my office he delicately placed his large hand on the middle of my back. I almost jumped out of my skin.

I also catch him out the corner of my eye staring at me when

I walk by his desk. He sits in a small cubicle a few doors outside my office. His long muscular dark body sits erect in front of the computer and I notice his eyes following me.

I find myself wanting to abort my mission and throw caution, danger, and trouble to the wind.

But I won't.

I can't.

I refuse.

In a few months he will be gone.

Out of my life.

No temptations.

No distractions.

Lord, give me the strength.

Chapter Twelve

The company receives a major announcement from Richard Goldstein, the President of GBS Television. Rap artist Jay-Z is performing at Radio City Music Hall. Our network has received complimentary VIP tickets to attend the show. Richard gives my department several tickets. I immediately decide not to attend. I don't have anyone to go with. Ashley has her performances with *The Lion King* and she can't afford to miss a show.

I give my assistant two tickets and since Quincy has been doing a great job thus far, I give him two tickets.

On the day of the concert everyone in the office is gleaming. They are all talking about the show. It is all over the radio. The newspapers cover the event like it is the biggest thing to hit New York City. It is a huge deal in the music industry.

Quincy taps on my door. His tall muscular frame is standing in my doorway. His bald head is only a few inches from the top of it.

"I'm sorry to bother you, but I want to ask you something." His deep voice reverberates.

"Sure. Come on in." I lean back in my leather chair.

"I want to thank you for the tickets. I really do appreciate it," he says as I watch his long body slide into the chair in front of my desk. "I have a little problem."

"Okay, what is it?" I ask, a little perplexed.

"I have two tickets, but unfortunately I don't have anyone to go with me. None of my friends are able to go or they already have tickets."

"I see."

"I know you are not going, but I was thinking maybe we could go together. It would at least allow me the opportunity to have a full uninterrupted one-on-one conversation with you. And I haven't had any extensive amount of time to really get to know my boss."

I am taken aback by his request.

I can't believe he has the audacity—the balls—to ask me out.

It is a bold and daring move on his part.

I am turned on by it.

He is making moves many men in my age range dare not even consider. Most of them are too intimidated by my success or they are hangers-on. They want the free perks that come with dating me and my job.

The free concerts.

The free movie tickets.

The grand openings.

Ugh!

Quincy doesn't seem to be threatened or bothered by it.

"Can I think about it and get back to you later, Quincy?"

"Sure. No problem. I know you are extremely busy."

I don't have anything on my calendar for the evening. I cleared it because I knew everyone will be at the concert. It will allow me the opportunity to leave work early and catch up on some other things, like a much-needed spa treatment.

Throughout the day I am torn about what to do. I will be attending the concert with Quincy—an intern who is a sexy and fine young man.

In public.

Where everyone will see us together.

Most of the employees know I am gay. It's not a secret, but I don't mix my personal life with my professional life. And I know everyone at GBS will be whispering if they see me with Quincy. As much as GBS is a great place to work, there is still the element of gossipmongers lingering throughout the company.

I also need to think about what to wear. I did not plan on attending the concert so the John Varvatos suit and Murray zip boots I wore to work are not appropriate for a Hip Hop concert.

It is nearing three o'clock. The concert is at eight. I still have time to run out and grab something quick from Bloomingdale's.

What the hell. It will be fun. I mean, this is innocent. It isn't a date. Besides, I could get to know Quincy more. I could find out his aspirations and how far he wants to go in this business. I could be a mentor to him, I tell myself.

I call Quincy back into my office. "Yes, I will go with you," I tell him.

"Oh man. This is great." The smile on his face is priceless. He lights up the entire room with his dazzling smile. He is more excited than I. He bolts out of my office and I swear he throws his hands in the air like he just scored two points for his basketball team.

I tell my assistant I am leaving the office for the rest of the day.

I rush to Bloomingdale's where I purchase a pair of True Religion jeans, a deep blue Prada shirt, and some gray suede Prada sneakers.

I must admit I am going to look fly.

I want to at least look age-appropriate, but not too much older than Quincy.

I still have time to get home.

Shower.

Change.

And mentally prepare.

I call a car service to take me to the concert.

When the car drops me off in front of Radio City it is ten minutes to eight.

Perfect.

Quincy is standing patiently like a dark knight in the urban jungle.

He has changed clothes from his office attire of slacks and a button-down dress shirt. He has on an Ed Hardy T-shirt with a sky blue blazer, some Rock and Republic jeans, a pair of crisp white Nike Air sneakers, and a blue New York Yankees fitted baseball cap.

He definitely looks like a sports star.

I notice the many women walking by staring at him.

Damn, he is handsome.

He beams with enthusiasm when I get out of the car. He rushes over and greets me as I step onto the sidewalk.

"Check you out!" Quincy grins.

I brush my shoulders and do a b-boy stance.

Quincy doubles over in laughter.

"And, look at you, fly guy," I say.

Quincy steps back and does a little spin.

"You know I got to have my swag game on."

I smile.

"It's going to be a crazy concert. You ready?" Quincy asks.

"I'm a big Jay-Z fan. I'm definitely ready."

"You're a Jay-Z fan? I would've never guessed it."

"Don't sleep, Quincy. I may be a little older, but I'm a true Hip Hop fan."

"Let me find out my boss is a Hip Hop head," he laughs.

"H to the iz-o, V to iz-a," I chant.

Quincy throws his head back and lets out a loud bellowing laugh.

He is so sexy.

Already he is making me feel comfortable and at ease. Maybe because there is no pressure. It makes the evening that much more enticing.

Chapter Thirteen

The concert was exhilarating. It was everything it was hyped up to be. I couldn't believe I had that much fun. Everyone in the audience stood or danced the entire concert. It was definitely a party inside of Radio City.

"Would you like to get some coffee or tea?" Quincy asks after the concert.

"Sure, why not." I glance at my watch. It's a little after eleven and past my bedtime. I figure it will be great to enjoy the nice summer evening. I am still in a festive mood and I don't want the night to end.

Everything is perfect.

"We can go to The Pink Tea Cup," I suggest. It's a small quaint place and I know it will be open late.

"That sounds great." Quincy smiles.

We hop in a cab and head to the West Village.

We enter the restaurant and find ourselves to be the only two customers. I glance at my watch and look at the hours posted on the wall behind the register. "Y'all barely made it. We close in thirty minutes," the plump waitress says.

"We just want some coffee," I say.

"Oh, great, 'cause all we got left in the kitchen is some meat-loaf and mashed potatoes." She hobbles from behind the counter, smiling, looking us up and down. "Y'all can take a seat any-where." She points to the empty chairs.

After we are seated Quincy keeps bringing up the highlights of the concert's performance. "Did you see when Foxy Brown came out?" He gleams. "That was bananas. And, what about Memphis Bleek and Beyoncé? Whoo-hoo! That was a great concert."

"Yes, it was." I smile. "Jay-Z pulled off an amazing show. I had a great time."

"Thank you for coming with me. I almost didn't think you would. I mean, you being my boss."

I smile and start biting my lip.

"I have to tell you again, you look really good." He beams.

"Thank you."

"I would love to . . ."

"So, is that two coffees?" The waitress interrupts Quincy. Her hand is on her hip and her hair is falling from its uneven bun.

"One coffee and one tea," he responds.

Quincy glances back at me. I look into his sparkling brown eyes. I am afraid of what he was going to say.

My heart is racing.

I feel a little perspiration under my arms.

I desperately want to hear it. Maybe it's best not to let him say anything.

"Listen, Quincy, you are doing a great job in the depart-ment. And . . ."

"Thank you, but I need for you to listen to me," he cuts me off. Quincy slides his chair close to me. Instantly my body be-comes flustered. The heat rushes from the bottom of my feet to the top of my head in a nanosecond.

Quincy leans his body forward. He cups my hand in his. I almost jerk it away. I've never been with a man who displayed public affection. I was caught off-guard.

He looks me in my eyes and smiles. "I really had a great time with you tonight. As a matter of fact, I have been thinking about you ever since I met you. When I walked in your office I couldn't contain my excitement. I have never met such a beautiful, smart, and powerful man who turns me on. I have prayed for a man like you."

I turn my head away. I don't want him to know that I have been thinking the same thing about him.

I, too, have prayed for someone like him.

He reaches for my face and gently turns it back toward him.

My heart is pounding.

My fingers begin to tremble.

I want to take my hand away.

We are in public.

People can see us, but I am enjoying holding his large dark hands.

"Quincy, I am your boss."

"I know. But I am very attracted to you."

"I am also much older than you. I am thirty-eight."

"I don't mind."

"But I do. This is flattering and you are definitely a handsome young man. But we have to maintain a professional relationship." I reluctantly pull my hand away from him.

"Chase, all I want is to . . ." And Quincy leans forward and kisses me. My eyes grow wide. My heart is trying to escape my chest. Then I feel his soft succulent lips. They make me quiver. I try to pull away but Quincy pushes forward and will not release me. I stop resisting and allow myself to be free. I suck his lips and tongue.

When he pulls away from me I find myself still wanting more of him.

"I have been wanting to do that for a long time." He kisses my hand.

"Quincy, we really have to be careful. This can get tricky."

"Anything you want, I want."

I smile at him. "Yes, that sounds great, but you are leaving at the end of the summer."

"But I am coming back home after I graduate. I can see myself with you."

"You are going a little too fast." I pat his hands.

"You know, I told my good friend E. Lynn Harris about you."

"Oh really," I say, shocked. I am surprised he has been discussing me. "I didn't know you knew E. Lynn. I am a big fan of his works."

"I am too. I've read every book." Quincy's eyes light up. "I met him in Los Angeles while he was promoting his book *I Say a Little Prayer*." He starts laughing. "You should have seen me. Here I am, this huge tall black dude trying to be inconspicuous in Eso Won Bookstore. The place is barely as big as this restaurant and it was packed with women. I think I was one of three black dudes in there. I was ducking and dodging trying to hide in between the bookshelves."

I let out a big snorting laugh. "I can see you now trying to hide."

"It was hysterical." Quincy laughs. "After the signing I had to wait almost two hours because every woman wanted to have their books signed and talk personally with E. Lynn. I just kept picking up various books pretending like I was there for some other reason. When the crowd finally left I eased over to E. Lynn and told him I loved his books.

"He told me, 'Thank you.' I couldn't believe I was there talking with the man that helped me to discover who I was sexually. I told him I had to meet him. 'I struggled for a long time with who I am and after reading *Invisible Life* it literally spoke to me. I felt as if there was someone else out there who understood what I was dealing with,' I told E. Lynn.

" 'I am honored and humbled,' E. Lynn said. 'Do you play basketball?' he asked.

" 'Yeah, I play for Stanford.'

"He was like, 'You're Quincy Thornberry.' I was shocked he knew who I was. I mean, he knew my name. Then E. Lynn told me he was a huge college sports fan and followed every team and its players. He even quoted my stats. I was very impressed. I couldn't believe he knew as much as he did about sports, especially me. Man, E. Lynn was so cool.

"He asked if I was busy that evening and if I would like to join him for dinner. I was blown away. I couldn't believe this was happening to me. I was like, 'Hell yeah, I can join you for dinner.' We talked for nearly six hours that evening. He was so nice and so open. He didn't have to go out of his way and talk with me. I know how celebrities can be, but he was the complete opposite. Ever since that day we have been friends. E. Lynn gave me his personal numbers and e-mail and told me, 'Don't be afraid to reach out. I know what you're going through.' We speak at least twice a week on the phone, and once a week via e-mail. E. Lynn has become someone I can talk with and he understands me."

"Wow!" I say. "It's really nice to have someone like that to support and encourage you. True friends are hard to find."

"Yeah, you're right." Quincy grabs my hand. "I told him how I felt about you and how impressed I was to see a black man in charge, one who is smart and rose to the top of a major company."

"Why, thank you, Quincy." I stare into his eyes taking all of him in. My mind is telling me to think rationally, but my body is screaming for sexual attention.

He grins at me.

I take a sip of my coffee.
I am trying to contain my enthusiasm.
My insides are fluttering.
I feel like a college boy.
I shouldn't be doing this.
I can't do this.
I must end this.
I will not let it go any further.
I can't.
Why not?
It's wrong.
Why?
I hate Ashley.

"Let's get out of here," Quincy says. He lays a ten-dollar bill on the table and slides his hand into mine. I stand and he leads me out of the door.

He steps into the street and hails a taxi. Quincy opens the door and I step inside. He climbs in next to me.

"One-hundred Thirty-ninth Street and Adam Clayton Powell." I give the driver my home address.

Maybe I can do this. It's just for the summer. I won't get caught up.

Chapter Fourteen

From the moment we walk into my condo Quincy pins me against the front door, kissing me from the top of my head to my neck.

His lips land delicately perfect.

Gentle.

We begin tearing off each other's clothes.

Shirts.

Pants.

Underwear.

Revealing our naked bodies.

Quincy's dark chocolate body is flawless.

Beautiful.

Absolute perfection.

All six-foot four-inches of him is made of muscles.

They are in places I didn't even know existed.

His muscles are huge, even the one standing long and strong between his legs. His large black massive dick pierces the air. The entire mass of erect hardness has one thick long vein protruding along it.

I approach him wanting to savor his scent.
I nuzzle my nose into his neck.
Inhaling.
His chest.
Inhaling.
His stomach.
Inhaling.
His back.
It's intoxicating.
His smooth black skin smells like rich cocoa butter.
Homemade from the roots of the earth.
Pure ingredients.
Natural.
We embrace. Holding each other. Refusing to let go.
We've been waiting for this moment.
This time.
He gently places his mouth on mines.
His kisses send chills through my body.
He then nibbles on my neck and ears.
Tongue flickering in a circular motion.
After circle.
After circle.
Slowly.
Slower.
He sucks on my earlobes and whispers all the things he wants to do to me. "I want to make love to every part of your body," he says. "I want to suck your dick and taste your juices. I want to eat your ass. Then I want to put my entire dick inside you."

I want him baaad!!!

He grabs my hand and leads me to the sofa. Quincy is taking control.

Commanding.

Dominating.

Powerfully.

And I let him.

He throws my legs over his shoulders and grabs my throbbing hard dick. He commences to whisper to it. Quincy speaks to the head.

Yes, he does.

In between each lick he talks to my throbbing erection like he owns it. "This is my dick," he whispers. "I am going suck your dick and swallow your balls. I don't want you to hold back. Let your juices flow. I want all them on my face. Then, I am going to fuck you like you've never been fucked before."

His head goes up.

Then down.

Then up.

Then down.

I push my entire dick in the back of his throat.

He slurps.

Then rotates his head around.

And around.

And around.

Oh my gosh!

I feel myself ready to cum.

He sucks and slurps faster.

Stronger.

I moan to the heavens. This man is my angel and he helps me to see the streets paved with gold. I see the pearly gates and know there is a God.

Before the juices can rush out of me he flips me over and grips my ass.

He smacks the hell out of it!

He gets down on his knees and puts his face in between my cheeks and takes a big whiff. And then he says, "I am going to stick my tongue deep inside you."

I force my weak body off the sofa and run into the kitchen.

I grab a can of whipped cream from the refrigerator and tell him to enjoy. He eats my ass for a good half hour and I love every minute of it.

Quincy's tongue is magical.

He then sprays the whipped cream all over his black thick dick. I kneel before him and begin licking his dick head.

I slowly work my mouth around the girth of his pulsating erection.

With each suction Quincy moans and his body shakes.

He grabs the back of my head and helps to ease me further down the shaft of his throbbing dick.

"Oh, shit!" Quincy yells and doubles over.

He pulls away from me. "You're trying to make me cum already? Not so fast."

He lifts me toward him and kisses me deeply.

He lays me on the sofa and spreads my legs. He grabs one of the patterned throw pillows and puts it under my ass.

I am ready.

Willing.

And Lord knows needy.

It's been a long time since a man has been inside me and I want Quincy to plow me.

Thrust himself inside me and never stop pounding.

That's what I need.

"Where's your condoms and lube?" he asks.

I point toward the bedroom. "Down the hall and to the left. The top drawer of the nightstand next to the bed."

I watch Quincy's naked body saunter out of the room.

Fat bubble ass.

Huge calf muscles.

Strong back.

DAMN!

DAMN!

DAMN!

His body is amazing.

Quincy returns with a smirk on his face.

Lube and condom in his right hand.

He rips open the gold magnum wrapper and eases the condom over his long dark dick.

He squeezes the bottle of lube and the clear liquid drips on the top of his fat erection. He strokes himself, smearing the lube over the shaft and the head.

He then lifts my legs and drips some of the cool lube on my ass. He takes his middle finger and slowly works the slippery gooey liquid in and out of me.

My head falls back and I close my eyes. I let out a low moan. I then gyrate my body, working in sync with his hand.

He pours a little more lube.

I am ready.

He leans in and kisses me.

Deeply.

Playing with my tongue.

Exploring my mouth.

He reaches down and slowly puts the tip of his dick head inside me.

I flinch.

He takes it out.

He slowly maneuvers the head inside me again.

I relax.

"You want more?" Quincy asks.

I nod my head.

He knows I am hungry.

I need to be fed.

Each time he inches a little more in and then pulls out.

"Please, Quincy," I beg. "Baby, please."

He grins at me. "That's right, beg for this dick," he demands.

"This time when I put it in I want you to work your body with me."

I do just what he commands.

I thrust.

Rotate.

Open my legs wider.

Quincy loves it.

He moves slow, then fast, and then slow again.

He rotates.

Dances.

And strokes his entire dick inside me.

My body starts to shake violently.

I moan loader.

Faster.

My breathing increases.

My chest is heaving up and down.

He muffles my screams with his juicy kisses.

"No more," my voice trembles. "Oh, this is so good."

"You like this?" He pumps faster.

"Yes . . . I . . . do," I say breathlessly.

"You want me to stop?" He is going faster and faster. His breathing grows rapid.

"No, no, no, don't stop," I pant.

"Baby, you feel so good," Quincy says. "Oh, baby, this is mines?"

"Yes, yes, yes!" I say.

"I can get it whenever I want?" I feel Quincy's body jerking.

"Yes. Anytime." I move my body in sync with his.

He pumps faster.

Deeper.

He moans loudly and throws his head back.

Pumping faster.

Faster.

Faster.

Then he releases his hot juices.
His sweaty body goes limp and he collapses on top of me.
I kiss his neck and ears.
Quincy is breathing heavily. "That was good!" he says.
I stroke his wet back and steamy head.
"Now it's your turn." He grabs my dick and smiles at me.

Chapter Fifteen

My prayers have been answered. All of my dreams have become a reality.

There is a man in my life.

And his name is Quincy.

I am overjoyed.

Happy.

Loved.

I cannot believe it's with a younger man.

I keep thinking I am going to wake up and realize it's a dream.

This is one of our reality shows and the scripted plot is part of the grand scheme.

But it isn't.

For the next month and a half I am with Quincy.

Every morning.

We wake up together. Our naked bodies entwined. Legs and arms entangled. Refusing to let go and be free. Our bodies warm and sticky from the love juices smeared on our chests, stomachs, and crotches from our night of passion.

In the afternoon.

We work silently and discreetly, not giving away our secret. We snatch glimpses of each other. Smiling. Winking. We both agree to maintain our professionalism. No time together, alone. Only if it's an arranged meeting. No outside lunches together. No fraternizing. I am his boss. He is my intern.

Then at night.

We make dinner together. Chopping, cutting, searing, and plating. Eating from one plate, sharing our food cooked from our hands. Our love. We curl in one another's arms on the sofa. Flipping through the channels. Caressing, stroking, and kissing. We fall asleep wrapped in our world.

When we are not together I find myself thinking of him constantly. Yearning for his deep voice. The gentleness of his strong arms. The greeting of his juicy lips.

Then we reunite later and laugh, smile, constantly grabbing hands, touching, and kissing.

His affectionate manner is extremely comforting.

Endearing.

Longed.

On some weekends, when he is not playing basketball at the local courts, we explore the city, going everywhere from Central Park to SoHo to Harlem.

Every other weekend we take long romantic walks in Central Park. We start in the early afternoon, walking from One-hundred Tenth Street to the middle of the park. We stop at the summer stage. We take in the featured weekend concert, events like Dwele, Erykah Badu, Jill Scott, and Ledisi.

My type of music.

We dance and sing with the crowd.

Waving our hands in the air.

And Quincy drapes his long muscular arm over my shoulder.

I reach up and put mine around his.

We rock from side to side with Quincy pulling me close to him.

In the middle of the park among thousands of people I completely let go of my inhibitions. I feel a gravitational pull so strong I know it's a love that binds me closer to Quincy.

After we explore mature grown-up music, Quincy drags me to Virgin Records in Times Square to share his version of lyrical geniuses.

Jeezy.

Lil Wayne.

Drake.

Gucci Mane.

Young Dro.

He even updates my iPod with these inspired great musical selections.

I put them on my iPod under the playlist—UHM, OKAY!

One Sunday we sat in the Studio Museum of Harlem for two hours just observing the paintings and sculptures. Whenever I ventured off to a different part of the museum admiring a piece of art Quincy would gently brush against me, or bump my shoulder then smile and wink at me.

After leaving the museum Quincy took me to Best Buy department store. He was trying to convince me to buy a Wii video game. "I don't play games," I said as he attempted to teach me how to play the basketball video game on display.

"Come on. Give it a try." Quincy jumped, and moved his hands and arms quickly from left to right, then up and down with the game's remote.

"You're an expert at this." I clumsily jerked and twisted from left to right.

"I have one at home and at school," he said, maneuvering swiftly and precisely.

I couldn't quite get the hang of it. My coordination was off. I was stumbling around the showroom making a fool of myself. I was moving my arms left instead of right to dribble and shoot. "I am too old for this," I said, frustrated. I wanted to throw the remote control across the store.

Quincy laughed and said, "You're never too old to have fun." He then grabbed me. He put the remote back in my hand, stood behind me, reached his arms around and placed them on mine, guiding my hands and arms. "Just take your time, baby. Slow down," he said in my ear.

I bought the game and now I am addicted. I play when I come home from work. It's totally relaxing.

Besides, I need the practice because Quincy is extremely competitive. "You don't want none of this," he yells every time he scores. "I'm the king up in here."

I shake my head and put on my game face. "This is my kingdom," I yell back. "Get off me and watch this drop in your face!" I score.

Fun.

Lots of fun.

And, Quincy loves eating dishes from varied cultures.

Indian.

Ethiopian.

Spanish.

French.

Italian.

And we explore restaurant after restaurant.

Feeding one another off each other's plates.

"Here baby, try this." Quincy scoops up a forkful of food and feeds me.

At the Ethiopian restaurant it's customary to eat with your hands. So when the dishes arrived Quincy gathered the meat, vegetables, and bread between his fingers, reached across the table, and put his hand in my mouth. I slowly licked and sucked the food out of his hand. My head moving back and forth, then round and round. "You didn't get all of it," he said. "There is some left on my fingers."

I opened my mouth and Quincy fed each finger to me one at a time until I captured all the leftover food and juices.

This turned Quincy on.

As well as me.

We rush home after dinner and finish devouring one another.

For dessert.

Quincy is the quintessential lover.

Making love with him is like dew drops on a summer morning.

Perfect.

He makes love to every part of my body.

From the balls of my feet to the top of my head.

Quincy's warm mouth succulently explores places that have been completely left desolate. Like a roving inquisitor Quincy reminds me what making love is all about.

It isn't fast.

Quick.

Or painful.

He is tender.

Passionate.

Gentle.

He whispers in my ear with each stroke.

We work our bodies together in perfect rhythm.

Having multiple orgasms in one night. Something I'd never experienced with any man.

I also enjoy giving oral pleasure and satisfying him. I gently place his massive erect dick in my mouth and taste his juices.

He is sweet like nectar.

Whenever his pulsating dick jerks and he wants to pull out of my mouth I push his hands away and swallow all of him.

He returns the favor.

His tongue flickers around the head of my dick then he licks and sucks every inch of me.

He won't stop until I let go, shooting my juices in his mouth.

He loves tasting and telling me, "Give me more. I want to taste all of you."

Then he crawls on his hands and knees, arching his back, lifting his fat bubble ass, wanting me to stroke him as he does me.

I can't and don't get enough of Quincy.

My mojo has been restored. I am refreshed and replenished.

Every day I get my fill of Quincy.

The most generous lover I have ever known.

My days are easy.

I am floating.

Stress-free.

Youthful.

I am in love.

Chapter Sixteen

"Chase, what is going on with you?" Ashley calls me right before lunch. I've been so caught up in Quincy I forgot, well actually, just have been too ashamed to tell her. I really don't want to hear her mouth of how she was right.

"You're acting different," she says.

I chuckle. "Nothing is going on. Just work."

"Boy, I know you. I've haven't hung out with you in weeks. We haven't done any of our weekend brunches."

"I'm just . . . busy." I smile.

"Are you fucking your intern?"

I start choking and coughing into the phone.

"I knew it!" she screams. "Oh my gosh! How long have you been fucking him?"

I hesitate a few moments before I say anything. "It's been two months."

"What! And you didn't even tell me?"

"I was planning to, but everything happened so fast."

"You are something else," she laughs. "I told you that you were a cougay. Now, fill me in."

I laugh and shake my head. I proceed to get my ace-in-the-hole caught up on all the details of my and Quincy's relationship.

After twenty minutes Ashley lets out a long sigh. "Wow! I can't believe all this has been going on for two months and you didn't even tell me. That is very shaday adieu."

Did she just call me shady? I pull the phone away from my ear and look at it.

Yup, she sure did.

Thanks to Ashley's good friend, Kenya, who came up with the catchy phrase. Kenya is a freelance writer and she put it in a story she wrote on black gay life. The gay lingo caught on like wildfire in the gay community, and especially amongst women. Now, Ashley loves saying it every chance she gets.

"Ashley, you know I am not shaday adieu. You are my best friend. I just didn't want to hear you say that you were right."

"Well, damn, I was!"

I laugh. "See, that's why I didn't say anything."

"He is working you over!" I hear her snap her fingers into the phone.

"We are working each other over. Thank you."

"So, when is his last day?"

"In two weeks," I sigh. "I am trying not to think about it. Ashley, I am in love with him."

"Oooh, chile! Not you saying you're in love. You are sprung. He must have some good dick."

"You're silly." I gaze up into the ceiling. "But for real, Ashley, he's so different from every other guy I've been with. He's smart, intelligent, fun, affectionate, and focused."

"Does he have a brother? Hell, any single available friends?"

"Girl, you are crazy!"

"No, I am serious!"

"Ashley, I'm trying to have a serious conversation with you about my feelings for Quincy."

"I am too. Can your best friend get a hookup?"

"I'll call you later. I have a lot of work to catch up on. I have this upcoming award show and I really need to get the budget together."

"All right, boy. But, I am happy for you, Chase," Ashley says.

"Thank you."

"But I am serious. See if he has any friends."

"Good-bye, Ashley."

I shake my head and grab the menu book from my bottom desk drawer. I call Tony's DiNapoli restaurant and place an order for delivery.

Quincy pops in my head. The image of him smiling at me with his dazzling eyes and hearty chuckle brings a smile to my face.

His soft touches.

His soft breathing when we are sleeping together.

His morning kisses.

His evening kisses.

We've planned to spend the last two weeks together before he leaves. I hate the thought of it, but I know he has to finish his last year at Stanford. I just wish he wasn't on another coast. Quincy keeps reassuring me we will work it out. He will fly home on the holidays to be with me. He's invited me to visit him, and to see some of his games at school, as well as those on the road.

My office phone rings. The food delivery is downstairs. I have to go down to pick it up. Security doesn't allow anyone upstairs who is not an employee of GBS Television.

As I am walking down the hall toward the elevator bank a deep melodic voice calls my name.

"Mr. Kennedy," the voice resonates.

I quickly turn.

"Quincy?" I glance around to see if anyone is looking at us. "What's going on? Do you need something?" I am truly happy to see him, but I maintain my composure. He strolls toward me with a huge grin on his face. He has his cell phone to his ear.

He is pure perfection as his tall muscular body makes his way up the hall.

Damn! I mumble to myself.

"I just want you to say hello to a good friend of mines." Quincy stands directly in front of me. His cologne rushes to my nostrils. His scent that I love to smell and hold fast in my memory fills my senses. Quincy hands me his cell phone.

I look at him curiously as I slowly take the phone from his hand.

He just smiles at me and nods.

"Hello?" I ask.

"Hello, Mr. Chase Kennedy. This is E. Lynn Harris."

I put my hand over my mouth. Excitement rushes over me.

"Hello, Mr. Harris. It's nice to meet you."

"It's nice meeting you, too. And, please, call me E. Lynn."

"Okay, E. Lynn." I gently punch Quincy in the arm. I am still trying to contain my enthusiasm. "I am a big fan of your work."

"Thank you, Chase. I really appreciate that. Quincy has told me a lot about you. I am coming to New York for some meetings next week. Hopefully we can all get together and grab something to eat."

"Yes. That would be great. I would love to."

"Good. Now, I love to eat, and I love me some soul food."

"Don't worry. I know the perfect place in Harlem. Miss Maude's Spoonbread. I highly recommend it."

"Well, good, Chase. I am looking forward to meeting you. Quincy is really in love with you. Every time we talk it's Chase this, and Chase that. He's my little brother, so I have to meet this man who has him smitten."

"I am flattered," I laugh. "Hey, if your schedule is permitting, maybe we can catch *The Lion King* on Broadway. I have a good friend who is in the play."

"Sounds like a plan. I will make some time for that."

"Great. It was wonderful speaking with you, E. Lynn."

"It was great chatting with you as well, Chase."

I shake my head and chuckle as I return the phone to Quincy.

"I have to go downstairs and get my food," I say. "I'll be right back."

"I'll be here waiting on you," Quincy whispers with a devilish grin on his face. He then places the phone to his ear and walks toward his cubicle.

Chapter Seventeen

When I make it back upstairs I look over to Quincy's cubicle and he is not there. I do a quick glance over at my assistant's desk. She is on the phone and typing on the computer.

Quincy is not there.

I do a scan down the hall.

I don't see Quincy anywhere.

I step into the copy room and he is not there.

I go to my office and plop in my chair.

I can't imagine where he has gone that quickly.

I remove my food from the white plastic bag. I peel off the white carton lid from the aluminum container. Steam rises from the chicken and pasta simmering inside. I open the other container, and inside is my zucchini fried chips. I tear open the plastic, holding my utensils, and take the fork and swirl some pasta around it.

I take a few bites and suddenly Quincy sticks his head inside my office and taps on my door. I wave him to come inside.

"Hey, Mr. Kennedy." Quincy walks in.

"Hey, Quincy. What's up?" I lay my fork down.

Quincy looks over his shoulder to see if anyone is around. "Thank you for talking with E. Lynn."

"No problem. I am glad I had the opportunity. He seems like a very nice person."

"I told you he was mad cool." Quincy slides his body in the chair in front of my desk. "He is so humble and easy to talk to."

"You should be happy to have a friend like him." I pick up a zucchini chip and toss it in my mouth. "You want some?"

"Naw, I'm good." Quincy leans back in the chair. He drops his head and folds his arms. "I can't believe I am leaving in a few weeks."

"I know. I've been thinking about that."

"You're still coming out to California the first week of September?" Quincy asks as he lifts his head.

"Of course. Nothing has changed."

"I really hope this school year goes fast." Quincy unfolds his arms and puts his hands on his lap. "I can't wait to come back home to you and to start working. Thanks for the hookup on the job in the talent department."

"No problem," I say. "You're very smart. You will do very well over there. Besides, I got to keep you close by."

Quincy snickers.

"And this year will go by faster than you think," I say. "But you got to stay focused on your grades and basketball. No distractions." I stand and walk from behind my desk in front of Quincy.

"I got it," Quincy says, looking up at me. "I know what I have to do. I am just so happy and sad at the same time."

"Yeah, I know how you feel." I step behind Quincy and walk toward my door. I peer out looking left then right. I push the door closed.

Quincy stands and turns. He puts his hands in his pockets. "You don't know how much you mean to me."

I slowly move toward Quincy. I feel my heart beginning to race. I want to rush into his arms.

Kiss him.

Make passionate love to him right here in my office.

But I stop in my tracks. My eyes follow his hands as he pulls them from his pockets. In his right hand is a black velvet box.

My heart is pounding.

Leaping.

Thumping.

Quincy opens the box, revealing a blinding diamond ring.

I can't speak.

Words have escaped my memory.

I shake my head.

I'm breathing heavy.

"Chase, I love you." Quincy moves closer. "I've never met a man who made me feel as whole and complete as you do. My heart beats joy because of your touch. It beats happiness because of your smile. It beats peace because of your love." Quincy stands directly in front of me. "I know you are my soul mate."

I am still unable to move.

Say anything.

My eyes are transfixed by the ring.

"I want to give you this ring as a symbol of my trust and commitment. A symbol of our love." Quincy takes the ring from the box. "You have me. I'm yours. I just want you to be mines." He takes my left hand and places the ring on my ring finger.

"I don't know what to say," I stammer and start biting my lip.

"Just say you're mines."

I gaze up into Quincy's eyes.

They are soft.

Welcoming.

I look back down at the ring on my finger.

Can I do this?

Do I want to do this?

He's only twenty-two.

I'm thirty-eight.

He's leaving in two weeks.

I'm scared.

Very scared.

I look up and hear a melodious voice say, *Love is patient. It is kind. It bears all things, believes all things, hopes all things and endures all things. You are love and it is being reciprocated.*

I close my eyes.

Take a deep breath.

Slowly exhale.

And, I say, "Yes, Quincy. I will be yours."

I wrap my arms around him and we embrace.

I hear our hearts sing in unison.

Thump. (*LOVE*)

Thump. (*LOVE*)

Thump. (*LOVE*)

Thump. (*LOVE*)

Chapter Eighteen

I can't stop looking at this huge diamond ring on my finger. I am flabbergasted.

I mean, really.

Really!

Really?

WOW!

I can't even finish my lunch. My appetite is gone.

I go the restroom and profile in the mirror, staring at the ring.

Placing my hand on my chest.

Then setting it on the sink.

I hold my hand up in front of my face.

I lean in.

Staring at the seven diamonds.

The white platinum band.

Is this real?

Is this happening to me?

Love has finally found me. In the body of a twenty-two-year-old. A fine, gorgeous, and beautiful twenty-two-year-old.

That night, while we are lying in bed, Quincy and I are discussing him leaving. I can't believe how fast the time has flown. To me it was just yesterday I was sitting at lunch with him discussing his internship. Admiring and lusting after him.

Now here he is naked in my bed. He's my man.

My lover.

My friend.

"I don't want to leave you," Quincy says as he strokes my head.

I sigh and then smile. "You're always with me," I say. I hold up my hand displaying the shiny diamonds. "You know you shouldn't have done this. How can you afford a ring like this?" I ask.

"I told you my mom is head of human resources at Macy's. So, I used her discount." Quincy winks at me.

My heart begins to race. "You used your mother's discount?" I turn and look at him. "So does she know you bought a ring for a man? For me?" I put my hand on my chest.

"Yeah, she knows. I told you, me and my mother are very close. I tell her everything."

"She knows about us?" I ask.

"She can't wait to meet you." Quincy smiles.

"Are you serious?"

"Very."

"Uhm, okay," I say. I am apprehensive. I have never met any of my boyfriends' or, should I say, any of my lovers' mothers.

"She already likes you," Quincy says. "I told her everything about you. E. Lynn even talked to her."

"You've been discussing me with everyone?"

"Yeah. I don't keep secrets, Chase. Why are you shocked?"

"It's just I never, I mean, I haven't . . ." I don't know what to say. How to formulate the right words to explain to Quincy my past lives of being someone's secret. Somebody's nobody. I take a deep breath.

"What is it?" Quincy asks. "Did I do something wrong?"

"No," I say. "I've just never been with someone who loves me as much as you do, and talks about me with his family and friends. I find it very flattering."

"That's just me. I thought it was normal and everybody did it. Especially for the person they love."

I lean in and kiss Quincy. Pulling and gently biting his bottom lip.

"Boy, you're about to get me started," Quincy laughs and places my hand on his rising thick erection.

"You are going to wear me out," I say. "I need to start playing basketball with you so I can get my stamina up."

"Speaking of basketball, you're still coming tomorrow afternoon?" Quincy asks.

"Coming where?" I look at Quincy inquisitively. "Ashley and I are going down to SoHo to do some shopping and grab lunch."

"Our tournament is tomorrow, remember? You are supposed to come and watch me play." Quincy props himself up on his elbows.

"I thought the tournament was next week." I put my hands behind my head.

"No, it's tomorrow," Quincy says. "Your age is starting to show. You need some ginkgo biloba." He laughs out loud.

I thrust the pillow from beneath me and hit him with it. "You love my old ass."

"Of course I do. *If I didn't like it, then I wouldn't have put a ring on it*," Quincy sings.

"Oh, so now you think you're Beyoncé?"

"Hey, I mean that is my girl."

"Well, how about that one about my love finally coming along?" I say.

"Who is that?" Quincy screws up his face.

"Etta James," I say condescendingly.

"Oh, you mean that old woman Beyoncé played in the movie *Cadillac Records*."

I shake my head. "Yes, the *woman's* song Beyoncé sang for President Obama's inauguration."

"Anyway." Quincy climbed his naked body out of the bed and walked toward the bathroom. "Are you coming tomorrow to see me play? I am going to win us the championship." Quincy pretends he's dribbling a ball and throws his hands in the air as if he is shooting it into a basket.

"Yeah, but I got to bring Ashley. She will kill me if I cancel on her."

"Bring her." Quincy yells from the bathroom. "There will be lots of young boys there. She will have a good time."

I burst out laughing. In less than three months Quincy has already figured out Ashley and I didn't even have to tell him.

Chapter Nineteen

The next morning I awake to the wonderful smell of bacon, eggs, and pancakes wafting through my condo. I yawn and stretch my arms across the bed hoping to find Quincy, but smile, knowing he's up and cooking.

I rub my eyes and glance at the clock.

It's nine-fifteen.

I've got to call Ashley and let her know there has been a change of plans. I know she is already up deciding on her costume and wig for the day.

Just as I reach for my iPhone on the nightstand, Quincy saunters into the bedroom wearing only a white chef's apron that says, *Do The Cook.*

"Good morning," he says, carrying a tray full of steaming food.

"Good morning." I smile. I sit up and hoist the pillows behind me against the headboard.

Quincy places the tray on my lap. He leans in and kisses me on the forehead. "Breakfast in bed," he says.

"Thank you, baby."

I pick up the glass of orange juice and take a sip. I then take a strawberry and feed it to Quincy. He takes a bite and then kisses me on the mouth. I lick the juice from his full lips.

"You better eat," Quincy says as he turns and walks out of the room.

"You're not joining me?" I ask.

"Yeah. I am going to get my tray. I'll be back."

I take a bite of the pancakes that Quincy has topped with chopped bananas.

Delicious.

My man can cook.

Damn it!

Just as I am about to take another bite my cell phone rings.

Speak of the devil.

"Hey, Ashley," I say. "I was just about to call you."

"Boy, I didn't think you were going to answer the phone. I was ready to leave a message."

"Why wouldn't I answer the phone?" I say in between bites of my eggs.

"Quincy may have had your legs tied up in a knot over your head and behind your back."

"Ashley, you're crazy."

"But, I'm telling the truth."

"Anyway," I say, taking a sip of orange juice. "How would you like to go to a basketball game today instead of SoHo?"

"Oh lawd," Ashley says.

"I forgot Quincy's team is playing in a tournament this weekend. I promised him I would come. Besides, I have something I need to show you." I hold up my hand that is showcasing my new diamond ring.

"What do you have to show me?"

"You'll see." I smile.

"Chase, you are really wearing me out right now," she huffs.

"I guarantee you'll love it."

"Whatever, Chase. And, why do I have to be dragged along to your commitment to your boyfriend?"

"Come on, Ashley. There will be some young tenders at the game. And, you can meet some of Quincy's friends."

Silence.

Longer silence.

"Hello? Ashley, are you there?" I ask.

"What time does the game start?" Ashley asks, trying to sound irritated.

I chuckle.

"The game starts at two."

"Well, hell, that means I got to do a complete change. Boy, let me go and I will be at your house by one."

"Good-bye, Ashley. I'll see you at one."

Chapter Twenty

I hop in the shower after breakfast in bed with Quincy. He rushed out of the house to get to Brooklyn so he could warm up with his team. But, of course we had to get a quickie in before he left.

Some foreplay.

Some sucking.

Stroking.

And ejaculation.

As I am coming out of the shower I hear my doorbell ringing.

And ringing.

And ringing.

I wrap a towel around my waist and rush into the living room. "Hold on!" I yell. "I'm coming!"

Quincy probably forgot his key again. He always runs out of the house and then minutes later he is ringing and knocking on the door for me to let him in.

He talks about me needing some ginkgo biloba.

He is the forgetful one.

"You're always forgetting your key," I say as I open the door. "I am going to put it on a necklace so that . . ."

And there he is.

Standing tall.

Regal.

With a smirk on his face.

Trent Campbell.

"Hello, Chase," Trent says. "I would have used my key, but it no longer works." He holds up the key that once unlocked the door to our home.

Our love shack.

But, I changed the locks, babe.

"So, are you going to invite me in?"

I am standing in shock, dripping wet. My left hand gripping the towel wrapped around me.

My right hand still holding the doorknob.

Clinching it for dear life.

Wanting to slam the door shut.

But my heart is pounding.

My body is tense.

"Trent, hey, sure, come in," I say. He waltzes past me. His cologne lingers under my nose. He still smells the same. His scent is undeniable. Tangy with a sharp sting but sweet and alluring.

Trent makes his way to the sofa. I follow behind him.

"So, I get no love?" Trent stretches his arms wide.

I give him a half-hearted embrace. He pulls me closer. I resist and step back.

"I'll be right back," I say, avoiding eye contact. "I just got out of the shower."

"You look great, Chase," Trent says.

"Thanks," I say. "You look different." His lean muscular frame is thinner. His mustache and goatee are missing. He's clean-shaven. His curly locks are thicker and longer.

I dash into the bedroom scrambling to find my sweat pants.

I can't believe he is here.

He just strolls in like he was just here yesterday.

It's been three years and he expects me to throw myself at him.

He walked out.

He left me.

FUCK HIM!

I come back into the living room and Trent is making his way toward the kitchen.

"I see you changed things around." He points toward the sofa and chair.

"No," I say. "You changed things around."

"You're not happy to see me?" Trent asks.

"I just was not expecting you. Why didn't you call?"

"I wanted to surprise you. And, I told you that I was coming home and wanted to see you."

"Yeah, but you should have called first. Coming unannounced . . . well, it's not cool." I make my way to the chair and sit.

He would have gotten a big surprise if he would have arrived a little earlier.

My new man, Quincy.

"You're making it seem like I am unwelcome." Trent sits on the sofa across from me.

"Hmmm," I say.

Every emotion and feeling I thought I would have seeing Trent after all this time.

Nothing.

Absolutely, nothing.

Don't feel a thing.

Actually, I do feel something.

"You know, Trent, three years ago, I was in love with you. I would have done anything for you. As a matter of fact, I did do anything for you. I gave my time, energy, and home to you. I let you in." I point to my heart.

"I appreciate that," Trent says.

"Oh, so, I should feel honored that you appreciate my love?"

"Well, what else do you want me to say?"

I stand and walk toward Trent. His eyes follow me.

"You never apologized for the tacky and sorry-ass way you left me! You never once acknowledged me or my feelings." I'm spitting my words at him like daggers.

I wish they were.

Trent stands and opens his mouth.

I cut him off. "And you walk in here like I am supposed to forget everything as if it never happened." I am standing directly in his face.

Unmoved.

Steeled.

Defiant.

Strong.

"Chase, I am really sorry. I didn't mean to hurt you," Trent says and takes a few steps back. "The way I handled it was wrong, but it was the best way I knew how then. I am a different man today. The man you see right here in front of you is not that immature and selfish man. Africa has changed me."

"Good for you, Trent," I say and walk toward the door and open it. "I've changed, too. And, I didn't have to leave the country to figure that out."

Trent is staring at me with his mouth wide open.

"I'm happy. I'm in love. I've moved on. And, so should you." I wave him toward the open door.

Trent slowly walks across the room. His face looks drained as if the blood has left him and already made it to the street.

"I am very sorry," Trent says as he stands in the doorway.

"I am, too." I slam the door.

I look at my ring and smile.

It feels good to be in love.

Chapter Twenty-one

"Oh my gosh! I can't believe Trent just came to your house unannounced," Ashley yells. We are in the back of the Lincoln sedan car service headed to Brooklyn. "That motherfucker got a lot of nerve. I wish I would have been there." I stare at Ashley while she adjusts her short cropped blond wig on her head. "I would have given him a piece of my mind."

"You know what, Ashley? I didn't feel anything for him. I thought seeing Trent would bring back all those old feelings. But it didn't."

"Well, it's about time you're over that loser. Ugh! I don't know what ever you saw in him anyway. I can't stand them high-yellow light-skinned Negroes." Ashley frowns. "Especially those with their pedigrees and letters after their names. They think they are better than everyone else. Negro, please! You still black just like me, and living on Park Avenue ain't shit." She sucks her teeth and then tugs at her large breasts spilling from her Yves St. Laurent T-shirt. She purposely ripped it down the front exposing her massive cleavage.

"Ashley, what the hell do you have on?" I pull on her snug fitting T-shirt.

"What? You don't like my outfit?" She arches her back and pokes her chest out further.

"You're dressed like we're going to a rap video. Those shorts can't get any shorter. You'll give everybody a full view of the moon." I point to her ass cheeks peeking beneath the material.

"Boy, this is the newest trend."

"Yeah, and you don't need to be copying it. And, do you have on a bra?"

"A bra?" Ashley snaps her head back. "It's the summer. Who the hell wears a bra in this hundred-degree heat?"

I put my head in my hands.

"Lord, give me the strength," I mumble.

All of a sudden Ashley lets out a loud squeal. I jerk my head at her. The driver swerves and nearly sideswipes another car. He looks in the rearview mirror with wide eyes.

"What's wrong, Ashley?" I yell.

"Boy, look at that diamond ring on your finger! That is some serious bling!"

I laugh. "Girl, you scared me and the driver." I point to his shocked reflection in the mirror.

"Sorry, Mr. Driver," Ashley purrs, licking her lips at him.

The driver smiles and winks at her.

That damn Ashley.

"Quincy gave you that ring, didn't he?" Ashley put her hand over her mouth.

"Yeah. He gave it to me yesterday at work."

Ashley starts rocking back and forth and stomping her feet.

"Girl, calm down," I say, glancing at the driver, who is still looking at us in the rearview mirror.

Well, he's looking at Ashley's jiggling breasts, which I swear are about to pop out if she bounces any harder.

Ashley grabs my hand and thrusts it toward her face. She leans in and starts counting, "One, two, three, four, five, six, seven BIG-ASS DIAMONDS. You. Better. Work!" She waves her finger.

A huge grin spreads across my face. "It's serious, Ashley. We've moved a step further into our relationship."

"Boy, this is marriage. Quincy got you on lock!"

I snatch my hand away. "We got each other on lock."

"I am so happy for you, Chase." Ashley reaches over and gives me a hug. "This is what I am talking about. You got yourself a keeper. See, I told you about them young boys. But, naw, you didn't want to listen to me."

"Okay, okay," I laugh. "Yes, you were right. Yes, I should have listened to you a long time ago. But, I wasn't ready. You know me, Ashley. I am a little slow. Old-fashioned."

"Well, it's a new decade and century. You better keep up and get with the program." Ashley snaps her fingers. "The days of sitting on the porch and talking all night are over. It's all about get it, hit it, and if it's good, then keep it."

"I'm learning. But I'm still taking it slow," I say. "I'm taking my old-fashioned ways with me."

"Okay, Mr. Old Fogey. But when we get to Brooklyn you better make sure Quincy introduces me to all his friends."

"Let me find out you're trying to get a diamond ring." I lift my hand and wave it in Ashley's face.

"Hell naw! I don't need a ring. Just some good steady dick."

Ashley and I burst out laughing.

Along with the driver.

Chapter Twenty-two

When we arrive in Brooklyn, at Prospect Park, an enormous crowd has already gathered. It looks as if all of Brooklyn is at the basketball court.

Hood dudes with their fresh white sneakers. Printed T-shirts and sagging shorts. Profiling and mean-mugging the outsiders. Giving fist pounds and daps to their boys.

Fab ghetto girls with their too-tight blouses and short shorts. It looks like every girl got the memo to rock the ass cutters with their Christian Louboutin heels and oversized purses. Door-knocker earrings dangling from their ears. And, every chick had hair—black, blond, red, auburn, chocolate, and platinum.

Yes, this was Brooklyn.

In the summertime.

I missed it sometimes.

Late night parties on Eastern Parkway.

Caribbean music blaring.

Jamaicans.

Haitians.

Guyanese.

Barbadians.

The island people represent with their thick accents and thick bodies.

It's hard to miss them strutting down the ave in their bright colorful clothes—red, yellow, orange, and green.

Rainbows on the streets.

Then there is Junior's Restaurant downtown.

The smell of cheesecake stirs in your stomach.

Yeah, if I could get away with making one of my interns walk from midtown Manhattan to downtown Brooklyn for a slice of cheesecake with strawberries, I would do it.

Who Wants to Work for Chase?

Ashley and I make our way through the crowd. Squeezing and sliding through bodies and bodies of dark, brown, and yellow skin waiting for the tournament to begin.

As we get closer to the court music is thumping from the huge speakers surrounding the basketball court. The deejay has the crowd rocking and bopping. Heads are nodding and people are reciting the rhymes filtering the air.

Then the sounds of Brooklyn's own infamous Queen Bee comes blaring through the speakers, singing about not being afraid of the dick anymore.

Ashley throws her hands in the air, waving them back and forth. She starts pumping her way through the crowd in her five-inch Christian Louboutin heels, chanting the lyrics.

A line of girls follow suit, waving their hands in the air and dipping their asses low to the ground.

The guys start hooting and hollering. "Go 'head, baby girl! Rock that shit!"

My mouth falls open.

I stare at Ashley in disbelief. She is shaking her shoulders, winding her ass with her cheeks winking as she twirls from side to side.

The deejay screams through the microphone, "Pop that thang! Rock that thang! Awww, shucks now, Brooklyn! Mami is out there doing her thang!"

Her voluptuous titties are bouncing.

And bouncing.

And bouncing.

With no support.

A group of young guys with platinum and gold chains swinging on their necks and wrists encircle Ashley and start throwing dollar bills at her.

And, like the true diva she is, she squats lower and lower. Bounces harder and harder. She scoops up the money with each dip. Stuffing the greenbacks in her shirt.

My Ashley.

The beat changes and so does Ashley. She wiggles her way around the young guys and struts toward me smiling from ear to ear.

I see Quincy jogging across the court toward us. He has changed into his black basketball shorts and white jersey with a red number eight printed large on his chest. He's laughing and pointing at Ashley.

"Did you see me?" Ashley boasts, pointing at the crowd. The guys are still cheering and clapping.

"I saw you out there doing your thang!" Quincy gives her a high five.

"Please, don't encourage her," I say.

"Boy, please, I am just having fun," Ashley says.

"But, you're too old to be out there popping and dropping it like it's hot," I say. "Especially shaking your girls with no bra on." I point to her breasts. Her nipples are perky and poking through the thin material.

"You're just jealous." Ashley pulls the crumpled bills out of

her T-shirt. "Besides, you're only as old as you think you are."
She licks her fingers and starts counting her money.

"And let me guess, you're seventeen?" I say.

Ashley rolls her eyes. "Boy, I am twenty-five, at the least.
That's my industry age."

I give her the side-eye.

"I made it rain out there." Ashley continues counting the
bills.

"It was more like a drizzle," Quincy says. We burst out
laughing.

Ashley gives us the side-eye.

"Forget y'all. I made two hundred sixty-seven dollars." She
waves the money in our face. "And, I wasn't even trying hard."

I shake my head.

"The game is getting ready to start," Quincy says. "I got
you guys a spot up front so you can see me in full action."

"Well, let's go. I need to be in the V.I.P. section anyway."
Ashley teases her coif. She then takes out her compact mirror
and daps some bright red lipstick on her lips.

"You are a mess," Quincy chuckles and leads us through the
crowd. We follow him to the seats at center court.

"I love you," Ashley squeals and throws her arms around
Quincy. "This is perfect."

We are smack dab in the center of it all.

The action.

The muscular.

Tall.

Dark.

Light.

Mocha-colored men running back and forth up and down
the court in their shorts and jerseys.

Nothing can get past us.

Well, nothing can get past Ashley.

"Oh my, look at number twelve." Ashley fans herself with

her hand. "Damn! Number three is foine! No, wait, look at number fifteen." She points at the tall, curly-headed Rick Fox look-alike. "Today is my day." Ashley shifts in her seat.

"Yes, Ashley, today is your day," I say.

The game starts with Quincy's team, Bed-Stuy's Finest, paired against the Crown Heights Hustlers.

They are some rough-looking guys.

Scars on their bodies.

I'm not sure if they are gunshot or knife wounds.

They have tattoos on their necks.

Hands.

And arms.

With their babies' mamas' names.

Numbers.

Streets.

Scriptures scribbled on every available piece of skin.

I'm a little nervous for Quincy and his team. They are some pretty boys.

Clean cut.

Smooth skin.

Manicured.

I hope they don't get rough out there.

The young girls standing behind us scream the player's names and numbers.

I hear a few constantly yelling, "Hey, number eight! I want your Thornberry!"

I start to stand up and put my hand in the air and yell, "He's mine, bitches! Back the fuck up!"

But, I reason against it. I don't think Quincy would appreciate the embarrassment.

Neither would I.

The referee blows the whistle and starts the game.

Quincy is in the starting lineup.

He looks over at me and winks.

I smile and do a slight nod.

I don't want to give myself away.

But, it's obvious Quincy doesn't mind.

Two tall guys are in the center of the court waiting for the referee to toss the ball in the air.

The official gives the go-ahead and the referee releases the ball. It is loose in the air. Quincy's teammate gets the height on the other guy and he hits the ball far right.

The two teams scramble for the ball, going back and forth, ripping it from each other.

The men push and dribble past one another.

They are dipping, turning, and faking left then right.

The curly headed Rick Fox look-alike gets the ball and he is sprinting down the court.

He thrusts the ball hard to Quincy, who is standing under the hoop.

He catches the ball.

Leaps in the air.

He looks like a gazelle.

Graceful.

Swift.

Effortless.

Soaring high.

And, with a slight spin he slam dunks it.

He hangs on to the rim, swinging back and forth.

He lets go and falls to the ground on his feet.

The crowd erupts.

I jump up with my hands in the air and scream, "YEEEEAAAAHHHHH!!!!"

The announcer on the microphone yells, "Oh, no!!! Thornberry starts the game with a dunk! This is going to be one of those games!"

And it was one of those games.

I can't contain myself watching Quincy run up and down the court slamming the ball in the basket.

Blocking shots.

And dribbling like a true champion.

Yeah, he earned his basketball spot at Stanford.

The end of the game is a nail biter. The score is Bed-Stuy's Finest, 58, and the Crown Heights Hustlers, 56.

It is thirty seconds left in the game.

The Crown Heights Hustlers have the ball. The giant lanky guy with bad skin sprints up the center and does a pump fake. He rushes the basket with a lay-up.

He scores two points.

The game is tied.

Bed-Stuy's Finest has the ball.

Rick Fox's look-alike is dribbling the ball down the court.

He is yelling and pointing at his teammates, "Get in position! Get in position!"

Quincy is being blocked by a big stocky guy who is twice his size. He definitely needs to be playing football. I didn't know basketball players looked like linebackers.

Quincy breaks free. He jerks right and then crosses in front of the Rick Fox look-alike.

He passes the ball to Quincy. He dribbles past the defense.

The crowd is on their feet.

Everyone's screaming.

My heart is pounding.

Ashley is gripping my arm.

Quincy does a finger-roll, releasing the ball in the air toward the basket.

One of the guys goes up and tries to slap the ball out of Quincy's hands.

He misses.

The ball hits the edge of the rim.

All of the players are looking up, watching to see if the ball is going to drop in the net.

Ashley grips my arm harder.

I can't look.

I turn away.

Then I hear an eruption of cheers. Ashley starts jumping up and down. "He did it! The ball went in!" Ashley screams.

I turn and see people rushing the court and the players.

The team is leaping around hugging one another with Quincy in the middle.

Ashley and I hug.

All of a sudden I see Quincy breaking through the melee coming toward me. He has a huge smile on his face. He stretches his arms wide and I rush into him.

We embrace.

Rocking from side to side.

"Congratulations," I say.

"I told you I was going to do this," Quincy says. "This was for you, baby."

I want to reach up and kiss him.

BADLY!!!!

"I love you, Chase," he whispers in my ear.

"I love you, too, Quincy," I say.

Reluctantly we let each other go.

His sweat is on my head, neck, and arms.

"Come on. I want you to meet my dad," Quincy says.

I step back and look at him, shocked. "Your dad is here?"

"Yeah. He came to the game. He's right over there." Quincy points to the other side of the basketball court.

I'm nervous.

Shaking.

Scared.

I'm not sure if I am ready to meet his parents.

His dad.

The man who's been in and out of Quincy's life, but he so desperately wants to have a relationship with.

"Don't worry. He'll like you. He's cool." Quincy notices my apprehension.

I take a deep breath.

I can do this, I say to myself. *I have to do this.*

"Let me tell Ashley we'll be back," I say.

Quincy points behind me. I turn and she is all up in one of Quincy's teammate's face.

The Rick Fox look-alike.

She's giggling and placing her hand over her chest.

Trying to act bashful.

He's grinning and staring into her cleavage.

I step next to Ashley and tell her I will be right back.

"Okay, okay." She waves her hand at me dismissively. She doesn't even turn to acknowledge me standing next to her.

I follow Quincy through the crowd. Guys are patting him on the back and congratulating him on winning the game. Girls are screaming his name, "Hey, Thornberry! We love you!"

With each step my feet feel heavy.

My heart is pounding and echoing throughout my entire body.

The closer we get I feel anxious.

We are a few feet away.

Now steps.

His father's back is toward us.

WOW! From behind Quincy's father looks just like him. They are exactly the same height, build, and color. One would easily mistake them for the same person, or perhaps brothers.

When we reach his father, he turns, and Quincy excitedly says, "This is my dad, Lenny Givens!"

We stare into each other's eyes.

Shocked.

I can't breathe.

The air has escaped me.
Everything around me stops.
I don't hear the yelling.
Or screaming.
My mind rushes back to when I was eighteen years old.
Lying in Lenny's bed.
The first man I gave myself to.
The first man I fell in love with.

Chapter Twenty-three

Lenny.

Lenny.

Lenny.

It has been eighteen years since I last saw Lenny Givens.

He is dark.

Sexy.

And, oh so fine.

Six-feet four-inches of smooth black skin.

Has a body like the rocks of the project buildings.

Sturdy.

And, as black as Lenny is, he has the prettiest eyes.

Light brown.

You couldn't help but stare at him. They're mesmerizing. I got lost in them.

His pearly white teeth gleamed when he smiled.

His huge massive hands swallowed mine, and he used to have wavy hair all around his head. I swear all he did was brush his hair and wear a doo-rag all the time.

When Lenny walked it wasn't like the other men.

Naw.

He was cool.

Too cool.

He strolled.

It was like he was gliding on air and his sneakers dared not touch the ground.

I yearned for him.

Desperately.

Lenny was a legend in our area.

All-star basketball player.

Recruited to the University of North Carolina.

Traveled overseas.

He did things young boys and young girls in the hood only dream about.

Every day I would watch Lenny as he gallantly strolled the streets, going to the corner bodega.

The basketball court.

The Chinese restaurant.

Everywhere he was, my eyes followed.

I watched as Lenny seduced the young girls in our hood.

They loved him.

He was older.

Mature.

Very mature.

He would take the anxious girls back to his sex nest.

A queen-sized bed with animal print sheets and matching comforter.

Dim red lights.

Slow music playing in the background.

Wine glasses.

That is what I imagined it to be like.

And I discovered I was right.

When Lenny chose me he knew I had not been touched by

another man yet. He said he could smell it. I'd just turned eighteen. I always knew I was gay, but I never been with a man. I came close in college, but I was too scared.

I didn't want my first experience to be with a white boy.

In Nashville, Tennessee.

I met some black guys.

But, I kept thinking.

Wondering.

Imaging myself being with Lenny.

When I came home for summer break I bumped into Lenny at the corner bodega.

"What's up, college boy?" Lenny's voice stung my ears.

I felt my stomach turn.

My hands shook.

Light perspiration hit my forehead.

"What's up, Lenny," I said.

Still trying to register he was really speaking to me.

"How long you back home?" He stepped closer to me. I smelled his sweet musk and hint of cologne.

"Just for a few months. I go back in August." I breathed deeply.

In.

Then out.

Taking Lenny inside my lungs.

"What are you doing later?" Lenny asked.

"No plans."

"Why don't you come through?"

Stunned.

Lenny's deep voice was so hard it scared me into his bed. He talked in my ear every time he stroked my innocence with his massive blackness. I had never seen anything like it before. It looked foreign and ugly. It had a lot of veins protruding from it. I knew it wouldn't fit inside me, but he told me not to worry. He said he would be gentle and take his time. He told me that he was going to help break me in for the other boys that would want to stick their things in me. Unfortunately, none would be like his. Lenny was my first and I would always yearn for it.

I believed everything he told me because he said I was special. "You're the only guy I've done this with," Lenny said as we lay in his bed under the leopard print sheets. I believed him. "I've been watching you as you watch me. I've been waiting for this for a long time," Lenny said.

I had too.

"We have to keep this as our secret," Lenny said, stroking my head.

"I know," I said. "I won't say anything."

I never said anything.

I never mentioned our relationship to anyone.

Lenny taught me how to do things I didn't know grown men did with one another. Things I dare not speak about, not even to my own best friend, Ashley.

How to touch.

Tease.

Massage.

Suck.

Lick.

Arch.

Receive.

Clinch.

Hold.

Release.

Grind.

Slow.

Fast.

Control.

For two years I was in bliss. Unspeakable pleasure.

Happiness.

When I went home for Thanksgiving, Christmas, spring break,

and the summer, I spent my time sneaking in and out of Lenny's apartment.

I belonged to Lenny and he was mine.

So I thought.

I was twenty years old when I returned home after my junior year of college. I found out Lenny had also been sexing a twenty-two-year-old young woman who moved from our neighborhood. She was eighteen when they started fucking.

And she had a four-year-old son.

Lenny was the father.

I went to his house to confront him, but those eyes and that voice lured me to his bed. I let him take me one last time.

One last painful time.

He whispers my name with each stroke.

Loud.

Louder.

And louder.

"Chase!" Quincy taps me on my back.

I look around and remember where I am. I gaze at the sea of faces spattered throughout Prospect Park. The crowd is still cheering, "BED-STUY! BED-STUY!"

I look at Quincy.

His lips are moving.

I finally hear him saying, "Chase! This is my dad, Lenny Givens."

I turn to his father. Lenny's light brown eyes are wide. His large dark hand is extended toward me.

"Nice to meet you, Chase," his father says.

Quincy puts his hand on my shoulder. "What's **wrong?**" He stares into my eyes.

"Nothing. Why?" I say and shake my head. I reach for Lenny's hand.

Quincy points to my mouth. "You're biting your lip and it's bleeding."

A Tribute

By James Earl Hardy

Different sides of the same coin: that's how many viewed E. and me over the years. To an extent, they were right: We're both Black Same Gender Loving men; we made our mark on the publishing world around the same time; and we document the underrepresented and misunderstood lives of Black gay/bisexual men. But our relationship was much more complex than that simplistic description.

We met at a reading/signing at A Different Light bookstore in late spring '94; he was promoting *Just As I Am* and the reissue of *Invisible Life*. After getting my copies signed, I asked if he would read my debut novel, *B-Boy Blues,* and if he liked it, provide a jacket blurb. I came prepared—I had the galley with me. He saw and mouthed the subtitle—"A seriously sexy, fiercely funny, Black-on-Black love story"—and his eyes grew wide. He emphatically said yes. I didn't expect to hear from him for weeks since he was on his first major tour but I received a phone call a few days later. His initial reaction: "Oh, James Earl! This is *sizzling!*" Then he added, "I could *never* write anything like this—but I'm glad you did, because we need it." He welcomed me into the literary fold with open arms; he knew that we were hungry for work that spoke to us. And he had a generosity of spirit that was unmatched: after *B-Boy* bowed later that year, I encountered quite a few readers who picked up the novel because E. mentioned it when asked to recommend other authors.

Traveling the country to promote *B-Boy,* I was privileged to observe just how much of a publishing phenomenon he had become; it wasn't only the sisters on the A train in New York City (or those brothers attempting to camouflage their book's cover) that had caught E. Lynn fever. Back then, it wasn't an exaggeration to state that we were indeed invisible; Blackness was very much a straight thing, gayness a white thing. And the most high-profile image representing Black SGL life was the documentary *Paris Is Burning.* Into this vacuum stepped a man spinning tales of heartbreak and healing, packing in hundreds of people at Barnes & Noble and Borders as if he were a rock star. We'd never seen that type of excitement, those types of crowds for a Black male *or* gay author before. He was bringing folks together who didn't read the same books—and those who didn't read *at all.* As the testimonials revealed, he was helping families break their "don't ask, don't tell" silence around homosexuality and begin building bridges of communication and understanding between straight and gay African Americans. It was common to see more than one tear shed during those question and answer periods, and for mothers to embrace and thank him for reuniting them with their SGL sons. He was respected like a dignitary, revered like royalty (and in many respects, he was).

Given that we were the most popular Black SGL authors at that time, some couldn't help but compare us. But we would laugh out loud about folks thinking we were enemies; I was pegged the younger upstart attempting to upstage his mentor (as he joked about the manufactured rivalry, referencing his favorite film, *All About Eve:* "I guess that would make you Eve Harrington and me Margo Channing!"). We knew there was room for more than one Negro Homo in the literary universe; too bad some of our fans refused to see this, believing that in order to compliment one they had to diss the other. We had to remind them that it's okay to have your favorite author but he shouldn't be your favorite because another author *isn't;* confiding in one of us that "I like you better than . . ." is an insult, for you're not lifting either of us up if you have to put one of us down.

Being such a beloved figure made him a target for criticism, much of it unfounded and vicious. Some blasted him for not being gay or Black enough (I've often been accused of the reverse); some Black SGL folks felt he had sold out by also focusing on the lives of heterosexual sisters. While the accusations did bother him, he rarely addressed them publically. He heeded the advice he gave me when I was attacked for writing a story in which Black men were the center of their own universe and not bit players in the worlds of white gays or Black heterosexuals: don't get wrapped up in the politics and melodrama. "The most important part of this experience *has* to be what you create. And if it's not bringing you joy, then why do it?" And you could tell he received immeasurable joy from Raymond Tyler, Jr., John "Basil" Henderson, and the dozens of other characters he gave life to; the man *glowed.* He found his passion in life, something many of us aren't lucky enough to discover and follow.

E. was one of the industry's best-selling and most prolific authors. But he was also an ambassador for Black SGL people, taking our stories and our voices into venues and spaces we weren't before. Not only did he do us proud, he encouraged us to be proud of ourselves. *Invisible Life* and *Just As I Am* were the lifelines that many, conflicted over their sexuality—and doubtful that they were worthy of love—needed. And, by publishing *Invisible Life* himself and selling it out of the trunk of his car, he was a shining example of naming and claiming ourselves by any means necessary, of not waiting for someone else to do it. He didn't listen to the naysayers who viewed his leaving his corporate job to write a Black gay novel as unwise. His stepping out on faith inspired me and many of the Black authors we have today, regardless of sexual orientation, to do it, too.

There will be those who bite, mimic, imitate, and copy his storytelling technique and style, but no one will ever be able to reproduce or repeat it, or have the cultural impact he had. I thank God that I was blessed to know and fellowship with him, and in the process be a witness to history. I lost a friend, a colleague, a big brother, my fraternal twin. He was born to do what he did and he did it like no other—and my life, our lives are so much richer, fuller, and better because he did.

Is It Still Jood to Ya?

James Earl Hardy

August 13, 2003, 12:23 P.M.

"Man . . . you crazy."

Angel said it twice—and not because Raheim didn't hear him the first time. Angel just could not believe what *he* was hearing. His outbursts raised the eyebrows and drew curious glances from a couple of the other diners. They were having lunch at The Pink Tea Cup, a soul food spot in Greenwich Village.

Raheim shrugged. "I ain't crazy."

"Then what you call it? You drivin' the ex that you don't want to be an ex no more to the airport to go mess around with some other dude!"

"They ain't gonna be messin' around."

Angel *glared* at him like he was crazy.

"He's gonna be singin' on his new record, that's all," Raheim argued.

"You keep tellin' yourself that."

"They gonna do a duet, or somethin'."

"He's gonna be spendin' how many days there?"

"Five."

"Right. They gonna be doin' a duet one of them days and a *whole* lotta somethin' on the other four."

"He ain't never been to the ATL, so they gonna be sight-seein', too."

"I bet." Angel leaned in. "You wanna get back together with him or not?"

"You know I do."

"Then how you gonna just hand him over to the competition?"

"He ain't my competition."

"Homie got serious dibbs on ya boi. It ain't no coincidence that he dedicated a song to him on one of his CDs."

"Whatever. Little Bit ain't feelin' him like that."

Angel had to go there, *again.* "He ain't Little Bit no more, man. He left that name behind in the twentieth century."

Raheim's eyes darted to the left. He sucked his teeth.

"And how you know he ain't feelin' him like that? You asked him?"

"I don't have to ask. I know him."

"No, you don't. You tryin' to get next to a totally different person now."

"*I* know his heart," Raheim snapped. "That ain't changed."

"But his heart ain't what homie plans on pullin' and tuggin' on. And I've seen that dude in action: Brutha can sing, is hella-sexy, got charisma—and *azz.* Jazz was about to lose it at that concert, especially when he came over and sung to him, and then afterwards when he took a pic with him. But I couldn't get upset: he coulda sung *me* outa my drawers. And they gonna be singin' *to* each other? Man, I'm tellin' you, if I was you—"

"You *ain't* me, a'ight?"

Angel sighed. "A'ight." Angel's cell gonged. "It's Jazz. I'm gonna take this outside." He rose and walked several feet toward the restaurant's front entrance.

Raheim knew that everything Angel said made perfect sense.

Yes, there was the distinct possibility that this business trip could turn into pleasure; along with Mitchell's admission about the liner notes dedication, there was the mystery man Mitchell "spent the night with" in 1995 when Raheim was in L.A. making his first film. Mitchell never gave that mystery man a name but Raheim was pretty sure that Montee was him. But he certainly couldn't ask Mitchell not to go—they were getting to know each other again and hadn't even been on their first official date. Sure, they both attended the kindergarten graduation of Destiny, Mitchell's daughter; the high school honor roll induction ceremony of Errol, Raheim's son; and visited the Vietnam War Memorial in D.C. on Father's Day to pay respects to Mitchell's father, who was killed in combat in 1972. But they were always surrounded by their children (and others).

By volunteering to take him to the airport, Raheim wanted to send the message that he was indeed a different man from the one Mitchell was with years ago (there's no way the younger, jealous, possessive, territorial, self-absorbed Raheim would've supported him going—and he sure as hell wouldn't have taken him to the airport), and that he didn't feel threatened by Montee. Also, it would be Mitchell's first time flying since 9/11 and Raheim wanted to be there to see him off since Destiny would be with her grandparents in New Jersey and Errol was in Philly visiting Temple University with his best friends, Sidney and Monroe. Naturally, knowing that Raheim would be driving Mitchell to Newark scored him major points with both their children, who were more than eager to see their fathers reunite. But there was also an added bonus: the last familiar face Mitchell would see would be Raheim's, and Raheim was hoping that maybe his face would stay on Mitchell's mind all five days, preventing him from *going there* with Montee—if they hadn't already.

Angel returned. "Jazz said hay and to give you a message."

"What?"

"Pack a bag and follow him."

"What? Why would I do that?"

"Why? M-o-n-t-e-e."

"Man, I can't do that."

"Why not?"

"I wasn't invited!"

"You ain't joinin' their party. But you *can* try to spoil it."

"How?"

"By showin' up wherever they go—with a phyne mutha-fucka on ya arm."

"And I betcha Jazz knows a coupla bruthaz down in the ATL who fit the profile and will gladly play the part."

He held up his cell. "A couple? He can line you up with a brutha every day he down there."

Raheim laughed. "Jazz needs to stop watchin' soap operas; this ain't *Gays of Our Lives.*"

"You let Mitch go down there solo and it will be."

"I trust that whatever goes on down there is gonna stay down there."

"He ain't goin' to Vegas!" Angel shouted.

"He knows what's waitin' back home for him. So, even if they end up . . . doin' somethin' . . . I know it ain't gonna compare to what he knows we gonna have. You know what they say: 'If you love somebody, set 'em free.' "

Angel frowned. "Man, that's a song."

"And it's real life."

"I swear, you soundin' more and more like Dr. Phil every day."

They grinned.

Angel stirred his lemonade. "There's one thing you *gotta* do before he gets on that plane."

"What?"

"Tell him how you feel. And seal it with a kiss. At least you'll get a dibb in before Mista Montee."

Now, *that* Raheim planned to do. But he hadn't settled on *when* he'd make that move. He'd been playing the different scenarios over for days and each one had a serious con . . .

When he arrives at the house? No, that would be too soon.

When they're leaving for the airport? No, it might give Mitchell the impression that he expected it as a reward for giving him a lift.

Before they exit the car at the airport? No, he wanted to be toe to toe, eye to eye, face to face, in each other's arms when they shared what would be their first kiss in the twenty-first century.

After Mitchell checks in and before he goes through security? *Hell* no. Raheim had become much more comfortable in his own skin as a man who loves men, but not *that* comfortable. Unfortunately, that would be the ideal time to do it—especially since they would most certainly hug when saying good-bye. So, while he might not be ready to do something like it, he might have to get ready.

Of course, Mitchell could solve all of this by tackling Raheim (which, despite Raheim's taller and larger frame, wouldn't be hard to do when Raheim's very willing to be taken), tonguing him the fuck down only the way Mitchell knows how to (Raheim just *shivers* thinking about it) and, instead of heading to Atlanta, locking Raheim up in love for days (yeah, 'til the cops comes knockin').

Uh-huh, wishful thinking.

3:00 P.M.

This was the interview of Mitchell's lifetime.

He'd profiled your usual suspects in the celebrity department: singers (Alicia Keys), rappers (Jay-Z), actors (Alfre Woodard), sports figures (Venus and Serena Williams), models (Tyra Banks), dancers (Savion Glover), politicians (Maxine Waters), even porn stars (Tiger Tyson). Most were gracious and engaging; some were self-absorbed; and a few, downright obnoxious. Most were entertaining; some enlightening; and a few, totally clueless (in one case, the publicist was actually answering most of the questions for them). No matter who it was or what mood they were in, one thing remained the same: Mitchell never got caught up in their spotlight. Even with the heavy hitters like Patti LaBelle, Bill Cosby, and Sidney Poitier, he wasn't the least bit star-struck; he always left his fan hat at home.

Not this time. Mitchell was genuinely . . . well, *giddy* about his subject. He was so excited that he barely slept the night before and arrived at Jack's Joint, a restaurant in SoHo, a half-hour early so he could cool down before the interview.

But his palms became sweaty the moment the world's most high-profile Black SGL man—best-selling author E. Lynn Harris—breezed through the entrance.

Mitchell thought he'd be taller but that was because he looked up to him. E. Lynn was dressed in white. The smile was even more radiant in person.

"Mr. Crawford?"

"Yes," Mitchell croaked, the word stuck in his throat.

E. Lynn extended his hand. "So good to meet you."

"Believe me, the pleasure is mine. Thanks so much for taking the time to meet with me."

The maitre d' approached them. "Ah, Mr. Harris, so glad you'll be dining with us this afternoon."

"Thank you, Jonah."

"Your table is ready. If you and Mr. Crawford will come this way . . ."

They followed Jonah to a booth, hidden from the main dining hall.

E. Lynn settled inside. "Not only is the dessert here to die for—so is the view."

They turned toward the window as a very muscle-bound brutha, wearing just cargo shorts and sandals, bopped by.

"There's a New York Sports Club around the corner, and a modeling agency just a few doors down," E. Lynn explained. "I've received *lots* of inspiration, sitting right here."

"I bet. How many years have you been coming here?"

"At least seven."

"I'll certainly partake of the view. But I'll have to pass on the dessert."

"*You* cannot be on a diet."

"No."

"Then, please, you have to join me. You will not regret it—and I can indulge without feeling guilty."

Mitchell didn't regret it—the fudge brownie cheesecake *was* to die for. E. Lynn had a slice of sweet potato pie with a scoop of banana nut ice cream.

Mitchell figured the real juicy stuff would be revealed *after* the tape recorder was turned off—and it was. They were no longer interviewer and interviewee—just two bruthas shooting the breeze over a bottle of Dom Perignon. E. Lynn felt comfortable enough to disclose the names of one of the professional football players and an R&B singer he'd been involved with—as well as the melodrama that came along with it (which included clandestine meetings and baby mamas).

Mitchell didn't expect he'd be baring his own soul, but E. Lynn turned the tables and began interrogating him.

It all began after another of E.'s secrets was revealed: he wants to be a father. That, of course, led to Mitchell pulling out his wallet and going on and on *and on* about Destiny.

"*My*. She is a baby doll," E. expressed, like many before him. He then noticed the picture tucked behind the others that Mitchell wasn't showing him: Raheim and Errol, after Raheim received his G.E.D. "Now, who is *that* fine man?"

Mitchell chuckled. "My ex."

"He looks familiar."

"His name is Raheim Rivers. He's an actor/model."

E. Lynn connected the dots. "Right. The All-American man."

"Yes."

"I always heard stories that he was family." E. studied the pic. "His son?"

Mitchell nodded.

"He's definitely a chocolate chip off the old block."

They laughed.

"How long has he been your ex?"

"Four years."

"And when was this taken?"

"Seven months ago."

E.'s eyebrows rose. "Does he know you're carrying that picture around?"

"No."

"Then he doesn't know you're still carrying *him* around."

"Huh?"

"It's not just another memory, like the slideshow of Destiny. It's the man he is today. That means you're still carrying a torch for him, today. Does he know?"

"I . . . think he does."

"You think?"

"I'm sure he does."

"You're guessing. When do you plan on telling him?"

"I . . . I don't know."

"You better know soon. Is he in New York?"

"He is."

"Is he involved with someone else?"

"No."

"So, what are you waiting for?"

"Well . . ."

"Hold it. Before you get into *that*, let's start at the beginning— and get ourselves another round." He motioned for the waiter.

Mitchell started at the beginning—a decade ago, when they first met at Harry's bar (E. confessed he had some "really wild times" there). After nearly an hour, he'd recapped their history, leading up to Errol's fifteenth birthday party two months ago.

"Now, that is one rollercoaster of a relationship. It's the stuff that best-sellers are made of," E. observed.

"You have my permission to use it," Mitchell assured him.

"*Me?* Why can't *you* write it?"

"Me?"

"Yes, you."

"I couldn't do that."

"Why not? You *are* a writer. And a damn good one."

"How do you know?"

"Because of the way you approached our interview. You didn't ask me about things you could find in my bio or a press release. You asked questions I hoped others would have for years. In fact, I have a feeling that a lot of what we talked about won't end up in *Ebony*."

"Actually, there's a Black gay magazine in Atlanta, *Clikque*, that I'll be doing an article for, too."

"See. Insightful *and* resourceful. You should be running your own magazine. This was one of the best interviews I've ever done."

"Thanks. But I've never written fiction before."

"Join the club! I never thought I could, either. Besides, no one will tell this story better than you. Think about it. We can never have too many Black love stories."

Mitchell couldn't disagree with that.

"So, back to the question that led us down this road: what are you waiting for?"

"Things are . . . complicated."

"They don't have to be. Cook that man his favorite meal and invite him over this weekend."

"I can't. I'll be out of town."

"Oh? Where are you headed?"

"To Atlanta."

"Ah. Business, pleasure, or both?"

"Probably both."

"Of course. How can a Black man go to Atlanta on business and *not* find some pleasure?"

They laughed.

"Are you staying with a friend?"

"Yes."

"What kind of friend is he?"

"What kind?"

"Yes. Is he a friend"—E. Lynn leaned in with a smirk—"or a *friend?*"

Mitchell giggled. "He's a . . . special friend."

"Hmm . . . what's his name?"

"Montee Simms."

E. Lynn did a double take. "Montgomery?"

"Yes. Do you know him?"

"I do." He grinned. "You will not be able to resist that man. *Be-lieve* me."

"You and Montee?"

"We . . . shared something, for a brief time."

"How brief?"

"A few months. Many, *many* moons ago."

"What happened?"

"Well, this was before I became more . . . comfortable with myself. Montee was already there; he was *always* there. How could he not be, having parents who were bisexual? Being from Little Rock, we had a special connection, a lot in common. The people, the places, the schools. But . . . it wasn't enough."

"Did you love him?"

"I couldn't love him. I didn't know how and I didn't believe I was worthy of it. I was still trying to love myself. And, the truth was . . . I wasn't in a place to do either one. So we broke up. I told him, 'Whoever snags you will have captured some Heaven on earth.' I guess that lucky man is you."

"No."

"No? Then why else would you be taking this trip?"

"Montee and I have already discussed my situation. He knows I'm not in a space to pursue something with him."

"His head may know it, but his heart? He is a very passionate—and persistent—man. And, I'm sure Raheim is, too. I wouldn't want to be in your position."

"My position?"

"On one hand you have the love of your life; on the other . . . *Montgomery*. Torn between two bruthas. You go to Atlanta, and the game plan will change. You will have some choice to make."

Mitchell considered what he said. "You don't think I should go."

"I can't say. Only you know what's best for you, what'll be good for you. Maybe you and Montgomery *can* only be special friends. But this is really about you and Raheim—or whether there will be a you and Raheim again. Something is holding *you* back. Are you afraid?"

Mitchell sighed. "I am."

"You have every right to be. If you two give it another go, it'll be the third time. But it sounds like you two have something that many of us pray for. So . . . don't stop believing in love, Mitch, 'cause love won't stop believing in *you*." He raised his glass. "To love."

Mitchell followed suit. "To love."

Clink.

August 14, 2003, 3:55 P.M.

Raheim knew Mitchell would be preparing one of his favorites for their late lunch. And he was: fried chicken, succotash, and cornbread. So Raheim wore what he hoped was still an outfit Mitchell loved to see him in: a bright orange tank, orange and black checkered pants (which Mitchell purchased in Honolulu), and sandals.

The look on Mitchell's face when he opened the door told him he had.

Mitchell also enjoyed watching Raheim eat. They didn't say much during the meal; they didn't have to. As Mitchell wrapped up and stored the leftovers, Raheim loaded the dishwasher.

"That was *so* jood," Raheim raved.

"Thanks. Glad you enjoyed it."

"You should give my Moms the recipe; I know she'd love it."

"Doesn't she have one?"

"I don't ever remember her makin' it."

"I wouldn't know how to write it down. There is no recipe."

"There isn't?"

"No."

"Then how do you cook it?"

"By memory. And smells. I saw my mother and grand-mother make it so often."

"You should try to put it on paper. I might even try to make it."

"You?"

"Yeah, me. I do cook now, ya know?"

"Yes. Now, your version I would have to taste." Mitchell placed three containers in a brown paper bag. "Don't forget your to-go box."

"Ha, you know I won't. Thanks."

"You're welcome."

Raheim closed and started the dishwasher. He looked at his watch. "So, do you want to head out now? We can beat the rush hour traffic."

"Mmm, can we wait 'til 4:30? I'd like to see at least one episode of *Judge Judy*."

"That's fine."

They settled on the sofa in the great room, sitting just a couple of inches apart (as their glasses of lemonade were on the coffee table). They balked as the defendant claimed it wasn't his fault that he was involved in a crash with the plaintiff's car since (1) he didn't ask to drive the car, (2) he was doing the plaintiff a favor by running an errand, (3) he may have run a red light and caused the accident but the plaintiff has insurance and he should take care of any damage through that channel and, besides, (4) what kind of a family member sues another?

Mitchell and Raheim wore the same expression: *Boy, is he gonna get it!*

As Judge Judy was about to go in for the final kill . . . both the television and room light went off. Mitchell grabbed the remote and pressed power. Nothing. He got up and tried it manually. Nothing. Same for Raheim as he flicked the light switch.

"Hmm. Must be a short," Mitchell said, more to himself.

"Let me check the breakers," Raheim volunteered.

Raheim remembered where they were: in the front hall, just before you enter the living area. He opened the compartment and found the prong for the great room, moving it left then back to the right.

"Okay. Have they come back on?"

"No."

Then Raheim noticed that the floor lamp in the living room was off and the clock radio on the end table wasn't blinking. He flipped all six prongs under the first floor banner. Neither the lamp or the radio came on.

"How about now?" he called out again.

"Still nothing." Mitchell headed up the hall. "Don't tell me I'm about to leave town and I've got a burnout in that room."

"Looks like it may be the whole first floor."

Suddenly, there was a flurry of activity outside: cars honking, police sirens, and people chattering. They peered out the window. There was a teenager, a radio on his left shoulder, running in the street. *"Yo, it's a blackout! It's a blackout! The lights are out all over the city!"*

Mitchell and Raheim looked at each other in disbelief. Raheim followed Mitchell into the kitchen, where a small transistor radio sat on the window sill. Mitchell turned it on.

"If you're just tuning in, a blackout has hit New York City, Albany, Buffalo, Newark, Baltimore, Detroit, and three cities in Ohio: Toledo, Akron, and Cleveland. According to a Con Edison spokeswoman, a faulty or damaged grid at a plant in Syracuse, New York, appears to be the culprit. Energy officials speculate that, given the reach of this blackout, chances are total power will not be restored to all affected areas until early tomorrow morning."

Their first calls were to the women who brought them in this world. Raheim hit speed dial and #1 on his cell.

"Hi, darlin'."

"Hay Ma. You a'ight?"

"Yeah, just trying to get these remaining customers out of here so we can close up shop." She owns and operates a restaurant off 125th Street called the Chicken Kitchen.

"You need me to come there and help?"

"How are you gonna get here?"

"Drive."

"No, you're not. Folks don't know how to obey traffic signs and laws with the lights *on*. You just stay in Jersey. Are you at the airport or have you already dropped Mitchell off?"

"I'm still here in Brooklyn."

"Oh? You're still in Brooklyn?"

"Yeah. We never got the chance to leave."

"Hmm . . ."

"What?"

"Talk about divine intervention."

"Ma . . ."

"Well, what else *could* you call it? Have you called Errol?"

"Not yet. I will after you."

"And what about your father?"

"He's still asleep. He worked the night shift. I'll call him around six."

"Well, tell Mitchell I said hello."

"Moms says hey."

"Hi, Mrs. Rivers," Mitchell sang.

"He's *still* calling me 'Mrs. Rivers'; don't he know he can call me Mom by now?"

Raheim chuckled.

"Hmph. And after tonight, it'll once again be mother-*in-law*."

"Ma . . ."

She giggled. "You two have fun."

"Call me when you get home."

"I will. Love you."

"Love you, too."

"My turn," Mitchell announced. He didn't get the chance, though; his cell rang. The caller ID flashed: Mom. "Hello?"

"Hi, Daddy!"

"Hi, Sugar Plum. How are you?"

"I'm jood. How you?"

"I'm jood."

"Daddy, you sure?"

"Of course. Why do you ask?"

"Because, the lights went out."

"Yes, they did."

"And you by yourself."

"No, I'm not. Uncle Raheim is here."

"He is?"

"Yes."

"Joody! May I talk to him?"

"Hold on."

Mitchell pressed the loudspeaker button. He placed the phone on the counter, between them.

"Hay, Baby Doll."

"Hi, Uncle Raheim!"

"How you doin?"

"I'm doin' jood. How *you* doin'?"

"I'm jood. The lights out at Grandma's?"

"Uh-huh. Grandpa says we gonna camp out in the backyard if they don't come back on."

"Ooh, that sounds like fun."

"Uncle Raheim?"

"Yeah?"

"You gotta stay with Daddy."

Mitchell and Raheim's eyes met, then returned to the phone.

"Uh . . . you think I should?"

"Uh-huh. He can't be by himself. *Please?*"

"Okay. I will."

"Joody! You and Daddy can camp outside, too."

"*Daddy* is not camping outside," Mitchell interjected.

"You should, Daddy."

"We don't have a large backyard or a tent, like Grandma and Grandpa. So you have fun for me and Uncle Raheim."

"I will."

"And take care of Grandma and Grandpa."

"I will."

"Tell them I'll speak to them later."

"Okay. I love you Daddy."

"I love you, too, Sugar Plum."

"And Uncle Raheim?"

"Yeah, Baby Doll?"

"I love you, too!"

Raheim replied with her hallmark. "And I love you, too, times two!"

Destiny giggled.

At that very moment, their other child checked in. Raheim placed his cell on the counter.

"Hay son," Raheim answered, on speakerphone.

"Hey, Dad. How are you?"

"I'm jood. You?"

"Same."

"Where are you?"

"We just got back to Sid's aunt's house."

"Are the lights out there?"

"No. But you'd think they were. Some of these folks are trippin'."

"Why?"

"There's talk that it's a terrorist attack and the rest of the East Coast will be in darkness soon."

"Make sure y'all stay indoors until tomorrow."

"We will."

"How was the tour?"

"It was cool."

"So, did Temple move up on the list?"

"No. It's still coming in number eleven on the top ten."

"Ha, I'm sure Sid is tryin' to change that."

"Yeah. Looks like this trip made his mind up. At least he won't have to pay for room and board. His aunt has one really hot townhouse. Where are you?"

"I'm in Brooklyn. With Uncle Mitch."

"You are?"

"He is," Mitchell assured him.

"Cool beans." Errol knew full well what *this* meant. "Don't forget about the emergency kit; it will come in handy."

"Emergency kit?" Raheim asked.

"Yes. It has all the necessities for a family facing a crisis like this."

Raheim smiled. "My son saves the day."

Errol blushed. "Oh, that's Mom on the other line."

"Okay. We'll talk with you later."

"Okay. Love you both."

"Love you, too," Raheim and Mitchell responded together.

Silence.

Mitchell sighed. "Uh . . . let me show you the kit."

Raheim followed Mitchell into the kitchen. Mitchell opened the door to the utility closet. He pulled down the silver-pronged tassel attached to the light fixture, forgetting there was no electricity. They laughed.

"You want me to get that?" Raheim asked.

"Thanks."

Mitchell scooted out of his way. Raheim hunched down and lifted up the dark green milk crate. He placed it on the island. He went back for the twenty-four-count case of Nestle Pure Life water, placing it on the counter.

"What possessed him to do this?" Raheim inquired.

"Errol and I were watching *The Day After,* on the SciFi Channel."

"That's the nuclear bomb movie?"

"Yes."

"That was, like, twenty years ago."

"Mmm-hmm. It still gives me chills. He enjoyed it but thought it was dated. I couldn't blame him, since his generation hadn't faced a threat like that. But then, a week later, 9/11 happened. Those images after the Towers fell—they were similar to a nuclear winter. And when he discovered stationery from Goldman Sachs on our roof the next day, it clicked. He realized we have to be prepared for a natural—or unnatural—disaster."

Raheim surveyed the joods: Lay's potato chips, Rold Gold pretzels, SMARTFOOD caramel popcorn, a canister of Planters peanuts, Jolly Rancher hard candy, Werther's caramels, blueberry and raspberry Nutri-Grain cereal bars, Del Monte canned peaches, four cans of Campbell's chicken noodle soup, and a six pack of Canada Dry ginger ale.

And . . . "Ha, I don't have to ask who *these* are for." Raheim held up a box of Sun-Maid raisins.

"She's had her eye on that since he put it in there. That had to be a year ago. What's the expiration date?"

"August 25, 2003."

"Just in time."

"How often does E refresh the kit?"

"Every other month. With his own money."

"Really?"

"Yup. He sees it as part of his responsibility, being the oldest child in the home. He also has us doing a fire drill every other month."

"I bet Destiny loves that."

"She does. She's on whistle duty."

"Whistle duty?"

"It's her job to blow the whistle after Errol yells, 'Smoke!' And Errol times how long it takes us to get out of the house."

"How long does it usually take?"

"I think our personal best has been twenty-eight seconds. And that time, I was in the middle of brushing my teeth."

They laughed.

Raheim took stock of the non-food items: Kleenex tissue packs, utensils, a can opener, three flashlights, four candle sticks, two books of matches, batteries (AA, AAA, C, and D), Tylenol, Pepto-Bismol, Johnson & Johnson's baby oil, Band-Aids, peroxide, rubbing alcohol, cotton swabs, and something he hadn't seen in years: his mini-boom box, which his mother purchased for his sixteenth birthday. It had both a CD and dual cassette deck.

"Wow. I forgot all about this. Does this thing still work?"

"It did when Errol conducted his inventory last month."

Mitchell watched as Raheim examined the knobs and dials as if he were seeing them for the first time. He then checked the back panel; there were already batteries inside. He turned on the power. The volume was on full blast; they jumped back.

Raheim turned it down. "Oops, sorry. It's still one powerful little machine." He fiddled with the tuner and landed on (what was once) one of their songs: Toni Braxton's "Breathe Again."

They blushed.

Raheim spotted a small, rectangular manila folder. "What's this?"

"All the important papers: family contacts, home insurance, life insurance, medical insurance and history, lawyers."

"Wow, he left no stone unturned. The only thing missin' is some green."

Mitchell reached in and grabbed the two rolls of $1 coins, which totaled $20. "He thought of that, too."

"Well, the one thing he *couldn't* store in here is ice. I'll run out and get some. Anything else you want me to bring back?"

"I don't think so. Thanks to Errol, we're set."

"A'ight. I'll be Black."

Mitchell smiled; like *jood*, it was another one of Raheim's trademarks. He hadn't heard it . . . since the twentieth century. It made him tingle.

4:55 P.M.

Now that they were separated, each man immediately contacted those he knew would be the happiest about their being stuck together.

"I hope you're calling to tell me how much you—and Mitch—enjoyed that kiss good-bye," answered Angel.

"Nah. But I will be givin' you a full report about our jood-*night* kiss."

Angel almost tripped over his own feet. "Huh?"

"We didn't get to the airport, because of the blackout. So . . ."

"You'll be stayin' the night! Man, did you dodge a bullet or what?"

"I dodged a bullet?"

"Hell yeah. If he got on that plane, Montee woulda been gunnin' for you. But the universe was lookin' out."

"I guess. Where are you?"

"On Fifty-sixth street. And I got fifty-eight fuckin' more blocks to walk."

"Fifty-eight blocks? Just hop on a bus!"

"Man, you know how long those lines are? It's madness in these streets. By the time I wait to get on one and manage to *get* on one, I could be home."

"Make sure you drinkin' water, man. This heat is no joke."

"That's the only thing I'm carryin'. Left my briefcase at work."

"Cool. So you and Jazz ain't hookin' up tonight?"

"Nah. He's gotta head to Brooklyn to be with his moms.

Which means he's gotta walk over the Brooklyn Bridge. And you know Jazz—he don't like to walk *anywhere*."

Raheim snickered. "I *still* can't believe he wanted us to hop in a cab after hittin' the club—to go five blocks. And not even five city blocks."

"He's wearin' Aldo today, too. He'll probably stop off at Foot Locker and buy some kicks for that trek."

"If he can find one open."

"Knowing him, he will. Uh, you got your Pooquie pack?" That being a dark brown leather back pouch Raheim has had handy just in case a moment like this arrived. It contains a toothbrush, toothpaste, mouthwash, deodorant, four condoms, lube, massage oil, and a very bright pair of orange bikini briefs.

"You know I do. I'll be gettin' it out the car as soon as I get this ice."

"Jood. You better be ready: he ain't gonna be diggin' a trench in you, he's gonna be diggin' a canal!"

They laughed.

For Mitchell, it was B.D. and Gene, two of his best friends.

"*Ooooooooh,*" B.D. squealed. "It's gonna be Bed, Bath and Beyond tonight—and not necessarily in that order."

"Probably more *beyond* than anything else," added Gene. They were at Gene's apartment in Harlem, on speakerphone. "And we know who ain't gonna be happy about *this* turn of events."

"Uh-huh—*Montee,*" B.D. chirped. "Have you talked to him yet?"

"No."

"Well, don't tell him about Raheim," Gene advised. "It's bad enough you can't get there; knowing you'll be spending the night with *Pooquie* will make things worse."

"I feel sorry for Montee," B.D. admitted.

"Why?" Mitchell asked.

"Because, he's been diggin' on you for so long. And, now, on the very night he would finally be diggin' *in* you, the lights go out."

"You are just *so* disgusting," Gene snapped.

"What's disgusting about that? *You* were doing the very same thing an hour ago."

"Oh?" Mitchell inquired.

"Are you going to tell him with *whom* or do I get to spill those beans?" B.D. directed toward Gene.

Gene sucked his teeth. "Carl."

Mitchell was shocked. "*Carl?* When did he reenter the picture?"

"Apparently, two weeks ago. They're now neighbors—he moved in on the third floor."

"And before you say it, this doesn't mean *anything*," Gene argued.

"Of course it doesn't. It just so happens that you, like Mitch, have recently reunited with a very special man from your past—men you both met on the *same* night, in the *same* place."

He's right, Mitchell thought. "Wow. What a coincidence."

"That's no coincidence, hon. Like Shug Avery sang, 'God is tryin' to tell you *both* somethin'.' Looks like Babyface and I will be celebrating our tenth anniversary in February—and I'll be helping you two pick out color patterns for your weddings in June."

"*Oh puh-leeze*," Gene gagged.

Mitchell laughed. "Where is Babyface?"

"He's with Carl, getting some essentials. The Grinch has graciously offered us his apartment for the evening. And I don't have to tell you where *he* will be sleeping this evening."

"You have such a big ass mouth," Gene snarled, just like the Grinch.

"Is the pot calling into question the pigmentation of the kettle?" B.D. shot back.

"Anyway, instead of giving Pooquie a *piece*, you need to give him a serious piece of your mind."

"Like he can't do both?"

"Just because he *can* doesn't mean he *should*. Homie's got a lot of explainin' to do, a lot of apologizin' to do, and a lot of makin' up to do."

"Mmm-hmm, and the very best part of makin' up will be fillin' up each other's cups!"

5:27 P.M.

"Hello?"

"Hi, Mista."

"Hey, Mitch. Glad you called. Do you mind if we have drinks with a couple of friends tonight? I told them all about you and they heard your solo track and love your voice. They'll be leaving town tomorrow morning for a week to meet with Teena Marie. Cash Money just signed her, and we're hoping she'll do one of our songs."

"Well . . ."

"I know, you probably won't want to do anything since you'll be arriving around ten and you haven't flown in some time and may have a little jet lag, but you won't have to leave the house, they would be coming over, and I've told them they can only stay for an hour—"

"Montee?"

"Oh, I'm sorry. I'm just so excited. They don't have to come over. It's your call."

"Haven't you heard?"

"Heard what?"

Mitchell broke the news.

Montee was stunned. "You *gotta* be kidding?"

"I wish I was."

"*A blackout? Now?* Well, do they know how long it's gonna last? Maybe the lights will be back on time for you to make your flight."

"Anything's possible, but it doesn't look like it. The reports say the glitch in the system may not be fixed until the morning."

"Do they even know what happened?"

"They believe it was lightning."

"Lightning?"

"Yes. An electrical storm damaged a grid. The lights are off in Ontario, Canada, too."

"Canada? *Damn.* Well . . . I guess we'll have to play it by ear. You're not at the airport, are you?"

"I'm home."

"At least you won't be stuck sleeping in a terminal chair or on the floor. Are you home alone?"

Mitchell recalled Gene's warning. "Yes. Destiny is at her grandparents'. Errol is still in Philly."

"Ah. Wish I was there with you."

"Me, too."

"Well, I'll keep an eye on the news and just hope things turn around soon. Call if you need me."

"I will. Thanks."

5:50 P.M.

"It's *brutal* out there," Raheim reported, heading straight for the kitchen. "These two sistas almost came to blows over a liter of Deer Park."

"Almost?"

"Yeah. Sista with the natural was about to grab the last one on the shelf when Sista with the cherry blond weave bumped her out of the way and snatched it up."

"She didn't!"

"She did. Then Sista with the natural grabbed her by her weave and yanked her into a display of Hostess cakes and cupcakes."

"Then what happened?"

"I don't know. I was on my way out the door when Sista with the weave was bein' restrained by one of the employees—and pickin' Twinkie cream out of her hair."

"Mph. Some people can really get beside themselves in a crisis."

"Especially when you're told you can't buy something. Like with the water, there was a limit of one bag of ice per customer."

"So you went to four different stores?"

"Yeah."

"You didn't have to do that."

"I figured you'd need extra for the perishables."

"Thanks."

Mitchell already had most of those perishables in one of the coolers. "Do you want your to-go-joodies in here?"

"Nah. I'll be eatin' them in a few."

"In a few hours—or minutes?"

They laughed. Mitchell dumped two bags of ice inside the cooler with the food; Raheim handled the one that contained the beverages.

Raheim took off his backpack and pulled out his CD case. "You'll want to listen to these."

Mitchell unzipped it. The first few names didn't surprise him: Janet Jackson, Mary J. Blige, Sade, Donnie. The next few—Kem, Maysa, Ledisi, Norah Jones, Queen Latifah (post-rap)—a little. And then . . . "*Nancy Wilson?*"

Raheim chuckled. "Yeah, Nancy Wilson."

And not just any Nancy but her two-disc Capitol anthology. Mitchell was impressed *and* proud. "When did you start listening to her?"

"A couple of years ago. Even saw her in concert."

"You did? With who?"

"My pops."

"Are these his CDs?"

"Nah. Ain't no way he'd let me borrow his. He's like, 'You'll enjoy them more if you have your *own* copy.'"

He has really become his father's son. "Do you have a favorite Nancy song?"

He didn't hesitate with his reply. "'Can't Take My Eyes Off You.'"

Even if it wasn't his favorite, Mitchell loved hearing him say it—and Raheim loved the way it made Mitchell blush.

Mitchell then realized there wasn't a single rap CD in the bunch. Could this *really* be the same Raheim Errol Rivers who blasted "Gangsta Bitch" on repeat a decade ago?

Raheim snapped his fingers. "Damn. I forgot Jill Scott. She must be in the car stereo."

"I have her."

"Both of them?"

"But of course."

"*Jood*. That's my girl."

"Oh? I thought Janet was your girl?"

"She still is. They just occupy different places. Speakin' of our favorites . . ." Raheim pulled the present wrapped in gold paper out of his sack. "For you."

"For me? What's the occasion?"

"No occasion." Actually, that wasn't the truth: Raheim planned to give it to Mitchell at the airport. He believed it would be the perfect going-away present, something that would keep him on Mitchell's mind in Atlanta.

Mitchell hadn't received a gift from him in years. It gave him goosebumps. He stared at it.

"Open it."

He did. His expression took Raheim back to Christmas 1993, when he gave him a gold chain that spelled "Little Bit."

Mitchell was *stunned*. He attempted to speak twice but couldn't. Finally . . . "*Where* did you get this?" It was Aretha Franklin's *So Damn Happy*.

"I got my connections," Raheim boasted.

"That is some connection; this won't be released until next month."

"I know."

"Wow. What a wonderful surprise. Thanks."

"We can listen to it while I trounce you in Scrabble." Raheim pointed to the game sitting on the kitchen table.

"You think?"

"I know."

"You said that *two* months ago." They had played with Errol, who won. "And, in case you forgot, you came in *last* place."

"Not today."

"Ha, we shall see."

7:45 P.M.

The final score was 218–171, but Raheim didn't mind losing. As they drank, snacked, and debated whether a foreign word like "muchacho" and the hyphenated "work-study" could be used, Raheim sensed the wall between them coming down. It felt so jood to see Mitchell have a jood time, humming and singing along with Aretha (who was on repeat for the third time), and laughing. Just like the jood old days . . .

And when Mitchell's left knee knocked against Raheim's right and it remained there for almost an hour, Raheim knew he'd made it to first base.

Which is why he began clearing the tiles off the board. "You wanna play again?"

"Really?"

"Yeah."

"Okay. But we should light the candles first; it'll be dark soon."

"A'ight."

They started in the living room. As Raheim struck a match to the apple-tini that sat in the center of the coffee table, his eye caught a stack of photos sitting on the far left.

"*Man.*"

"What is it?"

"Where did you get these?"

Mitchell came over. "Oh, I meant to give them to you the last time you were here. Destiny found them in a shoe box in the basement. I believe you were gathering them to create a collage."

Raheim plopped down on the sofa. Mitchell joined him. They were photos of Raheim's deceased best friend, Derrick "D. C." Carter: in front of his jeep; at a birthday party for his two-year-old daughter, Precious; sitting courtside at a Knicks game; with Treach of Naughty by Nature at a Dallas BBQ restaurant; on the boardwalk at Coney Island; and with Angel. The last one, with Raheim, was taken just hours before he was killed.

Raheim's breathing became heavier. He slightly lowered his head.

Mitchell leaned in closer and looped his left arm through Raheim's right. He rested his cheek on Raheim's shoulder blade. Raheim didn't know if he could count these gestures as getting to second base, but he did, anyway.

They sat like this for about fifteen minutes. Mitchell broke their silence. "I'm sorry."

Raheim lifted his head. "For what? *I'm* the one who is sorry."

"I meant . . . this probably wasn't the right time for you to see them."

"Actually, it is. Ten years. I just can't believe it's been ten years."

"Have you been to visit him in the last few years?"

"Nah."

"You plan to?"

"If you go with me." Raheim has been to D. C.'s grave only once—with Mitchell.

"Of course I will."

Raheim was glad he'd accompany him, but had to change the topic and the mood. "Uh . . . did you tell them you won't be taking the job?"

"I did."

"What did they say?"

"They were disappointed."

"I bet."

"I told them I could become a contributing editor."

"What did they say?"

"They'd rather I was a *consulting* editor."

"Ha, what's the difference?"

"If you're consulting, you still get an office—but no benefits."

"Are you gonna do it?"

"I am. It's what I've been doing since they brought me on board, anyway. But I'll only have to attend biweekly editorial meetings."

"Twice a week?"

"Twice a month."

"How are you gonna consult if you're only in the office twice a month?"

"I don't know, and frankly, I don't care, given what they'll be paying me. It's like I'll still be the editor in chief without the title, perks, bonuses, and long hours."

"Maybe that's their plan: make you love the job so much that you'll want to come on board full-time."

"Maybe, but this will be on a trial basis: I'll be signing a contract for one year and I can't consult with or write for other periodicals during that time."

"They want you on *lock*. Have you told Destiny yet?"

"Not yet."

"She's gonna be too happy. Are you sure this is what you want to do?"

"Yes. Why do you ask?"

"I know how happy you were about the offer and the chance to get back into the workforce."

"I was. But . . . the happy wore off."

They laughed.

"This is the best way for me to test those waters. It could've been a nightmare for all of us if I just jumped back in. It's a jood thing this is a start-up. I really needed these two months to think about it."

"And when does *Rise* rise?"

"November."

"Who's on the cover?"

"Can't tell you, it's a surprise."

"Oh, come on . . ."

"Don't you want to be surprised?"

"How surprised am I gonna be?"

"*Very.*"

"A'ight. I guess I can wait. Did you do the interview with them?"

"No. But I did attend the photo shoot."

"How was that?"

"It went smoothly—even with the photographer showing up forty-five minutes late."

"Now there's a switch."

"It's a jood thing the subject was very patient and humble."

"And what was the photographer's excuse for bein' so late?"

"Traffic."

"Right."

"He'll wish he didn't show up on the set at all when he sees that paycheck."

They laughed.

"Speaking of being on the set: Tell me about *your* shoot."

Raheim became a little more animated. "It was a *lot* of work. But it was also a *lot* of fun."

"It was a *lot* of fun?"

"Yeah. Why wouldn't it be?"

"I guess I didn't think it would be . . . a lot of fun for you."

Raheim knew what he meant. "It got . . . deep, sometimes. And it made me go to some deep places. But I didn't let it get to me; I couldn't. It was his story, not mine. Besides, I was glad to be workin', and workin' on somethin' important. Not many people know about Glenn, especially Black folks, and they should."

"My aunt Ruth remembers him. She used to be a Dodgers fan. She always felt there was *something* different about him. Now she knows what it was."

"And, this was my first movie in three years and it took me out of the steam heat for six weeks. It felt more like a vacation than a job."

"That's what Destiny thought when she got your postcard. It's tacked to her bulletin board."

"They should have some stills for us next week. Wait 'til you see me."

"Don't tell me they put you in an Afro wig, bell-bottoms, and platform shoes."

"Three out of three."

"Oh, no! Did the Afro at least *look* like the real thing?"

"It did. Nothin' like the ones they wore in *The Jacksons: An American Dream*."

"Even your son could tell those were fake, and he was only six when we watched the miniseries."

"The same producers are thinking of doing the Larry Levan story. They want me to play him."

"Wow. That would be juicy. Have you ever spun on the tables before?"

"Yeah. Way back in the day. I rocked a few parties."

"You'll have to talk to Gene. He knew him."

"He did?"

"Yup. He could probably tell you things the producers don't know. The Paradise Garage was like a second home to him."

"Damn, Gene is older than dirt."

"No, he's older than *light*."

They chuckled.

"You better not let *him* hear you say that."

"Hmph, *he*'s said that. I tell ya: first Glenn Burke; Larry Levan may be next. You're gonna have the market cornered on Negro homo bios. Who else is on the list? Bayard Rustin? James Baldwin? *Sylvester?*"

"Funny."

"Actually, I don't think you as Sylvester would be funny. Look at Ving Rhames in *Holiday Heart*. I bet *he* never thought he'd play a role like it. You never know."

"*You* know that ain't *never* happenin'."

"Well, *you* never thought you'd play a closeted pro-baseball player."

Jood point.

"You may have the lead on a few other Negro homo roles. I put in a jood word for you with E. Lynn."

"Harris?"

"Yup."

"When?"

"Yesterday. I interviewed him."

"Cool. Which book is comin' to the screen?"

"They're still working out those details. He recognized you."

"From where?"

"From the picture. In my wallet."

Mitchell didn't mean to disclose that bit of information; he was a little embarrassed. But he shouldn't have been, since Raheim started carrying around a picture of him after Raheim and his ex, Simon, broke up last December. Besides, Raheim didn't need that kind of confirmation to know Mitchell had been carrying him around—the man had been literally raising his son the past four years.

But Raheim could tell it was awkward for him, so he steered them in another direction, again. "It's just about dark. We should light the other candles so we're not bumpin' into walls."

Mitchell appreciated the save. "Jood idea."

11:25 P.M.

Even with the setting of the sun, the house was still humid. So they camped out in the basement, bringing most of the joodies and the boom box with them. Raheim strategically positioned the three battery operated night lights (one propped up behind the futon, the other two on tv tables) so that they formed a triangle.

"You have a jood eye," Mitchell complimented. "If this acting thing doesn't work out, you could be a lighting designer or stage manager."

Raheim chuckled. "I guess I picked up more than a paycheck bein' on location all these years."

Game Two was close for a while—they were both ahead by a few points several times—but Mitchell pulled it out: 239–222. Again, Raheim didn't mind. Mitchell was *glowing*—he never thought he'd see that shine on his face, in his eyes, in his smile again. You'd think they were guzzling champagne all night, seeing how bubbly he was.

With their sandals off and only one of the lights on, they faced each other, bent knees touching. Raheim's left arm extended across the futon just inches above Mitchell's back. Mitchell waved a church fan with his right, providing them with a little breeze and giving them yet another reason to sit close.

So Raheim knew it was the perfect time to ask . . .

"Can I hear some Jill Scott?"

"Sure." Mitchell prepared to stand.

Raheim's hand dropped down and caught his left shoulder. "No. We don't need the CD."

"How else are we going to listen to her?"

"Easy. I know Jilly from Philly can't sing 'A Long Walk' like you."

It was Raheim's favorite Jill Scott song. He often fantasized about Mitchell serenading him with it.

Mitchell blushed. He, too, also fantasized about performing it for Raheim.

The song truly captured this moment; Raheim was *here*, Mitchell was *pleased* and he really did *dig* his company. So much so that, when Mitchell was suggesting they take that long walk a third time, folding his hands into Raheim's seemed like the natural thing to do.

Third base, accomplished.

That final *"Come on"* was Raheim's cue. He leaned in. Mitchell did too.

They dived in—and *landed*.

When they *kissed* . . . it was the Fourth of July, the Macy's Fireworks Spectacular. Like the first time.

Was it Raheim's imagination running away from him, or did Mitchell's lips *still* taste like honey?

It wasn't.

Was it Mitchell's imagination running away with him, or did Raheim's lips *still* taste like Hershey's chocolate Kisses?

Again, it wasn't.

Raheim grasped Mitchell by the waist and pulled him into his arms. Mitchell clutched Raheim's bald head.

They settled back, settled down, and settled into each other, never once breaking their lip lock.

They kissed. And kissed. And *kissed*.

When their lips finally parted, they were, like that first time, out of breath.

Mitchell almost recommended they pull out the futon but quickly nixed that since this would (1) disturb their mood and (2) ruin the cramped yet comfy closeness they were sharing.

So his right cheek claimed its rightful place on Raheim's left pec, taking in his scent. And Raheim breathed in the aroma of strawberries, emanating from Mitchell's locs.

They *exhaled*. Raheim hit a home run. And he was home.

August 15, 2003, 7:55 A.M.

They didn't have a jood night's sleep—it was a jood night's slumber.

Mitchell woke to his locs being caressed. He lifted his head and smiled. "Jood morning."

"That it is."

Smack. Smack Smack. Smack Smack Smack.

Mitchell reached to turn on the radio. "Let's see if the world is still on pause."

"Well, it looks like many New Yorkers will not be returning to work today, as power has only been restored to pockets of Manhattan and Long Island. The only borough no longer in the dark is Staten Island. Con Edison projected that the entire city and surrounding areas would have electricity by one A.M. this morning; now that time has been moved to one P.M. this afternoon."

Mitchell sucked his teeth as he turned down the volume. "And pretty soon they'll be adding another twelve hours to the delay."

"They ain't called *Con* Ed for nothin'."

"Indeed. So, you wanna have some breakfast?" He could hear and feel Raheim's stomach grumbling.

"Like you gotta ask?"

After they brushed their teeth and splashed cold water on their faces, Raheim sat on the floor, his back against the base of the futon; Mitchell was parked between his legs. As Jilly from Philly testified about, among other things, the jood lovin' she was getting from *her* Raheim (a reference that had them both grinning), they shared a package of Entenmann's white powdered mini-doughnuts (Mitchell fed Raheim the last few). They washed them down with orange juice.

They returned to their cramped yet comfortable quarters. Raheim ran his fingers through Mitchell's locs, something he'd longed to do for years. It *relaxed* Mitchell—so much so that he was drifting back to sleep, when . . .

"I wish we could go back."

Raheim's outburst startled Mitchell. "Go back? Go back where?"

"Just . . . go back. Remember when we first met?"

"How could I forget?"

"I was down there, yesterday."

"At Harry's?"

"What's left of it. They shut their doors."

"Did they? When?"

"Like a couple of months ago."

"Oh, no. Wait 'til Gene hears that. He'll be in mourning for weeks, if not months. That bar was his *other* second home. I wonder why it closed."

"Why else? Gentrification."

"They must've raised their rent threefold. I bet that area really is another world now. I haven't walked that runway down to the pier in years."

"Believe me, you wouldn't recognize it."

"What brought you to the Village?"

"I . . . just went to see."

"Went to see what?"

"To see . . . us."

"Us?"

"Yeah."

"And . . . did you?"

"I did. There was this couple. Hangin' out near the Path station, on Christopher."

Mitchell giggled. "Pooquie and Little Bit, the sequel?"

Raheim hadn't heard his nickname come out of Mitchell's mouth since . . . well, the twentieth century. Mitchell wasn't calling *him* Pooquie, but it still gave him the chills. "Yup. Except this Pooquie had a head full of twists and this Little Bit was bald."

"Did your namesake have on your favorite b-boy outfit?"

"Yeah. A wife-beater, black Sean John jeans, and, of course, Timbs."

"And mine?"

"He musta just come from the office, 'cause he still had on his corporate gear: navy blue slacks, white shirt, powder blue striped tie, black shoes."

"Opposites still attract."

"When they looked at each other. Held hands. Held each other. And kissed . . . it was like summer of ninety-three all over again."

"How long did you watch them?"

"For, like, a half hour. I wanted to go up to 'em."

"What would you have said?"

"To . . . really hold on to what they got. To . . . let him love you."

Smack. Smack Smack. Smack Smack Smack.

With *that* door opened, Raheim decided to walk through it. "Uh . . . are you still angry with me?"

Mitchell didn't miss a beat. "I haven't been angry with you since the twentieth century."

"That long?"

"Yes. Why, you *want* me to be angry with you?"

"Nah. I guess . . . I just couldn't blame you if you still were."

Mitchell sighed heavily. "I don't know if I should say this . . ."

"If you don't know, that means you *should*. It's probably somethin' I need to hear."

"It . . . it wasn't a nice thing to think. It wouldn't be a nice thing to say out loud."

"You can tell me."

"Well . . . I wished you were dead."

Raheim wasn't expecting to hear *that*. "Whoa."

"Told you it wasn't nice."

"Guess I don't have to ask why."

"Maybe you do. Not because of what you did."

"No?"

"No. I . . . I guess I felt it would be easier for me to go on without you if you were no longer around. You . . . you *were* dead to me, in a way. But I think it might've been easier for me to accept your . . . being gone if you were *really* gone. At least then I could grieve, and move on. But knowing you were out there, with . . . someone . . . I couldn't just grieve and move on. There was . . . I guess . . . a chance. Hope. And hoping was so painful."

"I know that feeling."

Silence.

Raheim squeezed him. "I'm sorry, Baby."

Baby. No one has ever called him that the way Raheim has. It was *so* jood to hear it; it gave him the chills. And while he knew Raheim was sorry, seeing him say it with his eyes was the assurance he needed. "I know."

Raheim *squeezed* him. "You won't be feelin' that again."

Smack.

11:15 A.M.

It was all about *the quiet*. A sound they hadn't heard in years, a sound they could only hear together. Listening to their heartbeats bounce off each other, breathing in unison. They lay there, still as a statue, as if someone were capturing them on a canvas.

Then something disturbed *the quiet*. It wasn't their cell phones vibrating; neither one had a charge left.

Raheim turned his head in the noise's direction. "You hear that?"

Mitchell strained to make it out. "I do. What is it?"

"The dishwasher."

They smiled. It was time to get out of their sweaty, sticky clothes so they could *get* sweaty and sticky.

Mitchell led Raheim by the hand upstairs, to the master bath. Raheim turned on both nozzles, adjusting the temperature and choosing "jet stream" on the shower head. He watched Mitchell pin his hair back and cover it with a shower cap, then undress standing in front of the mirror. Mitchell watched Raheim do the same.

Mitchell wasn't surprised Raheim was still tight and defined—after all, jood Black don't crack—but Raheim *was* surprised how much tighter and defined Mitchell was. Errol mentioned he was working out more; Raheim liked the results.

Raheim eased behind him. Mitchell titled his head up, and to the right.

Smack. Smack Smack. Smack Smack Smack.

Raheim ushered Mitchell in. Mitchell allowed the water to cascade down his neck, chest, and thighs. Raheim hunched down, wrapping his right arm around Mitchell's waist and lathering him up with his left. Raheim spent the most time pulling on and polishing his dick, causing Mitchell to grind back on Raheim's dick, which grew longer and thicker between Mitchell's cheeks.

Then Mitchell turned so Raheim could do his back; of course, his azz got the most attention. The tip of Raheim's middle finger wiggled its way inside him.

Mitchell grabbed Raheim's shoulders. *"Sssss, oh."*

Raheim gently but forcefully pushed his way in. Deeper . . .

"Ooh," Mitchell shrieked.

. . . and deeper . . .

"Ooh."

. . . and *deeper* . . .

"Mmmm," both Mitchell and Raheim growled.

When it was Raheim's turn to get lathered up, Mitchell dropped the soap. "Oops."

As Raheim bent over to pick it up, Mitchell smacked him on his right azz cheek so hard that Raheim jumped a foot forward. Mitchell laughed.

"A'ight, a'ight. Turna*butt* is fair play," Raheim promised.

He didn't lay one smack on Mitchell's ass; he whacked him a dozen times, six on each bun. No, Mitchell didn't complain—he just got even.

While spreading lots of icing on Raheim's cakes, he also let his finger do the wiggling up inside Raheim—*and* his tongue do the licking on Raheim's left nipple. Raheim huffed and puffed in ecstasy.

As the water washed away the remaining foam and funk, Raheim leaned against the shower wall with Mitchell in his arms, their tongues slow dancing.

12:15 P.M.

After getting nice and clean, they got down and dirty.

They collapsed on the bed—jostling and jerking. They twisted into a 69, feasting on the other's meat, sucking and swallowing and sopping each other up.

Then Raheim assumed the position: on his knees, palms planted on the bed, azz tooted up and out. This could only mean one thing: It was time for Mitchell to bury his face all up in Pooquie's place.

Raheim's azz has a distinct geometric pattern, and before he got to tonguin', Mitchell had to inspect the joods. It appeared that his basketball booty was phatter and plumper—and, no doubt, juicier. Mitchell pinched it, poked it, prodded it. Naturally, that wasn't enough for Raheim.

"*C'mon, Little Bit, don't tease me,*" he pleaded.

The fluttering, the flittering, the flickeration around and on the hole was . . . *indescribable.* Raheim squealed and squirmed with delight, yet Mitchell had to hold him down so he wouldn't escape.

"You *begged* me for it, so keep your azz still!" Mitchell barked.

Raheim obeyed.

The tongue pushed its way in, almost as solid as a finger. Then it folded inward, like a closing book. Then it opened up and twisted around and around and *around.*

With Mitchell getting all tongue-tied up in him, Raheim got all tongue-tied and *imploded;* his dick sprung a serious leak. He was definitely ready for his rump to be rammed—and Mitchell was just the man, the *only* man, to do it.

There happened to be two condoms and two packs of lube on the night table, which Mitchell was planning to take to Atlanta. Raheim grabbed one of each and threw them over his left shoulder. The condom landed on the left cheek, the lube on the right. Mitchell dabbed just a few drops of the lube on Raheim's chocolate-covered berry (Raheim had one of those self-lubricating azzez) and suited up.

"I'm about to take the Pooquie Plunge," Mitchell announced to himself. He'd dreamed this day would come again—it had been exactly four years, three months, two weeks, five days, seven hours, and (give or take) thirty-five minutes since he last took that plunge. He had to say it out loud to make sure he *wasn't* dreaming.

Raheim humped up against the dick head. "Whatcha waitin' for? Come *on.*"

"You're so impatient, Pooquie. Don't you know *jood* things come to those who wait?" He slapped his dick against the azz.

"See, you ain't right. Got me all hot and horned up and—"

Mitchell plunged right on in.

"*Ooof!*" Raheim eeked. Mitchell's bum-rushing his way in was a surprise—but a welcome one. He missed that dick. The way Mitchell *fit*—it was like he'd never left.

And Raheim was *lovin'* it. "*Yeah, Little Bit, go on 'n' claim dat azz.*"

Mitchell was *lovin'* it, too. And he was *claimin'* it. He was on a mission; every stroke . . . no, *slam,* was delivered with precision and purpose. Raheim had a pretty jood idea what each hit meant. . . .

"*This* is for forging a check on my account . . ."

". . . and *this* is for lying about it."

"*This* is for stealing Destiny's piggy bank . . ."

". . . and *this* is for accusing Errol of taking it."

"*This* is for making me feel this was my fault . . ."

". . . and *this* is for not helping me see that it wasn't."

"*This* is for fucking up . . ."

". . . and *this* is for taking so long to get your fucking act together."

. . . and he was *lovin'* every slam. "*Damn, that dick is sick. Get it, Little Bit.*"

He didn't have to tell Mitchell *twice.*

Mitchell wanted to get it *all*—so he grabbed Raheim's ankles and flipped all 220 pounds of him on his back, threw those thick legs back, and plowed back in.

"*Mph, go on 'n' get gangsta wit' it, Little Bit, yeah.*"

Mitchell did. He dove down quicker and drove in harder. As he knocked, the bed rocked.

"*Oh oh oh oh,*" Raheim wept.

Mitchell was committing assault and battery on that azz, but there's no way Raheim would report it to the police and file a report.

Mitchell could tell he was hitting *that* spot: Raheim's eyes rolled back, his calves tightened around Mitchell's neck, and he began speaking in *un*-Holy tongues.

And as Mitchell whipped his dick out, all he could muster was an *"Oh, shit!"* as his gusher blew.

"Oh no, oh no, oh no," Raheim whimpered between short breaths. He was now sitting up. They both watched in amazement as Raheim's dick did its own thing: Without Raheim's hand yankin' or Mitchell lips puckin', the juice just oozed out, all over the shaft, for a full two minutes.

After they caught a few breaths, Mitchell reached for the towels they dropped on the carpet. He wiped himself, then Raheim.

Raheim quivered at just the touch. *"Ah."* He was still experiencing aftershocks from his eruption.

"Was that your first time?" Mitchell queried.

"Yeah."

"Guess your dick has a mind of its own."

They laughed.

"Woo. Thanks, Baby. That was *better* than jood."

"That was better than jood, *times two. I* should be thanking *you.*"

"You *will* be. Turnabutt *is* fair play."

And it proved to be just that, twenty minutes later.

1:05 P.M.

Mitchell also assumed the position, but faced the foot of the bed. This is because Raheim wished to lean back against the headboard and take all that azz in. Because he's small and slender in stature, you can't help but notice how huge Mitchell's azz is—bumped up, bumped out, and ready to be bumped. Whoever came up with "junk in the trunk" must've had his backside in mind. Raheim thought he'd never see it again, in all its glory, like this. So he needed just a few minutes to silently say . . . *Thank You* to whoever or whatever made Mitchell and this moment possible.

But after those few minutes were up, he *pounced*: grabbing it with both hands, spreading those mounds, and chowing down.

"*Oh, Pooquie,*" Mitchell cried out. "*Eat that azz.*"

Raheim fulfilled his command. He savored Mitchell's flavor: caramel cream, with a dash of almond. Raheim was immediately reminded of just how potent it was: It sent a shock through his system. "*Day-um.* You givin' me a sugar rush, Little Bit."

Mitchell also put a rush *on* him: throwing that azz back full force, smothering him. Raheim didn't care: If he was gonna die, at least it would happen doing one of his favorite things.

After some more jood eatin' in Little Bit's hood, Raheim felt that vibration on his fingertips, the signal that Mitchell was achin' to be taken: the azz started buzzin', calling his name. Plus, Mitchell let his hair down; yeah, he wanted to let it *all* hang out. He didn't have to, but Raheim decided to make sure he was reading Mitchell right.

"You want me to tag that azz?" he whispered in Mitchell's right ear.

"Uh-huh."

"What cha say?"

"*Yes, Pooquie, tag that azz.*"

Glad. Ly.

Raheim was already covered, the dick set to go. But he didn't intend on just running up in and running through it, like Mitchell had; he wanted to take it *slo mo.* He'd been dreaming of getting back here for so long and planned on enjoying *every second.*

So he popped his head in—and popped it out, just to make sure he had Mitchell's undivided attention.

He did.

"*Mph,*" Mitchell moaned.

He popped back in—and popped back out.

"*Mph,*" Mitchell moaned again, louder.

He popped back in—Mitchell inhaled, bracing for yet another withdrawal—but Raheim stayed. He then employed the two strokes forward, one stroke back method.

Uh-uh. Uh.

Uh-uh. Uh.

Uh-uh. Uh.

Mitchell got the message: Every time Raheim *pulled* back, he *pushed* back. Mitchell's call of "*Oh*" on the downstroke and Raheim's response of "*Yeah*" on the upstroke blended as their pace gradually picked up.

"*Come on, now, give it to me, baby,*" Raheim almost harmonized like Rick James, his tongue darting in and out of Mitchell's ear.

Mitchell honored his request and began bouncing back on the dick, his tresses bobbing. Raheim bopped forward, accenting each thrust with a swat on Mitchell's azz.

"*Oh yeah, Pooquie, slap it and tap it.*"

Glad. Ly.

Raheim couldn't play it cool anymore: He latched on to Mitchell's waist and began punching the dick up in him. The harder and faster he pumped, the higher and lighter Mitchell's whistle-like groan became. Mitchell continued to gyrate and grind, arching back to kiss him.

Then Raheim hit Mitchell's spot, a spot no other man has ever found. This caused Mitchell to hit an octave that made Raheim's ears pop, pushing them closer to poppin'.

"*Ah, Baby, I'm cumin', I'm cumin', I'm cumin',*" Raheim shouted, slipping out of Mitchell.

Mitchell turned to face him. "*Mph, me too. Ooh-ooh-ooh-ooh.*"

With both hands milking his dick, Raheim blew his top all over his left thigh. As he held on to Raheim's shoulders, Mitchell released onto Raheim's right thigh.

Was it jood sex? No. Was it *better* than jood sex? No. They had just made some better than jood *love*. The tears in their eyes were the proof.

2:15 P.M.

Spent and sent, they settled into a spoon, Raheim bear-hugging Mitchell from behind. They enjoyed more of *the quiet*. Once again, Raheim interrupted it. . . .

"This is better than goin' to Disney World."

Mitchell peered over his right shoulder. "Have you ever been?"

"No."

"Then how do you know it's better?"

"'Cause. I do."

Silence.

"I guess there's only one way to find out if it really *is* better than goin' to Disney World." Raheim grinned. "Let's go."

"To Disney World?"

"Yeah."

"When?"

"Now."

Mitchell turned completely around. "Now?"

"Yeah."

"We can't just *go* to Disney World."

"Why not?"

"Because . . . it's not something you do on the spur of the moment."

"Why not?"

"For one thing, it's something that you plan."

"We plannin' it right now."

"Second, it's the dead of summer. I'm sure the crowds are crazy."

"Ain't no place on earth has crowds as crazy as New York during rush hour."

"Third, airfare would be ridiculously high."

"We can probably find one of those last-minute specials on-line."

"Fourth, we wouldn't be able to find a vacant hotel room in the entire *state* of Florida."

"There's got to be somethin' available."

"And, fifth, do you know how much that will cost?"

"I got a little mad money."

"I can't let you do that."

There he goes again, being the practical one. Raheim missed that voice of reason. "I *want* to do it."

"I know you want to, but . . . there are more important things you can do with it."

"Like, leave it in the bank?"

"Right."

"Well, what could be more important than treatin' my family to a vacation?" He hugged him tighter. "If anybody needs it the most, *deserves* it the most, it's you. And the kids will *love* it."

A smile slowly formed across Mitchell's face. "They're not the only ones."

The house phone rang. Mitchell reached for the receiver with his left hand. "Hello?"

"Hi, Daddy!"

"Hey, Sugar Plum. How are you today?"

"I'm jood. How you?"

"I'm . . ." Mitchell tried to prevent Raheim from snacking on his neck. ". . . better than jood."

"Oh, joody!"

"Are the lights back on?"

"Uh-huh."

"Did you camp outside last night?"

"Uh-huh. I counted the stars, Daddy."

"Really? How many did you count?"

"Twenty-six!"

"Now, that's a lot of stars."

"Is Uncle Raheim still there?"

"He is."

"Ooh. May I speak to him?"

"Of course."

Raheim took the receiver. "Hay, Baby Doll."

"Hi, Uncle Raheim!"

"How you be?"

"I be jood. How *you* be?"

He grinned at her father. "I be *better* than jood, too."

"Joody. Did you and Daddy have a jood time?"

"Yeah, we did."

"Is Daddy still taking his trip?"

"I don't know. You'll have to ask him."

"I don't want him to go."

"No. Why?"

"Because, I want us to take a trip together."

"You do?"

"Uh-huh."

"Well, I guess you'll have to ask Daddy about that."

"I'm askin' *you.*"

Raheim was blindsided by Baby Doll. "Uh. Well . . ." Raheim nudged Mitchell. "I'd love to take a trip with you and Daddy."

"And don't forget Errol."

"Of course. Errol, too."

"If Daddy doesn't go to Georgia, we all can be together this weekend."

"Well . . . I'll try to talk Daddy into it, okay?"

"Joody!"

"Where's Grandma and Grandpa?"

"They on the porch, with Auntie Ruth."

"Well, you tell them all I said hello."

"I will."

"And give your grandma and auntie Ruth a kiss from me."

"I will. Uncle Raheim, tell Daddy I'll talk to him later. And that I love him."

"Okay. I will. I love you, Baby Doll."

"And I love you, too, times two!"

"Jood-bye."

"Jood-bye."

Mitchell hung up the receiver. "I swear, she can hear the word 'Disney World' being said miles away."

The phone rang again.

Raheim pointed to it. "And so can my son."

"No, this cannot be . . ." Mitchell answered it. "Hello?"

"Hey, Uncle Mitch."

Mitchell was flabbergasted. He nodded yes at Raheim. "Hey there, Mista. How are you today?"

"I'm jood. How are *you?*"

"I'm doing jood."

"I bet," Errol snickered under his breath.

But it was loud enough for Mitchell to hear. "What did you say?"

"Nothing."

"Uh-huh." Errol knew that *sumthin' sumthin'* went down over the past twenty-four hours. "How are *you?*"

"I'm jood. I tried reaching you and Dad on your cells."

"They're charging. How was your night?"

"It was cool. We played Scrabble and watched *Harry Potter.*"

"Did you win?"

"But of course."

"I beat your father in Scrabble last night, too."

"Ha, of course you did."

"Your son is ragging on your Scrabble skills," Mitchell informed Raheim.

Raheim spoke into the phone. "He'll be beggin' for mercy when we play again."

Errol laughed. "Is he still picking me up today?"

"He wants to know if you're still coming to get him. . . ."

Raheim nodded. "Yeah. I'll call when I'm on my way."

"He'll let you know when he's on the road."

"Cool beans. Are you coming with him?"

Now Mitchell got blindsided. "Uh, I . . . I don't know."

"You're still going to Atlanta?"

"I . . . I haven't decided yet."

"Oh." Errol wasn't hiding his disappointment.

"I'll make a decision soon. I will let you know."

"Okay. Talk to you later. Love you both."

"We love you, too. Bye."

Mitchell returned to his spot on Raheim's chest.

"Well . . . ," Mitchell breathed.

"Well . . . ," Raheim repeated.

Silence.

"There's probably a T-shirt and shorts you can wear. In that middle drawer. On the right."

That was always Raheim's side of the bureau. *He didn't take my clothes out?*

"While you search the Web for a family package . . . I'll make that phone call."

Raheim wanted to leap out of bed and do a happy dance, but controlled himself.

Mitchell peered up at him. "So . . . let's go get our kids."

"Yeah. Let's."

Smack.

November 18, 2009, 8:00 P.M.

DJ: Yo, welcome to Da Spot! This is DJ Korrupt—and I am *hyped!* I've been trying to get tonight's guests on this show forever. The problem was getting them in the same room. No doubt they are buzy men—buzy representin' *us*. They are the Black gay community's power couple. So, for this special ninety-minute segment, I want to welcome Oscar nominee Raheim Rivers and his hubby, *New York Times* best-selling author Mitchell Crawford. Evening, gents, and thanks for agreeing to appear on the show. . . .

Mitchell: Thanks for the invite, DJ. Glad we could finally connect.

Raheim: Yeah, now you can stop harassing us.

[Laughter]

DJ: Ya know, I had to stay on it. I was beginning to think y'all didn't want to do this small-time webcast blog, bein' in the big leagues.

Raheim: We're in the big leagues?

DJ: Come on, y'all don't have to be modest. Just the other night, you two were on *Entertainment Tonight*.

Mitchell: *Raheim* was on *ET*, they just included some video footage of the family as an afterthought.

DJ: Right. it was just *some* video footage—at the White House with the First Family! Not many of us will have that experience. Now, I didn't plan to get to this topic until later on but since we're there, what do you each think of President Obama's claim that he is a "fierce advocate" for the gay community? It's been a year since the election—is he living up to the title?

Raheim: Ha, you are just jumping right into the pot!

Mitchell: Before I answer, first let me tell you that you *are* the big leagues. Your forum means so much to Black SGL people across the globe.

DJ: Thanks, Mitch. I appreciate that.

Mitchell: And we appreciate you and all you do. So thanks to you, for also representin'. I also want to address this notion that there is such a thing as "the gay community." When people say that, what they usually mean is the *white* gay community, since the faces projected to represent gay and lesbian in this society are white ones. But there are many gay and lesbian commmuni*ties*—geographic, political, cultural, social, ethnic, religious, even sexual.

DJ: A'ight, Professor Crawford!

Mitchell: Same goes for "the black community." That is, the Black *presumably* heterosexual community. But where is it? Where are its headquarters? Who is the President, the Executive Director, the CEO? What is its agenda? And how come I didn't get a membership application?

[Laughter]

Mitchell: Saying that there is *a* singular community of people who all share melanin or sexual orientation allows others to treat that particular group as a monolith. It also erases those people who are both Black *and* gay. For, if these two distinct communities do exist, can we be a part of both or do we have to choose?

DJ: I get what you're saying.

Mitchell: But back to President Obama. The short answer is no, he is not living up to that self-proclaimed title. The long answer: How could he? It was a campaign slogan. So I didn't and don't expect him to wave a magic wand and change things overnight—but that's what some Same Gender Loving people, particularly those of the Caucasian persuasion, expect.

DJ: No you did *not* just say *Caucasian persuasion!*

[Laughter]

Mitchell: I find all the righteous indignation and hand-wringing from white gays and lesbians to be so fake. You expect him to undo DOMA and DADT, and push ENDA through just like that? And, *he's* responsible for our marriage rights being voted away in Maine? Now, he isn't doing what he *could* do: for one, ordering that DADT dismissals be stopped. Those witchhunts are a waste of taxpayer dollars and are destroying lives. Avowed white supremacists can serve openly but *not* gays and lesbians? But saying that "Hillary would've done X, Y, and Z by now"—as if she's done *anything* except walk in a pride parade or two—or, "I'll be voting Republican in 2012"—and you know many of them did in 2008 anyway—tells me you are naïve, delusional, and/or not savvy when it comes to politics.

Raheim: I feel it's too early to be blasting the President as a failure. Look at what he inherited and what he has to try and clean up. And I said *try* and clean up 'cause there's no guarantee he'll be able to fix things. We waited two hundred plus years for a Black man to take the wheel; many of us never thought we'd live to see this day. So I'm willing to give him the benefit of the doubt.

DJ: Given his slow response to gay and lesbian issues, was it difficult for you all to accept the invitation to the White House?

Raheim: The President called—you think we weren't going to go?

[Laughter]

DJ: But in giving him the benefit of the doubt, aren't you ignoring that he believes marriage should remain a sacred union between a man and a woman?

Mitchell: Well, that's what he's saying *today*.

DJ: So you believe that he does support marriage equality but won't publically for political reasons?

Mitchell: I don't believe he cares that much about it one way or another but, because he is a politician, has to take a particular stand that scores him the most points. A decade ago, saying he supported it didn't mean much; but today, it does. The Sean Insanitys, Bill O'Lie-lys, and Rush Limbigots would love to hang the "homo lover" sign around his neck, too.

Raheim: *They* would just love to hang him up by his neck, *period.*

DJ: You know it. You got a way with words, Mitchell. Sean Insanity. I gotta use that one!

[Laughter]

Mitchell: I just wish he wouldn't use religion as a crutch. Even if he honestly believes that, in hetero marriages, "God is in the mix," why even say that? Does that mean the unions of SGL people aren't or can't be blessed by God? Folks said similar things about couples like *his* parents forty-plus years ago, that this so-called sacred institution would be tainted by legalizing interracial marriages.

DJ: Doesn't his using that as a crutch mean he's not a friend of gays and lesbians?

Mitchell: If he's not our friend, does that mean he's our enemy? The president is not standing in the way of our being a couple and living our lives. If he were actively pushing anti-gay laws and propositions, it'd be a different story. And our support doesn't solely depend on where he stands on this one issue. And we don't agree with everything he says or does. You couldn't with any politician.

DJ: Speaking of that so-called sacred institution, you two were officially married in June 2005 in Boston.

Mitchell: Yes.

DJ: I remember seeing that photo of you with your son and daughter. Was that one of, if not *the* happiest day of your lives?

Mitchell: Most definitely one of. Right up there with the birth of our children.

Raheim: And the night we met.

DJ: *Ooh*, the night y'all met. We're gonna get to that in a minute. But back to the wedding: who proposed?

Raheim: I did.

DJ: Was it a surprise, Mitchell?

Mitchell: It was such a surprise that I fainted.

[Laughter]

DJ: You didn't really faint!

Raheim: He did.

DJ: Why did you faint?

Mitchell: Because I never expected him to do it. I figured that if it happened, I'd be the one getting down on one knee.

DJ: Why, 'cause he's not romantic?

Mitchell: Raheim is *very* romantic, always has been. But you have to have an openness about your life and be comfortable in your own skin to take that kind of step. The first three years of our relationship, his family, including his son, didn't know who I really was and what I really meant to him. And given how freaked out he was over my best friends' getting married in '94, I assumed that if anyone would pop the question, it would be me.

DJ: How freaked out were you?

Raheim: Man, I made the mistake of telling him that, since I am uncomfortable attending a gay wedding, that he shouldn't attend either.

DJ: Not attend his best friends' wedding? You was trippin'!

Raheim: I was.

Mitchell: So for him to go from hiding me and hiding us to holding me and holding us up was major.

DJ: I take it you said yes.

Mitchell: After I came to in his arms, yes.

[Laughter]

DJ: Did he put an engagement ring on your finger?

Mitchell: He did.

DJ: And was it a Rock of Gibraltar?

Mitchell [chuckles]: It was.

DJ: Did you go on a honeymoon?

Mitchell: Yes. To the Virgin Islands.

DJ: Nice. How long were you there?

Raheim: Six days.

DJ: Huh. There was a whole lotta baby-makin' goin' on down there!

[Laughter]

DJ: How did your children feel about your getting married?

Mitchell: They were all for it. I've known Errol for most his life; we met when he was five. I think he always knew we were a couple and saw the love between us. So it was easy for him to love me and love us together, and see us as a family. And Destiny has always loved herself some Raheim; he named her and she has a smile for him that she doesn't wear for anyone else.

DJ: We always hear about gay and lesbian teens getting grief for who they are but we never hear about the children of gays and lesbians and what they go through. Have your kids had to face homophobia?

Raheim: Yeah. Before we got married we talked about there being people who hate us for no other reason than we exist, who think we shouldn't love each other or be raising them. We deal with it [homophobia] as a family because when you tell our daughter that she has faggot fathers or try to pick a fight with our son, you are attacking all of us.

Mitchell: Anyone who has stepped to us in the wrong way has learned very quickly that if you fuck with my family, I will fuck over you.

[Hoots, hollers and applause]

Mitchell: I'm sorry, Destiny. Daddy cursed—twice—but it was very necessary.

Raheim: While I've gotten less gangsta over the years, he's gotten more gangsta.

DJ: And who usually steps to you all the wrong way? Blacks? Whites?

Mitchell: Most of the slights and indignities we receive come from folks with melanin.

DJ: Does that bother you more because it comes from folks who know what it's like to be discriminated against?

Mitchell: It doesn't bother me *more*; it just disappoints me. I don't subscribe to the misguided notion that just because a particular group knows what bigotry feels like means they won't act in a similar manner towards others. In fact it's very condescending; there's a "You people ought to know better" tone to many discussions surrounding homophobia in Black America, and that finger-wagging is often coming from white gays and lesbians who are doing less than *nothing* to challenge racism in themselves and others. Well, Black folks have just as much right to be prejudiced as anyone else. Sad fact, but true. That's what makes one human; their faults and foibles. Of course, just because it may be a natural human occurrence throughout history doesn't mean it's acceptable. It is *disgusting* that Bernice King is pissing on her father *and* his legacy.

DJ: Isn't that something? And now she heads the group that Bayard Rustin, a Black *gay* man, helped create.

Mitchell: She is pimping her lineage, holding it up as justification for her bigotry. You want to stand on the side of Bull Connor and George Wallace? That's your thang, do what you wanna do. Just don't insult our intelligence or attempt to speak for a man you never knew. You don't know what he'd think about SGL people marrying or whether the gay rights movement is parallel to the Freedom Movement. But I do believe the woman who gave birth to you, the woman he shared most of his adult life with, the woman who continued his work after he was taken from us, *would* know.

DJ: You are just droppin' the science, Mitchell. We're gonna let folks marinate on *that* and take a break. We'll be right back.

DJ: This is DJ and you're listening to Da Spot. I'm back with my special guests Raheim Rivers and Mitchell Crawford, the country's—if not the world's—premier Black male couple. Now, you have two children in total?

Raheim: Yeah. Our son, Raheim Errol the Third, is twenty-one; he's getting his master's at NYU in aeronautical engineering. And, our daughter, Destiny, is eleven; she just appeared in the Broadway musical, *Billy Elliot.*

DJ: Now, Raheim the Third is your biological son . . .

Raheim: Yup.

DJ: And Destiny is adopted.

Mitchell: Yes.

DJ: Given your public lives, there must be added pressure and stress on all of you. How do you balance the personal and the professional?

Mitchell: There's always going to be stress and pressure— you just have to make them work for you.

Raheim: Like my pops says, "Take it half a day at a time."

[Laughter]

DJ: Half a day at a time?

Raheim: Yeah. You're usually asleep for close to a third of it and spend almost another third just keeping your balance, getting from point A to B.

DJ: Who is the king of the castle?

Raheim: Depends on the day of the week.

[Laughter]

Mitchell: *And* the time of day.

[More laughter]

Raheim: No one rules the roost. We are a team. So there isn't this tug of war over control. And we know each other, we know who should take the lead in something, and don't trip about them doing it. That's a mistake some male couples make, that somebody has to be the boss, the man. . . .

DJ: That, like our boi Joe says, *"Somebody's* Gotta Be On Top."

[Laughter]

DJ: Let's go back to the night y'all met. Give us the when, where, and how.

Mitchell: We met at Harry's bar in the Village.

DJ: Get out! I don't remember seein' y'all there.

Raheim: Probably because we never went back after that night.

[Laughter]

DJ: You remember the date?

Mitchell: June 5, 1993.

DJ: Really?

Raheim: Yup.

DJ: Wow. How do you remember that exact date?

Mitchell: How could we not?

Raheim: Turns out it's also our son's birthday.

DJ: Sweet. So, if you remember the exact date, you gotta remember the first time you saw each other. [Pause] Now, see, y'all should've seen the look they just gave each other. Like it was yesterday, huh? [Pause] See, now they're noddin' and grinnin' like crazy, done got even closer, and holdin' the other's hand tighter. A'ight, let's hear it.

Mitchell: I spotted him coming into the bar.

DJ: You remember what he was wearing?

Mitchell: A green cap, green-striped form-fitting shirt, and khakis tucked inside his Timbs.

DJ: *Day-um!* You had him on ex-ray!

[Laughter]

Mitchell: I did.

DJ: How 'bout you, Raheim?

Raheim: Light brown shirt, brown sandals, and stone-washed jeans that fit him *perfectly*.

DJ: Ha, we know what *you* was after!

[Laughter]

DJ: How long after did y'all know *this is it?*

Mitchell: Three or four months.

DJ: Did it just sneak up on you?

Raheim: Hell yeah. I didn't go looking for it. I was too busy bein' a Mac, just tryin' to get me some. I wasn't even thinking about fallin' in love. Even when I was all in it and it was staring me in my face, I tried to wave it off, ignore it. Even my moms saw it.

DJ: Did she?

Raheim: Yeah. She saw I was mopin' around, had no appetite, playin' nothin' but quiet storm music. She asked, "Are you in love?" And it *hit* me.

DJ: *Bam!*

[Laughter]

Mitchell: It was definitely lust at first sight. I didn't think something else would grow out of it. Which proves that you really can't judge a book by its cover.

DJ: So you two have been goin' strong ever since.

Mitchell: We broke up in '99 and reunited in '03.

DJ: Really? What happened?

Raheim: My addiction took over my life.

DJ: Oh, your gambling?

Raheim: Yeah.

DJ: I'm sure there must be listeners who are or know someone who is going through the same thing. Can you talk a little about it?

Raheim [sighs]: I just got caught up, man.

DJ: In?

Raheim: In being a celebrity, in wanting to be some-body. I lost myself and lost sight of what was really important. All that mattered was gettin' that high.

DJ: Ah. Your separation must've been really hard on the kids.

Raheim: My Baby held it all together for us; he did a better than jood job of protecting them.

DJ: I was just *waitin'* for you to say my favorite word!

[Laughter]

Raheim: Jood?

DJ: You know it. I see I have been sayin' it the right way. And it does mean better than good . . . ?

Raheim: Yup.

DJ: Cool. But I'm sorry, didn't think you'd use it discussing something so heavy. Go ahead.

Raheim: Uh, it was probably the hardest on me because I fucked up my life and almost fucked up my family's, too. Uh, sorry, Baby Doll. I shouldn't have cursed but, like with your daddy, it was the right word to use.

[Laughter]

DJ: I take it Baby Doll is what you call Destiny?

Raheim: Yeah.

DJ: Cute.

Raheim: The old saying that "You don't know what you got

'til it's gone," is so true. I was really in pain, physical pain those four years we were apart. That pain didn't disappear until we were back together.

DJ: Mitchell, did you believe that Raheim would conquer his addiction and you would reunite?

Mitchell: In my heart, I did. When he became sick, we became sick. I tried everything I could to help him get well but had to face the reality that the only way that would happen is if *he* wanted to get well. I did a lot of praying that he would.

DJ: You did an episode of *Intervention*, helping a family confront a woman about her gambling. Is that how you finally faced your addiction?

Raheim: No. I just had one of those lightbulb moments. Lookin' in the mirror . . . I *hated* what I saw. I knew I needed help. So I reached out to the one person who would know what I was going through.

DJ: Who was that?

Raheim: My pops. He's been clean and sober for twenty years.

DJ: And you?

Raheim: Nine years, seven months, and eleven days.

DJ: Congrats, man.

Raheim: Thanks.

DJ: Apart for four years. Ha, I know y'all made up for lost time!

[Laughter]

Mitchell: You can never really make it up. You can only make the best of the time you have now.

DJ: I noticed that neither of you have adopted the other's name, something that most gay and lesbian couples do. Is that because of your careers? Is it a political statement?

Raheim: Well . . . he's my Baby, he's my man. If you ask me, I'll tell you that. If I feel you need to know, I'll tell you. I don't have to take his name for you to know it. I walk it every day. I talk it every day. I live it every day. We are one but we are also our own men.

Mitchell: It's also about defining what being a couple means for us. The whole hyphenated thing . . . it's a little *too* traditional.

DJ: What do you mean?

Mitchell: Our mothers took our fathers' names in marriage but that doesn't mean SGL people have to adopt that tradition. We don't belong to each other, we don't own each other and that's what the hyphenated names signal to me.

DJ: Are your parents supportive of your marriage and the family you've created?

Raheim: No doubt. My moms has always been on board, even before I was. [Laughs]

DJ: What do you mean?

Raheim: Well, they say mothers always know. And she did. When I brought Mitchell into the picture as Errol's godfather, she saw right through it.

Mitchell: And it didn't help that you never brought another girl around after Errol's mother.

Raheim: Right. She loved Mitchell but I was so afraid of what she would say or do, whether our relationship would change that I couldn't see that she was happy for me—she saw how happy Mitchell made me and Errol. It took me some time but I finally got there.

DJ: How about your mom, Mitchell?

Mitchell: She's been in our corner from the start, too. I think her being so supportive is linked to losing her brother to AIDS in the eighties. He was afraid to be truthful about himself and almost died alone. So she made it easier for me to come out to her.

DJ: What about your fathers?

Mitchell: Well, my biological father was killed in Vietnam.

DJ: Sorry to hear that.

Mitchell: My mother remarried and my stepfather—well, I had to work on him.

DJ: Was he homophobic?

Mitchell: More heterosexist. He, like most hetero men, believed the world is supposed to spin on a heterosexual axis. For them, it's not that all men are born straight but they are *supposed* to be straight. And, of course, everything he knew about SGL people he learned from other straight folk.

DJ: The blind leading the blind.

Mitchell: Definitely. Today, he's an ally. He's also one of my biggest fans.

Raheim: My pops has come a long way in that department, too. At first he blamed himself for me not being straight.

DJ: Why did he blame himself?

Raheim: You know, that whole "If I was around, you wouldn't have turned out this way."

DJ: Isn't it amazing how many people still believe a myth like that today?

Raheim: Yeah. But it's easier to hold on to the myth when the truth forces you to question all you've been told or exposed to your whole life. Once he saw that his son was still his son and it didn't matter who he loved, he was able to face those hang-ups.

DJ: He must have because I have that ad you did with your father and son for the National Black Justice Coalition. For those not in the know, the NBJC came up with this tight campaign to fight homophobia in the Black community . . . uh, forgive me, Mitchell.

[Laughter]

Mitchell: No problem. We're used to saying it.

DJ: That'll be one hard habit to break. But they used real-life father and son pairs. In your case, it was three generations. How did that happen?

Raheim: They approached me through my agent. I was more than happy to do it.

DJ: Were you afraid that really putting it out there like that would have a negative impact on your career?

Raheim: I wouldn't want to be associated with or do business with anybody who felt that standing with my family in truth was a bad move.

DJ: *Tell it!*

[Laughter]

Raheim: It was something I had to do. There are too many families that are torn apart because of homophobia, and too much silence surrounding it. It's a crisis we can't afford to continue to overlook. Our hearts broke hearing about that little boy who killed himself after being bullied. What was his name, Baby?

Mitchell: Carl Joseph Walker-Hoover.

Raheim: His classmates were using "gay" as a weapon, to taunt him; now where did they learn that from? People aren't born prejudiced; they soak it up and then wring it out on others. I'm lucky that I have a father and son who respect and love me for all that I am. I hope the campaign encourages more of us to do the same. Well, I know it has; we've gotten lots of positive e-mail and feedback on the streets about it.

DJ: Did your father or son have any reservations about doing the promotion?

Raheim: Not at all. In fact, we all became members of the organization. It's one of the few groups out there that gives us a voice, so folks should definitely check them out and support them.

DJ: Have you been treated like a spokesperson for the bisexual community? Just saying that out loud made me realize how absurd it is.

[Laughter]

Raheim: I have. On one level, I don't mind it. Bisexuals aren't a very visible group so I understand why people zero in on me and want to ask questions. But, like with any other so-called fill-in-the-blank community, just because you've spoken to one of us doesn't mean you've spoken to all of us. This woman once asked me if I knew her brother in Des Moines who is bi. I had to keep myself from crackin' up.

DJ: Now, I would've cracked up on that. We're gonna take another break. Stay tuned 'cause there's more to come with Raheim and Mitchell.

DJ: Welcome back to Da Spot. I'm DJ Korrupt and we're still rappin' with Raheim Rivers and Mitchell Crawford. Let's talk about your careers. Raheim, you've got one impressive credit list as an actor.

Raheim: Thanks.

DJ: I mean, you've been a guest on so many television shows—and I ain't talkin' 'bout the usual slots reserved for us like Gangbanger #1 and Menacing Thug #2.

[Laughter]

DJ: *Desperate Housewives, The Wire, Without a Trace, NCIS, Half & Half, CSI: NY, Everybody Loves Raymond, Cold Case, The DL Chronicles.* And you are the *king* of the *Law & Order* franchise. I counted fifteen appearances, split among the original, *Criminal Intent,* and *SVU.*

Raheim: Dick Wolf has been jood to me.

DJ: I caught you on both *The No. 1 Ladies' Detective Agency* and *Meet The Browns* last night. Talk about two totally different universes!

[Laughter]

DJ: And *The Ex Factor* is in its second season, right?

Raheim: Right. On the FX Network. Monday nights at ten, EST.

DJ: Being an out and proud family man, has it been a challenge portraying a womanizer?

Raheim: Well, I played straight for more than half my life, so I had a lot of experience to draw from.

[Laughs]

Raheim: But seriously, it's called *acting* for a reason.

DJ: I understand your character wasn't written for a Black actor. Is that true?

Raheim: It is. One of the executive producers of the series knows my agent and thought of me. But I just knew it was a waste of time when I got to the audition; there were nothing but blond surfer boy types. So I was shocked when I was asked back for the second round—and even more shocked when I got the call the next day that I had the part.

DJ: The beauty of nontraditional casting.

Raheim: I suppose. I give them credit for seeing that someone white didn't have to play the role—and that they didn't have to "black it up" for me.

DJ: "Black it up?"

Raheim: Matt has the same name, same family background, same occupation, and the same character history he did when I first read for the part. And they haven't come to me with suggestions to make him more "ethnic."

DJ: You've actually been told by other producers or directors to "black it up"?

Raheim: Yup.

DJ: Damn. I guess I already know the answer to my next question: Have you experienced more racism or homophobia in your career?

Raheim: I'd say I've experienced more racism. White actors don't have to worry about whether they will fit the profile because they *are* the profile—over ninety percent of the roles out there are still written for them. And why wouldn't they be, since

198 / James Earl Hardy

over ninety percent of those roles are written by whites. We are still pegged into boxes, drawn as stereotypes or caricatures. There are very few multi-dimensional roles written for us. So wherever you can fit in, you have to get in.

DJ: Have you ever been asked, when playing a gay role, to "gay it up"?

Raheim: Ha, no. I doubt most actors hear that, since most gay characters are off the rails, just flaming out.

DJ: There's nothing wrong with gay characters who are; after all, those men exist.

Raheim: They do but they usually aren't there to add any depth to the story, only to keep the audience in stitches. And the audience isn't laughing *with* them—they're laughing *at* them. Instead of just telling the joke, they *are* the joke. That kind of gay man is not as threatening as one who looks, talks, dresses and acts like a so-called straight man.

DJ: Along those same lines, I would think that, being bisexual, you're probably less threatening to some in the biz.

Raheim: How?

DJ: You know, you're not gay *all* the way, you're in the middle, so they see you as half-straight.

[Laughter]

Raheim: I don't think they give it that much thought, DJ. We're talking about Follywood. If it's an issue at all, I'm sure it's that I'm not straight *all* the way.

DJ: Do you know or know of any closeted actors?

Raheim: Of course!

DJ: Do they speak to you about whether they should come out?

Raheim: A few do. Most are just terrified of being found out.

DJ: Can you give us a hint about one our audience would be pleased to know is family?

Raheim: Nah, can't do that.

DJ: C'mon, just one hint. I'm willing to bet it was at least *one* brutha in *Stomp The Yard*.

[Laughter]

Mitchell: Well, at *least* one.

DJ: Can't blame me for trying. What did you think about the whole Terrell Carter episode?

Raheim: Episode, that's a jood way of describing it. The man earns his bread and butter doing churchified plays; what did folks expect him to say when those compromising pics hit the Web?

DJ: "Yeah, it's me; so what?"

Raheim: Not everybody is ready for that, not everybody is up for that. There's a reason why the down-low exists. Men— *and* women—know that being open has consequences, and some don't want to deal with it.

DJ: You're dealing with it like a pro, from where I sit.

Raheim: Thanks. But I gotta admit that, if I hadn't met my Baby or fallen in love with somebody like him, I probably wouldn't be sittin' in this chair right now.

DJ: Is it hard being one of the only out Black performers?

Raheim: Not really. Because I'm not gay or straight, most folks just don't know how to approach it so they leave it alone. They don't believe bisexuality exists.

DJ: Do you think that's why, even with your profile and credentials, you are all but ignored by the gay press? I've seen more coverage on Mitchell in gay media than you.

Raheim: You'd have to ask them.

DJ: I mean, you are a man, a *Black* man, who is unapologetic about his love for another man, and you are a *working* actor, a notable actor. You should be on the cover of *The Advocate* and *Out*. Mitchell, any thoughts on that?

Mitchell: I think he'd have a better chance of being on the covers of gay magazines if he were a *straight* man playing gay or bisexual. We see how well it worked for Heath Ledger, Jake Gyllenhaal, Phillip Seymour Hoffman, and Sean Penn. They love to award heteros merit badges for having the "courage" to play gay. Even if you're an SGL celebrity, you're not guaranteed that kind of a spotlight. It took *Out* a whole year to put Wanda Sykes on the cover—and, naturally, she's on it with, among others, a straight woman, Cyndi Lauper.

DJ: I just love the way Wanda came out: at a rally, standing up for her rights. That's what I'm talkin' about! Raheim, did you know she was in the life?

Raheim: I heard rumors. I didn't meet her until after she came out publicly.

DJ: That was this year?

Raheim: Yeah. At a cocktail party thrown by Dustin Lance Black and Gus Van Zant.

DJ: Oh, I wanted to get to that next: how did it feel to go to the Oscars?

Raheim: That was one of the longest nights of my life—but also one of the sweetest.

DJ: Sweetest? Even though you didn't win?

Raheim: That's part of the reason why it was so sweet.

DJ: What do you mean?

Raheim: The Oscar carries a lot more weight in the industry than all the other awards. If I had won, folks would have projected onto me their expectations, what they would want my winning to signify.

DJ: You mean, "The first openly bisexual supporting actor winner."

Raheim: Yeah. Doesn't it sound crazy? And, everyone would have been watching to see if I could live up to the hype of being an "Oscar Winner." I wouldn't want to be under that kind of glare. But, since many felt it was a make-up nomination for being passed over for *Rebound* and even Vegas was giving me

20 to 1 odds, I knew I wouldn't win. So I didn't have to sweat it out in my seat. We could just go to the ceremony and have a jood time.

DJ: Did you have a jood time, Mitchell?

Raheim: No question. I got to meet Halle Berry, Julia Roberts, Samuel L. Jackson, and Morgan Freeman, and we hung out at the Governors Ball with Will & Jada.

DJ: I gotta say it was *jood* to see you two on the red carpet, a Black male couple. But most of the newscasts showed you from the chests up!

[Laughter]

Mitchell: *You* know why that was. We were holding hands. What made it so silly is that, just a month before, we were shown at the Screen Actors Guild Awards holding hands. Guess the Academy didn't want to broadcast *that* to a billion people.

DJ: What was that moment like when they got to your category?

Raheim: All I could think was, "Let's hurry up and get this over with."

DJ: Did you practice the smile the losers wear after the winner's name is called?

[Laughter]

Raheim: Nah. It wasn't that deep, DJ. I was just grateful to be invited to the party. You know when they say, "It's an honor just to be nominated?" Now I know what they mean by that, that it isn't just talk.

DJ: OK, one more Oscar question: where were you when you learned about the nomination?

Raheim: In bed with my Baby.

DJ: Really?

Raheim: We'd just gotten Destiny off to school and was settling in for a little more shut-eye when Errol came bouncing up the stairs screaming, "Dad, you got nominated!" We couldn't believe it. Then my phone started blowing up. The nod for *Weight of the World* was so unexpected that the Academy used a still from *Rebound.* [Chuckles]

DJ: But it was deserved, brutha. That was a powerful eight and a half minutes. You pulled a Judi Dench.

[Laughter]

DJ: How did it feel winning the Emmy and the SAG?

Raheim: Those meant so much to me; *Dodging Me* was my comeback role.

Mitchell: Remember, it was your *rebirth.*

Raheim: Right. I had put myself through a lot and come through a lot to get to that place, and poured everything I had in that performance.

DJ: You did, man. It's a cliché, but you hit a home run with that one.

Raheim: Thanks. After we couldn't find a distributor, I thought it would never see the light of day. I was *crushed.* But then HBO rescued it and they really promoted it well, hosting special screenings in Chelsea, WeHo, and the Castro the night it debuted.

Mitchell: The Homo Tour.

[Laughter]

Raheim: I was thrilled when I learned about both nominations. It feels jood when your peers recognize what you've done. Just being acknowledged like that would've been enough. But winning and having my Baby with me? That was more than I could've ever hoped for.

DJ: And were those *real* tears you shed at both ceremonies?

Raheim: They were. I wasn't pullin' a Glenn Beck.

[Laughter]

DJ: Do you have a favorite actor?

Raheim: Mmm, not really.

DJ: What about a favorite movie?

Raheim: Don't laugh—*First Blood.*

DJ: The Rambo flick?

Raheim: Yeah.

DJ: Why?

Raheim: Rambo was like a hero to me, growing up.

DJ: Really? Why?

Raheim: 'Cause he took no prisoners. Nothing could stop him, not even the National Guard. I guess I admired his drive and determination. And he didn't let anybody push him around.

Mitchell: He *loves* action flicks.

DJ: Do you?

Mitchell: Well, I like my action movies with a little more . . . depth. *Aliens, The Fugitive, Breakdown, Air Force One, Thelma & Louise.*

DJ: Are those your favorite films?

Mitchell: No. *Lady Sings the Blues* and *Imitation of Life.*

DJ: Wow—talk about different tastes. There must be a fight over the remote when y'all are trying to decide what movie to watch!

[Laughter]

Mitchell: Not at all. We appreciate each other's choices. It makes us appreciate each other *more.* It brings us closer to knowing the man we love better. You have to love him for who he is, not who you want him to be.

DJ: Is there a movie you both love?

Raheim and Mitchell: *Jackie's Back!*

[Laughter]

DJ: I don't think I know a single Black gay or bi man who *doesn't* love that movie.

Raheim: How could you not? Jenifer is da joint.

DJ: Do you have a favorite actor, Mitchell?

Mitchell: My huzman, of course!

[Laughter]

DJ: *Huz*man—I love it! We're gonna take another break. When we return, we'll put the spotlight on Mitchell and his writing life.

DJ: Welcome back to Da Spot. This is your boi, DJ Korrupt, and I'm here with my favorite couple in the world, Raheim Rivers and Mitchell Crawford. So, Mitchell, tell us how it feels to be a *New York Times* best-selling author?

Mitchell: I never had dreams of hitting the List, never even dreamed of writing a book. I'm not caught up in what it al-legedly represents—that I have *arrived,* that my work has value because it has been validated by this entity. It would still have value if I published it myself and it sold only one hundred copies. For me, a first-time novelist, the honor is that people appreciate and embrace what I've done.

DJ: Where did the idea for *You, Me and He* come from—besides the song?

[Laughter]

Mitchell: I interviewed E. Lynn Harris in the summer of '03 and he encouraged me to try my hand at fiction. I began kicking around a few ideas—including telling *our* story.

DJ: You should still do that story. Given how long y'all been together and how much y'all have been through, that'd be h-a-w-t!

[Laughter]

Mitchell: I decided that if I do tell that story, it wouldn't be in fictional form. Then a female friend of mine confided in me about her recent breakup with a guy who turned out to be gay. Her thing was: "How could I not tell? I have you for a friend." It got me thinking about how this DL nonsense has fueled the fears of too many hetero sistas, turning them into detectives, while demonizing Black SGL men. I had to write about it.

DJ: Many people point the finger at Oprah for having *you-know-who* on her show. Do you agree?

Mitchell: You can't blame J.L. for telling his story. The problem is that his story was held up as *the* down-low man's story and, because we are so invisible, *all* Black SGL men were tainted by it. I love Oprah but she allowed herself to be punked. "You mean there are men who are gay that pass as straight by getting married *and* they have sex with men on the side?" Puh-leeze. *That's. Not. News.* Like Raheim said, men and women have been creepin' since the beginning of time. And to tie that in with skyrocketing HIV rates in Black America as if there was a direct correlation was irresponsible. There is no proof down-low men are the culprits. There's . . . well, Daddy won't curse again, Destiny.

[Laughter]

Mitchell: So I will spell it out: there's a whole lot of f-u-c-k-i-n' goin' on, and down-low men ain't the only ones doin' it.

DJ: *Preach, Mitchell, preach!*

Mitchell: But, what a convenient scapegoat they make—for the CDC, which saw those numbers rising over two decades and didn't sound the alarm; for the media, which loves to portray Black men as sexual predators; and for the self-appointed Black leaders and self-annointed Jesus pimps, who found another excuse to fag bash. We'd be having a very different conversation right now regarding AIDS and homosexuality in Black America if that show and that racist *New York Times Magazine* story hadn't defined the issue and shaped the dialogue. So I hope *You, Me and He* has steered the convo in a more sensible direction.

DJ: Since you brought her up: I love Oprah, too, but it's interesting how she handles gay issues differently when the faces are Black and white. Jonathan Plummer is nothing but a cad and a snake, but she lets Ted Haggard get away with saying he's "a heterosexual with issues."

Mitchell: Indeed. Her tone and body language was much different for each man. *Ted,* like Jim McGreevey, was leading a down-low life, yet she was very respectful. But she didn't try to hide the contempt she had for Jonathan. Maybe it was because she and Terry are close friends.

DJ: E. Lynn gave you a jacket blurb; how did it feel to get his stamp of approval?

Mitchell: He gave me more than his stamp of approval; he was partly responsible for me getting signed by Simon & Schuster. I sent him the manuscript, hoping he'd give me some feedback. A week later, I was contacted by Manie Barron, an agent here in New York, who E. recommended as a rep. Manie made some editorial suggestions, I incorporated them and, three weeks later, we had a deal.

DJ: Wow. How long did that process take?

Mitchell: A month and a half.

DJ: Damn. Just from talking with other authors, that is not the way things usually go down.

Mitchell: Not at all. Just getting an agent is a job. And the waiting game after it has been sent out can be torturous and demoralizing. Even I was taken aback by some of the comments editors had.

DJ: Such as . . .

Mitchell: Well, one, who will remain nameless, asked: "I love the story, but can you make it more ghetto?"

DJ: They didn't!

Mitchell: They did.

[Laughter]

Mitchell: Since street lit is all the rage now, you're more likely to get an editor's attention if you've written one of those "It's Hard Out Here for a Pimp/Prostitute/Player/Player Hater" tales. But most of the editors we approached got it. I was in the right place, and approached the right people with the right project at the right time.

DJ: For those who haven't read or aren't familiar with *You*,

Me and He—and given all the talk about it over the past three years, how could you *not* be?—can you give them a breakdown of the story?

Mitchell: Sure. A woman discovers that her husband is gay—or, at least bisexual in his behavior—but instead of kicking him to the curb, invites the other man into their marriage.

DJ: *Literally.*

Mitchell [giggles]: Yes, *literally.*

DJ: I gotta say, I was expecting one thing when I started reading it and was blindsided more than once. You took the story in directions I never would have guessed it would go. Was that your goal?

Mitchell: Well, I knew that, given the title, many would assume that it would be one of those jilted sista heartbreak tales, this time with the low-down, down-low husband and his home-wrecking male piece as the villains. But even people who may fall into those categories are more complex than the moniker. And how often do we get to really hear the men's voices in these kinds of situations? Not very. I wanted to get past the sensational headlines and really explore the host of emotions people go through.

DJ: Do you think there are more Lynettes, the woman who makes this deal with her husband, than we think?

Mitchell: Of course. Women decide to stay with their cheating husbands every day after discovering their infidelity—and all of those husbands are *not* cheating with women.

DJ: But would those women give their husband the green light to continue the affair, *especially* if it's a man?

Mitchell: If you can envision it, it happens. I can see how some would argue that this is truly the stuff that fiction is made of. But think about it: if he's seeing another woman, you can compete. But a man? And, remember, there are women who *know* a man is gay or bisexual, but for whatever reason—he's a great guy, he treats them well, he takes care of them, she is un-lucky in love, she is pregnant, she believes she can "change" him, she is tired of being alone/lonely—marries them anyway.

DJ: I take it the majority of your audience is women.

Mitchell: I think so.

DJ: Have you, like E. Lynn, gotten criticized by gay/bi bruthas for writing a story for *them?*

Mitchell [giggles]: I have, but the criticism usually disap-pears once they actually read the book. This isn't just Lynette's story and I didn't tell it to lock in a hetero female audience. Her husband, Bryson, and his lover, Wilmington, get equal billing. It is more of a character study.

DJ: Ha, I wouldn't say that, 'cause not only can you tell a jood story, you write some damn jood sex scenes! *Woof!*

[Laughter]

DJ: I had to take a break a couple of times—if ya know what I mean!

[Howls and uncontrollable laughter]

Mitchell: You're too much, DJ.

DJ: No, *you're* too much! Where did you get the inspiration to write like that?

Raheim: Man, don't look at me!

[Laughter]

DJ: Come on, he had to get the inspiration from *somewhere!*

Mitchell: What people don't get is that the sex is just another component of the narrative. So I didn't approach it as "Oh, it's time for the sex—gotta get my raincoat ready!"

[Laughter]

Mitchell: And it isn't sex for sex's sake. It isn't there because I didn't know what else to do at that moment. It's germane to the story. But the fact that people are talking about it and it gets them hot—that means I succeeded in presenting it correctly. I'd never written about sex in this way before, so I didn't know if my approach would be effective.

DJ: Oh, it is effective all right, t-rust!

[Laughter]

DJ: The other thing I love about the book is that it is about Black people but you would never know it—they don't wear it on their sleeves, so to speak.

Mitchell: Now, *that* was deliberate. I wanted to write a novel the way whites are able to: never mentioning the race of the principals involved or race, period, so that the assumption is it's a white story. Some white writers believe not mentioning it means it isn't an issue but, of course, that's not the case. Like Toni Morrison once said, 'When white people aren't writing about race, they are writing about race.' But this time, that table is turned. You only know the main characters and their family members, friends, and co-workers are Black because *others* are identified by their race or ethnicity; theirs is never specifically stated or acknowledged. It has really turned a lot of white critics and readers out; they are not used to reading a story where they are on the outside looking in and whiteness is on the margins.

DJ: See, you gettin' all sage on us now. And with that Toni Morrison mane you got goin' on . . .

[Laughter]

DJ: Did you have to get Mtume's permission to use the song title?

Mitchell: No.

DJ: Really? I thought he woulda been makin' out like gangbusters, too.

Mitchell: If we had used lyrics from the song, he would have. But song titles are fair game. I'm sure he isn't sore about it: during the first few months of the book's release, the song jumped into the iTunes top 10.

DJ: Cha-ching!

[Laughter]

DJ: How has your life changed being an author?

Mitchell: I wouldn't really call myself an author; a novelist, yes. Toni and James Baldwin are authors. I'm just getting my feet wet. When I've had a few more under my belt, I'll feel more comfortable with the title. But my life hasn't really changed that much. The best thing about this new career path is that it has allowed me more freedom.

DJ: What kind?

Mitchell: Both artistic and financial. I've been able to continue freelance writing and can be *really* picky about what I do.

DJ: Your essay on Sylvester in *Rolling Stone* was so on point.

Mitchell: Thanks. My schedule only calls for me to be on the road a month and a few weekends each year. And I *love* being a stay-at-home dad. I don't miss the daily grind of a nine to five at all.

DJ: Now, we're gonna get *serious*: Where were you when you heard about E. Lynn's passing?

Mitchell: [sighs] I was standing in my kitchen. Errol was on his phone when the text came through. I couldn't believe it. I immediately called E.; I got his voicemail. Then I got a call from a mutual friend who lives in L.A., confirming it.

DJ: Did you attend his funeral?

Mitchell: I couldn't. But I did participate in the memorial held in New York, and read from *Mama Dearest* during E. Lynn Harris Day.

DJ: With him gone, a void exists in the literary world. Do you see yourself or anyone else filling his shoes?

Mitchell: Absolutely not. No other Black SGL writer will be able to reproduce the volume and consistency, or have that kind of cultural impact. Instead of looking for the next or a new E. Lynn Harris, folks need to be encouraging whoever they know that writes from our perspective to do their own thing. That's what *he* did. If it weren't for him, I wouldn't have taken that step.

DJ: And on those words of wisdom, we're gonna take another quick break. Be right back.

* * *

DJ: Welcome back to Da Spot. I'm your host DJ Korrupt and we're havin' ourselves a jood ol' time with our guests, power couple Raheim Rivers and Mitchell Crawford. Mitchell, are Toni Morrison and James Baldwin your favorite authors?

Mitchell: How'd you guess?

[Laughter]

DJ: Do you have a favorite book?

Mitchell: *Just Above My Head.* I pick it up at least once a year.

DJ: You, too? I think it's Jimmy's gay masterpiece, not *Giovanni's Room.* How 'bout you, Raheim?

Mitchell: My favorite book is *The Autobiography of Malcolm X.*

DJ: A favorite author?

Raheim: Who *you* think?

[Laughter]

DJ: Now we're gonna get *real* nosy.

Raheim: Uh-oh . . .

DJ: Do you have nicknames for each other—besides my Baby?

Raheim: Mos def. I've always called him Little Bit.

DJ: Ha, I don't even have to ask why.

[Laughter]

DJ: Mitchell?

Mitchell: His nickname is Pooquie.

DJ: The ever-famous Pookie. Like on *A Different World.*

Mitchell: No, it's spelled with a q-u instead of a k.

DJ: Ah, he's a special brand of Pooquie. And why that name?

Mitchell: I had a teddy bear—well, I still have it—that I would cuddle with when I was a kid. Cuddling with Raheim reminded me of those days—except that he is not furry or fuzzy like the original Pooquie.

[Laughter]

DJ: What did you think the first time you heard the nick-names?

Mitchell: I *loved* mine.

Raheim: I *hated* mine.

DJ: Why did you hate it?

Raheim: Honestly, it sounded . . . stupid.

[Laughter]

Raheim: But it grew on me.

DJ: Do you two have a song?

Raheim: We do. "Love Has Smiled On Us" by Nancy Wilson.

DJ: Why that song?

Raheim: We love Nancy and that song really sums up where we've been, where we are, and what road we're traveling together. We've had to start over twice; it wasn't smooth sailing the first or second go 'round. And being married is not a picnic, it's not a happily-ever-after thing. There's gonna be heartache; there's gonna be *heartbreak*. But it can still be better than jood.

DJ: If y'all could see the way they are *lookin'* at each other . . . *that's* what love is.

[Chuckles]

DJ: Do you ever take time away from the kids?

Raheim: Yeah. Sometimes *we* need a time out.

[Laughter]

DJ: What about time away from each other?

Mitchell: We usually get that when we're on the job, on the road. But if we need a moment, an hour, a day to be with ourselves, the other can sense it. With four people on four different schedules, things can get pretty hectic in our house. Last week, Raheim treated me to a day at the spa while he handled the household.

DJ: This one's for you, Mitchell. The man you're married to is bisexual. Are you afraid that he may one day decide he no longer wants to be with a man and leaves you for a woman?

Mitchell: What difference would it make if he left me for a

man or a woman? The heartbreak won't be less painful if it's a man, or more painful if it's a woman.

DJ: For some, it would be.

Mitchell: I think that's just silly. It's similar to those women who discover their husband or boyfriend is cheating on them— but not with another woman. "Oh my, he's a homo, what am I gonna do?" "What does this say about me?" "Wasn't I woman enough for him?"

DJ: Like in *You, Me and He.*

Mitchell: See. What do you do? You do the same thing you would do if it were another woman: *deal.* Don't make the infidelity about you when it should be about them, what they did wrong, their lack of character, their being deceitful. There are a host of reasons why Raheim could decide to up and leave, *tonight*: he's not feeling me, he's not feeling us, he's sick of the kids, he wants to experience the single life again, he's found someone younger, he's found Jesus, he's becoming a monk . . .

[Laughter]

Raheim: And you could do the same.

Mitchell: Right. Why spend time worrying about what could be? Anything is possible. I don't fret about the what *ifs;* I concentrate on the what *ares.*

DJ: I feel ya.

Mitchell: Also, I don't view or treat my relationship as a sporting event, or a competition. I remember when we began seeing each other exclusively and, at a party one night, we ran into his ex.

DJ: Ooh, fireworks!

Mitchell: Well, I'm sure that's what that interloper was hoping for.

DJ: No, you didn't call him an interloper!

[Laughter]

Mitchell: He knew damn well who I was, who I was there with, and decided to be touchy-feely with Raheim.

DJ: And you didn't go over and kick that ass?

[Laughter]

Mitchell: That would've been the un-classy thing to do.

DJ: Did you just make that word up?

[Laughter]

DJ: I like it.

Mitchell: Later that night, we talked about it. Raheim was surprised I didn't confront him; that was his ego talking. I told him that it wasn't my place to—he's *your* ex, not mine, it was your job to set him straight. And what did you say?

Raheim: "You wouldn't fight over me?"

Mitchell: And I said, "No, I wouldn't. But I will fight *for* you."

DJ: *Al-righty then!*

Raheim: And he's proven that, time and time again.

DJ: So why didn't you set him straight, Raheim?

Raheim: I tried to.

Mitchell: You didn't try hard enough.

Raheim: Okay, I admit, I wasn't tryin' hard enough. What can I say, I enjoyed the attention.

Mitchell: And while you weren't consciously encouraging it, *sub*consciously you would've loved to see us throw down over you.

Raheim: Yeah. I admit it. But I still woulda been goin' home with you.

DJ: *Aaah.* Y'all gonna make me sick over all that sugar.

[Laughter]

DJ: Do you fight?

Raheim: Of course we do. Not anything physical, but we get into it.

Mitchell: Anger is a healthy thing. The trick is not to display it in unhealthy ways. You should be able to disagree without tearing each other down.

DJ: Can you tell when the other is angry?

Raheim: He won't talk.

Mitchell: And *he* will pout.

Raheim: I don't pout.

Mitchell: Okay. He *broods*.

[Laughter]

DJ: Raheim, is Mitchell *The One?*

Raheim: No, he's my Number One.

DJ: Uh-huh. Mitchell, is Raheim *The One?*

Mitchell: No, he's the Right One.

DJ: Okay, y'all are workin' me!

[Laughter]

DJ: Any advice for bruthas out there who are in relationships or hoping to be in one—like yours truly?

Raheim: Hopin' ain't gonna make it happen.

[Laughter]

Raheim: Don't think you are going to find *The One*. There is no *one* person who can be everything you want and need. No one is perfect—including you. But you *can* come close to having everything you want and need. But that means you're gonna have to do the work. Being in a relationship is hard work, man, and you gotta work hard at it. Some folks think you can just be together and that's it. No, you gotta work hard at doin' *that*, too.

Mitchell: I believe too many of us think that love is all you need. We've got the love, but it takes so much more than that. It takes patience. And sacrifice. Sometimes you have to put what you want on the shelf. Some say they want to be in a relationship but are too self-involved, they don't know how to be selfless. It can't be about *you*; it's got to be about *us*. But you also have to be careful not to allow it to define you, that you don't get lost in it. It's a delicate balancing act.

Also, too many SGL men get caught up in gender roles. Instead of trying to be *the* man in the relationship, recognize that you are *a* man in the relationship. We have to fight the world to see and treat us like men, so why would you want to be in a dick-waving contest with the man you love?

DJ: *Hell-o!*

[Laughter]

DJ: I was having a discussion with a group of single friends this past weekend about this subject. We're all attractive, professional men in our late twenties/early thirties—and single. Any insight on why so many Black gay/bi men are single—unless they hook up with a white man?

Mitchell: Well . . . there are cultural factors working against us. Black male couples are rarely profiled or depicted; white men are still held up as the standard, so it isn't surprising some Black and other men of color gravitate toward white men since interracial/interethnic relationships are propagated as the rule, the ideal for us. If you don't see a thing it's hard to imagine you can possess or be that thing. But since there are so few visible examples for us to follow, *we* have to be our own role models.

DJ: Well, you two are *my* role models.

Raheim and Mitchell: Thanks.

DJ: One of my friends said the reason many of us are still single is that "We don't know what we want." Do you agree?

Mitchell: I don't know exactly what *he* meant, but there is some truth to that. And that's not just a Black gay thing; it's a people thing. Everyone has their List, the items we check off that a potential date or mate has to have. But sometimes that List gets in the way. For example, we say we want a man with a job—but frown down on the *type* of job he has. We say we want a man with a degree—but if he didn't go to an Ivy League or HBCU, he's not really learned. We're all entitled to our preferences but if you are *too* particular, you could always find yourself flying solo. While I didn't reject Raheim because he was a bike messenger, I didn't think he was relationship material because of it. I didn't think I could settle down with a man who doesn't have a high school diploma.

DJ: And look at y'all now.

Raheim: And I never thought I would *be* in a relationship with another man. That wasn't what I was taught to want in life, it wasn't what the boiz 'round my way were into. But you never know what life is gonna throw your way. If somebody had read my palm sixteen years ago and told me I'd be a father of two and married to another man, I woulda laughed in their face.

DJ: What would you say is the most important ingredient in a relationship?

Raheim: That would be the most important word in relationship: *relate*. Just don't get engaged to each other, get engaged with each other.

Mitchell: I agree. The devotion, the loyalty, the trust, the passion, the intimacy, the love can't flow freely or be nurtured if you aren't tuned in.

DJ: Alright. What's next for you two, career wise?

Raheim: I just signed on to star in a bio-pic about Benjamin Banneker.

DJ: Wow. A theatrical film?

Raheim: It'll be on Showtime.

DJ: He seems like an odd figure for a bio-pic. I mean, the brutha was a genius; he designed DC. But was his personal life juicy?

Raheim: Oh yeah. [snickers] He was gay.

DJ: *What?* Benjamin Banneker was *gay?*

Raheim: Yup.

DJ: You jokin'.

Raheim: Nope.

DJ: This is actually documented?

Raheim: Yeah. In letters. He doesn't say "I'm gay," but the correspondence points to him being intimate with men. And he was in love with someone who was not born a free man.

DJ: *Damn.* You *do* learn somethin' new every day. I should've made the connection before; I've never read anything about his personal life. That's always a dead giveaway. You know those "don't ask, don't tell" gatekeepers ain't gonna like *that*.

[Laughter]

DJ: What's next on the horizon for you, Mitchell?

Mitchell: Well, *You, Me and He* has been optioned. It could go before the cameras next year.

DJ: Great! Who optioned it?

Mitchell: Black Eyed Peas & Rice, a production company in Atlanta. It's run by a sista, Amelia Denson. She used to work at Dreamworks.

DJ: Did you write the script?

Mitchell: Yes.

DJ: Was that difficult, adapting your own work?

Mitchell: The difficult thing was taking off the novelist/journalist hat. The blueprint you use for crafting a screenplay is much different. You have a lot of ground to cover in a hundred pages and every element you believe is important in the book can't be transfered to the screen. Every scene has to be concise, and you can't have a character talking for paragraphs or pages. I did three drafts before I came up with something feasible *and* filmable. I have new-found respect for screenwriters; it may look easy but it's not.

DJ: Will it be shot in New York?

Mitchell: NYC and Jersey.

DJ: Who has been cast?

Mitchell: No one yet, but I'm hoping that Sanaa Lathan will sign on as Lynette.

DJ: I was about to say! She is the only actress I see in the role. What about Bry and Wil? Raheim, *you* would be a perfect Wil!

Raheim [chuckles]: How did I know you were gonna say that?

DJ: How about it?

Mitchell: Raheim has his heart set on playing Ashton, Bry's best friend.

DJ: Do you?

Raheim: Yeah.

DJ: I can see that, too. Regardless, you gotta play *somebody*. How could you not, in your Baby's movie?

Mitchell: I believe Bry and Wil will be played by unknowns, or rather actors who aren't well known to the public.

DJ: Why?

Mitchell: Because I want to avoid the "I don't be kissin' no man on the lips" syndrome that afflicts many Black, *allegedly* hetero actors.

DJ [laughs]: Gotcha. Would you consider gay and bisexual actors for the roles?

Mitchell: Certainly. Chances are those actors will be.

DJ: Are you working on a new book?

Mitchell: I am.

DJ: Jood. It's been three years. Your public is feenin'!

[Laughter]

Mitchell: I know. I had to push back the delivery date because of the film project. But I am almost done. It may be out the end of next year.

DJ: Is it a sequel to *You, Me and He*?

Mitchell: It is.

DJ: *Jood!*

[Laughter]

DJ: If you haven't read the book yet: *spoiler alert*. So cover your ears or turn down the volume for ten seconds. Do we find out who is the father of the baby?

Mitchell: Yes . . . and no.

DJ: Oh, see, you playin' with me!

Mitchell: That's all I can say, DJ. But I'll make sure you get a galley as soon as they're available. You'll have the scoop before the rest of the public.

DJ: Thanks, man. I appreciate that. Now, I heard thru the vyne you've been approached about doing your own reality show.

Raheim: Ha, that's news to us!

DJ: Would you do a reality show?

Raheim & Mitchell: *No!*

[Laughter]

DJ: Why not?

Raheim: No *Jon and Kate Plus 8* here.

[Laughter]

Mitchell: We wouldn't put our lives—especially our children's lives—on display like that. No matter how grounded you think you are, your life will become a three-ring circus because it won't be *your* life anymore. What many don't realize is that those shows are scripted; nothing just *happens*. You become a paid actor, your moves and thoughts dictated by a writer, a director, a network. His skills and judgement as a parent are definitely questionable, but I believe Jon realized all that too late. Unfortunately, you can't unring the bell.

Raheim: I *really* feel sorry for their kids. They are growing up with cameras in their faces; what happens when the cameras are turned off? How are they gonna handle *not* being on television? And, where's their money? Will they have to sue their parents, like Gary Coleman did? This is why we went back and forth on whether Destiny should start performing. Show business ain't easy on the adults; *I* know. It can crush a kid.

DJ: How did Destiny handle being on Broadway?

Mitchell: Very well. We're so proud of her—not only for the excellent work she did but for how focused and professional she was. We told her, "Have fun." That's what childhood is supposed to be about. You let us worry about the business and you just enjoy the show.

DJ: Does she have any projects coming up?

Mitchell: No. But she plans on winning *American Idol* in several years.

DJ: Ah, another Fantasia?

Mitchell: More Jennifer Hudson.

Raheim: She reminds us of Monica. A woman's voice in a young girl's body.

DJ: Does Raheim the Third have any artistic aspirations?

Raheim: Not at all. He plans on working for NASA and walking in space.

DJ: Sounds like y'all got it all. Is there anything you wish you had?

Raheim: Bill Gates's bank account.

[Laughter]

Mitchell: We're blessed to have the life we do and to have each other.

DJ: And *I'm* blessed to have shared this time with you. You gave me and the audience a lot to consider—and a lot to laugh about. Thanks so much for coming to Da Spot.

Raheim: Our pleasure, man. And thanks to you, DJ, for doin' you and letting us be a part of your world. This was a lot of fun.

DJ: I hope we can do it again real soon.

Mitchell: I'm sure we will. I bet I'll be getting a call right after you finish the sequel.

DJ: Ha, you know it! Continued success to you both and all the best for you as a couple and for your family.

Mitchell: Thanks much, DJ. And thanks to everyone out there for their love and support.

Raheim: And here's to you, DJ, in your quest for a huzman!

DJ: Man, thanks. Now, if y'all got any single friends, hook a brutha up!

[Laughter]

DJ: Thanks everyone for tuning in. Y'all be safe and stay blessed. Peace out!

A Tribute

By Stanley Bennett Clay

Originally published in *SWERV* magazine—Fall 2009 issue

> We don't have a lot of role models as black gay men. We tend to buy into the sleazy side rather than the romantic aspects of making love and being with someone, which is one of the things that always disappointed me about 'the life.' Everything's always based on sex rather than romance.
>
> —E. Lynn Harris, April 1996

What I will always remember about my friend Lynn is that he was hopefully romantic. A true Southern gentleman with an easy smile, the child of modest means became a literary force to be reckoned with, who redefined gay-straight alliances in the black community and shined a needed light—sometimes harshly but always with class and compassion—on the emotional and often difficult trajectory of black gay men seeing their full, visible selves for the first time.

Even though we had spoken on the phone several times previously, I first met Lynn face-to-face in February of 1996 during a scheduled interview for my magazine **SBC**. Black History Month was making its presence bodaciously known with record-breaking snowstorms in the East, chilling rainfalls on the deserts of Southern California, and a freak winter heat drought throughout the Lone Star State. Although it was 84 degrees in Dallas, the air was clear and clean.

The weather and the city reminded me of what I had not only heard, but also deduced on my own (through his writing and our phone conversations) about the best-selling author. He was a brother of great warmth who spoke honestly and clearly. His prose was simple and clean and his stories were sweet, old-fashioned bedtime tales for black homosexuals in search of fantasy, Mr. Right and themselves.

According to everyone I spoke to who knew or had met E. Lynn Harris, he was truly one of the last of the nice guys. And with more than 300,000 book sales up to that date, multiple Hollywood offers, and a cash flow that placed him in the upper one percentile of black authors, it was good to know that nice guys can finish first.

We met in the restaurant of his hotel, The Crescent Court, a lavishly appointed palace of Old World Southern charm in Dallas. He was in town for part of his book tour and also to attend the annual Black Gay and Lesbian Leadership Forum convention that, of course, I was attending.

The setting seemed apropos. Lynn was the epitome of old world Southern charm and what began as an interview between a magazine editor and a literary celebrity ended three hours later as a friendship that would last until death brought down the curtain.

After that, we talked often, about anything and everything—the men in our lives, our writing careers, family, friends, the latest hot gossip, the black gay scene, and spirituality. Lynn was a very spiritual guy and felt that the hand of God guided his career. Therefore he felt privileged to help others as part of his spiritual duty. When I asked him to read my second novel *In Search of Pretty Young Black Men* prior to its publication, not only did he read it in a matter of days, but he also offered to write a cover quote. His endorsement—he called it "brilliant"—boosted sales beyond my wildest imagination.

It was Lynn who referred me to producer Proteus Spann, who hired me to write the book and lyrics (along with Ashford and Simpson) for the Broadway-bound musical stage play version of *Invisible Life*. And it was with Lynn's blessings and vigorous endorsement that I was hired to write the screenplay adaptations of *Not a Day Goes By* and *I Say a Little Prayer*. When he heard that I had collaborated with Tina Andrews on a musical version of *Why Do Fools Fall in Love?* he called me up and wanted to see the proposal so that he could invest. He believed in investing in our community; our black community and our black LGBT community.

I did not until after his death find out about his homage to me in his final novel *Mama Dearest*. His reference to me as a prominent playwright whose work Yancey's mother Eva had appeared in was yet another wonderful gift from a man who gifted so many so often, with little fanfare, little fuss, little focus on himself, only for the smiles he knew he would engender. Lynn was an oxymoron. Modest, yet extravagant, timid yet boisterously jolly, at times a shrinking violet who never thought of himself as good enough, cute enough, worthy enough, deserving enough.

He was crushed by Hollywood's rejection of his screenplay for the remake of *Sparkle,* and he was resigned to the fact that he would never be a Toni Morrison or James Baldwin. Resigned, yes. He was fully aware that that sort of respect would elude him. That doesn't mean he was particularly happy about it. He was not angry. Anger was not his thing. He was saddened by it. And so he ate himself to death. A heart attack complicated by high blood pressure and the hardening of the arteries.

The coroner reported that E. Lynn Harris died of natural causes. Well, I beg to differ. There is nothing natural about a man dying at the age of fifty-four. It is a life cut terribly short; leaving devastated loved ones in its wake.

Losing Lynn brought back the pain of losing my own father, who died seventeen years ago at the tender age of sixty-four. He, like Lynn, was a gentle man who laughed easily, was generous beyond a fault, rarely raised his voice, and was universally loved. And, as in Lynn's case, a heart attack took him away from us. My father was my friend. The loss is indescribable. To this day, when I pass his picture on my mantle, I often break down in tears, but then recover, grateful for the gift I had in him, and the gift I continue to enjoy in his spiritual presence.

And so, even as I mourn the loss of E. Lynn, I must be grateful for the gift that he was, and the gift that his great and generous spirit is.

I cry and then I smile.

HOUSE OF JOHN

Love is never a plan.

Stanley Bennett Clay

Chapter One

One must take a good close look at oneself when one feels a need to assign blame for a failed relationship. It is so easy to self-identify as the victim and point elsewhere at the culprit when oftentimes, not always, the culprit is that pampered figure feeling sorry for him or herself in a rather biased mirror.

And the clown thing about it all is that one is narcissistic enough to think that somebody else really cares. News flash: No, nobody cares. They are annoyed. Annoyed at the blathering idiocy and the melodramatic flourishes. Why would one think that a drama queen update on one's piteous, self-created predicament of the heart would be of any interest to anyone else? Such emotional self-centeredness surely renders one pathetic and laughable and downright foolish.

And yes. I am that one. Throughout the years, I've been known to cry in alleys, curse lovers' mothers, blame God for good sex gone bad; been known for bad luck with good men, and good times spent too quickly and recognized as good times only when time has passed.

Before Sean, I had traversed the roads of romantic partnership with mixed results, some good, some bad, one as hot as a California hillside fire, most as insipid as drying paint.

But after Sean and I crashed and burned, I decided to totally give up on love, at least the romantic kind.

After Sean, I was both fortunate and unfortunate enough to have loving family and friends.

I am the oldest of six children. After forty-two years of marriage, my parents were still as giddy as newlyweds, unable to keep their hands off each other, staring at each other from across crowded rooms, glow-eyed with longings and secrets not to be known by anyone else, certainly not by their children, who would still have to be blind not to witness occasional hints of their—our parents'—senior citizen erotica.

Most of my siblings followed my parents' example, marrying compatibly, romantically, and stably.

Well, except for my sister Frankie. Francesca Templeton Chapelle DaSilva acquired and discarded husbands like wardrobe. Seasonally. The baby of the family, Frankie has had more exes, lovers, boyfriends, and fuck-buddies than all the rest of us combined.

Frankie is an actress. Not a star, but she makes a good living at it and has a recognizable face. She's had small parts in blockbusters and leading roles in low-budget film festival gems. Back in the day, she almost got a starring role in a big budget actioner opposite Will Smith when Halle Berry got sick and had to drop out. Jada Pinkett-Smith got the part instead. Although not the kind of doll to cry over spilt milk and lost parts, Frankie pitched a bitch behind that one, claiming nepotism had robbed her of her shot.

My name is Jesse. Jesse Templeton III. Named for my father and grandfather. Most people call me plain old Jesse, except for my immediate family. They all call me Junie, short for Junior, but since that was my dad's moniker, they had to come up with something a bit more frivolous to always remind me that I was Jesse the younger, Jesse the cuddly.

Well, anyway, when Sean and I broke up, I was a mellow thirty-eight-year-old, freelance photographer. I'm still a freelance photographer, am back to being mellow and, needless to say, no longer thirty-eight. I was born and have lived in Los Angeles all my life and possess the breezy, devil-may-care attitude to prove it, although a cynical side does occasionally rear its pointed little head from the sunny disposition of my native Disneyland. Life has actually been very good to me in spite of my romantic lamentations, and I've been very good to life, in spite of what went down between Sean and me.

I have to either thank or blame my sister Frankie for Sean. You see it all began right after Frankie lost that part to Jada. She was in between men and in between jobs, though there were prospects for both. Her third ex-husband, Alvin, was still sniffing around and Frankie had an audition for a recurring role on *Grey's Anatomy*, as a sex-obsessed nurse whose bedside manner went way beyond the call of duty—a real stretch.

She arrived early at the Warner Brothers Studio lot for her meeting with the producers. While waiting in the reception area, several actors—all black, all built, all fine—sat across from her, sides in hand, silently mouthing the printed dialogue.

Used to and appreciative of lip-smacking stares from all black, all built, all fine men (Wait a second. Let me clarify that. Not all black. Color never mattered to Frankie. She has always been an equal opportunity ho'. And I mean that in the most complimentary way.), baby sister was in her erogenous comfort zone surrounded by all this pretty-boy testosterone.

Sean Dawson particularly caught her eye, and hers his. Sean was more of a model than an actor. He was, quite frankly, too pretty for primetime, was more like one of those chocolate Ken dolls lying around in tight-fitting boxers and life-altering angst on daytime soap operas. You know, one of those perfectly chiseled, honey-colored morsels designed to give stay-at-home moms dominatrix fantasies and Madonna wet dreams, not to mention the willies and the envy he provoked among daytime, stay-at-home soap queens who fantasized about being him, having him, or killing him for being him. He was like Shamar was back in the day, what Eric Benet could have been if it wasn't for the Halle pothole.

But I digress.

I can only imagine Frankie's initial reaction to the beautiful face, so deep-chocolate-red-tanned that one could only think Caribbean—though he was straight out of Detroit—the stunning ear-length dreads, much like mine, that bounced around that perfectly chiseled face, and the goatee that circled his perfect smile.

Turns out both Frankie and Sean got the parts on *Grey's Anatomy* they had auditioned for, ended up working together, and before the end of their first day, Frankie had invited Sean out to dinner at the Porterhouse Bistro in Beverly Hills with hopes of serving up some dark chocolate poontang dessert back at her Miracle Mile condo.

Now, to hear Frankie tell it, it wasn't Sean's scant notice of her ample breasts heaving out of her low-cut halter that re-awakened her sleepy gaydar, but the hot-ass waiter whose walk-away from the table was stripped naked by Sean's keen and lustful eyes.

"How did an old E. Lynn Harris fan like me let that get past me?" she asked me later that night over the phone.

"You're slipping, doll."

"All those stares and goo-goo eyes he gave me on the audition?"

"Yeah?"

"Turns out boyfriend's a fan. Saw me when I guest-starred on *Girlfriends*. I'm trying to get me some dick and he wants a goddamn autograph. You're a top, right?"

"Frankie!"

"Well, I'm just asking, Junie. I'm pretty sure he's a bottom. I mean, the way he was checking out the waiter's crotch when he came back with our drinks."

"That doesn't mean anything, Frankie."

"So you *are* a top."

"Francesca, I am not having this conversation with you. You're my sister."

"Well, I'm only asking because it would be a shame to let all that phine piece of man go to waste. You should let your baby sister hook you up. I showed him your picture and he thinks you're cute."

"Oh God, Frankie, you showed him that picture of me at Andre's birthday party?"

"It's the only one I had of you on my phone."

"I look like a dork in that picture."

"You look like an intellectual in that picture. The dreads give you character; completely disguises your dorkiness."

"See?"

"Besides, he has dreads too. You guys would make a great couple."

"Really?"

"Trust."

"He really said that?"

"What?"

"That he thinks I'm cute."

"Actually, he said he thinks you're a cutie pie. And *he* is totally gorgeous, dreamy brown bedroom eyes, lashes almost as long as mine, a perfect thick-lip smile, perfect goatee, a cute tight ass, maybe six-feet, six-one, I'd say a hundred-and-seventy-five, you know, skinny in that hot kind of way, and at least a size eleven shoe."

Well, it had been a while since I had been out with anyone, and he did sound absolutely delicious and just my type, so after a few hems and haws, I decided to meet my sister's fan.

Sean Dawson turned out to be everything Frankie said he

234 / *Stanley Bennett Clay*

was and more, and before I knew it, we were lost in the thrall of a hot and heavy affair after one dinner date. Perhaps we jumped in too quickly, but when the sex is as good as it was between us, caution and careful study were abandoned quicker than college final studies for a frat house orgy. It didn't help that I had been celibate for eight months and had all this sexual tension built up inside ready to explode at the slightest touch, and it didn't help that Sean was a male nymph feasting at the banquet table of carnal delights like a happy glutton who never met a calorie he didn't like. For the next week, we devoured each other ravenously, took from and gave to each other with erotic abandon, ran through lube and condoms like ice cream and cake at a six-year-old's birthday party.

The fact that we were having sex morning, noon, and night, a schedule easily accommodated by our respective occupations as freelance photographer and freelance actor/model, made the decision to move in together an easy one if, what did not seem so at the time, a foolish one.

We had gotten to know each other's bodies before we got to know each other. You would think that at thirty-eight, I would have known better, but good dick and booty can blind the inner vision of a soothsayer.

Now don't get me wrong. I did love Sean, or would eventually come to love him, and he me. But during those first few weeks, lust was our master, and under its whip, we were happier than singing pickaninnies on Scarlett O'Hara's plantation.

So Sean moved from his tiny, over-priced West Hollywood single into my two-bedroom apartment in the fourplex I owned on Fourth Avenue, just south of Hancock Park. I bought the building with money I had won as a college contestant on *Wheel of Fortune* ages ago. At the time, I was a senior at UCLA. I also won three trips—Ireland, Tahiti, and Rio de Janeiro—which began my life-long love of travel.

Although I had a cleaning woman—Mrs. Tremaine—com-

ing in once a week, Sean's slovenly ways and total sense of dis-
array kept the apartment in such a mess that Mrs. Tremaine
threatened to quit, in spite of my best efforts to pick up after
Sean. I eventually got Sean straightened out on the domestic
front and he taught me how not to be so anal.

Then Sean got his big break. He booked the role of Denzel
Washington's younger brother in some big-budget action feature shooting in Munich, Germany, which was also starring
Brad Pitt. We celebrated with the best sex of our young romance,
and since he would be gone for eight weeks, we had to get in
enough high-powered lovemaking to sustain us through those
two months of abstinence.

Although I was so happy for him, seeing him off to Germany was like bidding farewell to a spouse being deployed to
Afghanistan. That's when I realized how truly much I loved Sean;
dropping him off at the airport, kissing him good-bye, hunger-
ing for one more taste of him, feel of him, filling him, him filling
me, missing him before he was even out of my sight.

There was a bittersweet consolation attached to our respective occupations that linked us in ways that words could not
describe. Sean was an actor and loved to be photographed, and
I was a damn good photographer. The art we created on cellu-
loid and framed, then hung on walls, perched on mantles, displayed bound like coffee-table picture books was good enough
to give me warmth, if not the full encompassing fire of his
flesh-and-blood presence that I craved nightly and daily and
nightly when I dreamed of him spooned naked in my arms, the
smell of his coconut-scented hair, thick, soft and twisted, my
raging hard-on sandwiched between his long lean thighs, his
soft ass hairs moistened by commingled jizzum and sweet man-
hole pucker sweat that made me shudder in my smiling sleep.

In his physical absence, my morning showers, ritualized by
masturbatory fantasies of him, were clear in my mind and my
heart and my loins; the taste of his mouth, the taste of his dick,

the taste of his ass while I twisted my nipples, slipped soapy fingers up my throbbing rectum and beat my meat with masochistic glee as I closed my eyes and joyously grimaced and strained at the thought of him sucking me down to my shaft and my balls, swallowing me whole with his mouth and his ass, and me shoving tongue, dick, fingers, and toys into that glorious, soft-hairy rimmed hole of his.

Coming home after long sessions of photographing cute, not-a-care-in-the world toddlers, wide-eyed starlet wannabees, plus-size divas who brushed aside rejections like so many failed diets, bad actors with a look, good actors without game, hapless hopeful dreamers of impossible, unstoppable dreams, I could not get to my solitude quick enough, to this love-hate relationship with his too very real absence and his fantasy presence.

Still, my professional voyeurism kept Sean and his sex clear in my mind, even as I toiled behind my cameras, but save for the occasional dip into my studio washroom to milk my barking hound and calm it down, I had to wait until the end of my professional day to fully appreciate and pleasure myself with the porn that looped inside my head.

I rushed home each night and allowed the very thought of him to work me into a frenzy ignited by his smiling face on glossy and matte eight-by-tens and those X-rated nude and sexy photographs of him I'd taken inside my head, the kind of photos I wish to God I had in hand, solo scenes on DVDs, scenes of me fucking and sucking and hungrily tossing the salad of my own private porn star.

But most real actors and models these days are funny that way, willing to stick a camera up their ass for a big studio film or a small independent feature by a distinguished director and perform full frontal nudity and simulated sex on a legitimate theatre stage, but loath to do so much as show nipples in anything X-rated, even if they're taken by friends and lovers. After all, friends can easily turn into foes and lovers don't last forever, or so they say. But pictures and videos do. Big tabloid bucks can turn anyone into a Judas and wreck a promising career before the promise is fulfilled.

And although I am a proud professional voyeur, exhibitionism was never my thing, though a less modest man with a body like mine would have been proud to put it on display, if I must say so myself.

And so the double frustrations of not having Sean here and relying on the images of our lovemaking that danced in my head were both maddening and delicious, and his absence made my heart grow desperately full of want and implacable desire. It was not enough that we spoke on the phone every other day. (With his fourteen-to-sixteen hour a day shooting schedule, not to mention all the stunt work he had to perform and the lines he had to learn, he just didn't have the time or energy for daily phone sex.) It was not enough that his deep baritone voice hit all my buttons trans-Atlantically. It wasn't enough that the meat hung in the butcher's shop while I starved with my face pressed up against the window. I was hungry for my man.

Had I become obsessive? Addicted? I'm afraid I had, and I cherished the sweet pain of my malady.

The Labor Day weekend was three weeks away and I had deliberately kept my schedule clear. My sister Frankie and I had planned to spend the weekend laid up at the beach in Oceanside, then come back on Monday in time for the annual family barbecue at our brother Andre's place in Cerritos.

"Hey, Doll."

"Hey, Big Bro."

"Listen, how set are you on Oceanside?"

"What do you mean?"

"I'm thinking about flying over to Germany."

"To see your man!"

"It's been three weeks, Frankie, and I don't think I can last much longer."

238 / *Stanley Bennett Clay*

"I heard that, but you know Mom is gonna kill you if you don't show up for the barbecue."

"I'm just going over there to get some sustenance, three or four days, then I'm flying right back, cheeks flush and full."

"I'm not even gonna touch that. So I know Sean is happy."

"Well, he doesn't know."

"Excuse me?"

"I'm going to surprise him."

"You sure you wanna do that, Junie?"

"What?"

"Just make sure you don't end up surprising *yourself.*"

Okay, I wasn't born yesterday, but baby sistah's ominous foreboding seemed just a little too Zane for my Barbara Cartland sense of romance.

Chapter Two

Fuck Barbara Cartland. Fuck Zane. And fuck Frankie. Why does she always have to be so damn right?

It was Labor Day weekend but it was as cold as hell sitting at that tiny table at that funky-ass sidewalk café in the center of Munich, down the street from the Bayererische Hof hotel where the film company had put Sean up, but I didn't care. I needed to be exiled to the cold, under a gray and gloomy sky, made to suffer for my foolishness, my naïveté, my stupid romantic notions.

As much as I tried to empty my head of that hellish tableau, it looped over and over inside my brain like a bad YouTube porn video. I should have known from the muffled moans on the other side of the door. Come on, did I really believe that those were cries of distress and that here I was, to save the day, to rescue my baby from some fucking Heath Ledger seizure? Who was I fooling other than me? Certainly not the pale pixy *fräulein,* who bowed diffidently in her crisp maid's uniform, easing discreetly past the scene of the slime, as oblivious to it as to a gentleman's fart. But no, me, I had to drop my bags right there where I stood, outside of his room, in the cathedral-ceilinged, Persian-rug-covered hallway, and I had to rush right in, burst right in, and save my man from a fate worse than death. So I deserved exactly what I observed.

Heroically, I body-slammed the door, but not even the ruckus of my crash landing could outdo the wild rhythmic cries of intolerable pain, pleasure, and bliss grunting from the wicked and wanton grimace of my lover's tongue-wagging, wide-stricken grin, as his eyes flamed with unearthly delight. There he was, slung doggy-style over the damask-covered, armless, Queen Anne settee, as white thighs smacked his brown caboose, pink-white knuckles twisted in his sweat-drenched dreads, snatching his head back and forth, up and down, side to side, and the three-legged white jockey furiously rode his black ass, a wild neighing mare bucking for the finish line.

There he was, punched, jabbed, and massaged with what looked like at least twelve inches of manhood, confirmed by the triple-X condom wrapper crumpled on the floor, whose length and girth I immediately envied.

But then I was too shocked and too turned on to know exactly what I felt, seeing what I was seeing, angling my head in disgust, figuring out how my slim little boy could take all of the knockwurst this Brad Pitt–looking dickmeister was poling him with. And who says white boys don't pack? Maybe it's a German thing.

God, if I only had my camera, which was packed away in one of the bags I had left in the hallway, I would have finally gotten on film the picture that I'd cum to a thousand times in my head.

Exhausted and spent but not yet done with his feeding, it took Sean a few more escalating grunts to realize that I was piled just inside the doorway like a sack of dirty laundry tossed down a chute to a cold basement floor. I was what he saw, huffing with anger, jealousy, want and desire, turned on and turned off, struggling to drag myself up from the floor where I had landed so doofusly. German Brad was too busy stretching my boy's asshole into a Diana Ross grin to notice my steamy pathetic vigil, my rise from the puddle and shame of raging tears and the throbbing hard-on that my anger and hurt could not control.

And then suddenly our eyes met in that frozen moment in time, Sean's and mine, and I could tell by his newly contorted face, transmogrified from savage lust to stinging dread and bewilderment, that I seemed to him a phantom, a blur, an unbelievable reality that shocked and frightened him into an orgasmic explosion, an explosion in foreboding sync with the ravishing rattling, the spastic throbbing of that loose-cannon, latex-wrapped white boy's missile exploding inside the jaws of his ass.

Spent and sweaty, the Brad clone collapsed on poor Sean. Sandwiched between the Nordic Adonis and the Queen Anne damask, stained with spit, sweat, and cum, Jackson Pollock smeared on pristine brocade, what was left of my man smiled up at me meekly with a pathetic smile that could not find an answer to my silent question, "Why is another motherfucker's dick up your ass?"

"Jesse, wait," Sean pleaded as I straightened myself, turned around, and walked out the door, "let me explain."

Yes. That's what I heard him say as I snatched up my bags in a Dominique Deveraux snit, as I marched grandly toward the elevator, dreads bouncing with fury, summoned it with the touch of an outraged finger, boarded it with my head held high, swung around to give him, wrapped in his cum-stained towel, leaning out of his doorway, an evil eye answer to his tearful reprise, "Let me explain, Jesse. Please, just let me explain."

And as the doors of the elevator shut coldly between us, I had resolved that he would be shut out of my life.

Still, as the elevator carried me down toward the street-level foyer, I saw him, the vision of him. I turned to it, and looked at it, all of it, the lips I would never kiss again. The dick I would never taste again, the beautiful ass I would never know again. The eyes my eyes would never see again.

My heart snapped the picture, but as the doors of the elevator opened wide to the bustling and anonymous foyer, my mind, the smarter of the two, burned the negative. And so there I was, freezing in a cold and heartless Germany, hovered over by dirty ghostly clouds, seated at a table at some dreary outdoor café, drinking bad coffee, luggage at my feet, wishing that I smoked, understanding why folks needed to smoke after something like this, wishing I did drugs, but scared by the very idea.

Still, the dank and the harrowing cold was not punishment enough. I truly needed to freeze my balls off, get whipped by the razor winds that purpled my ebony cheeks and chapped my chattering lips. I needed the flagellant elements to drag out my penance, make me painfully accountable for my stupid stupidity.

I turned on my phone for the first time since fleeing the scene where my immediate ex had been getting his cookies done. I erased the missed calls from his cell and presumably his hotel room. I called my airline instead and re-booked my flight back home, but they had nothing until the next day, so I found a room in some cold, tacky dive, strapped on my camera, and decided to make the best of my self-pity, my sentence in this city I shared with a man I never wanted to see again.

I found my way to the Dachau concentration camp site and took pictures of misery much greater than mine. At Englischer Garten I got pissy drunk on too many mugs of a German pilsner whose name I could not pronounce. I avoided the beautiful landscapes I had read about. I roamed the frigid streets that night in the seediest neighborhoods, donned dark glasses and a Goth-like demeanor. I did not want to experience anything that threatened to pull me out of my funk.

The next morning my head pounded like it had been beaten with a sledge hammer. I squinted listlessly as my shaking hand dug into my small carry-on and found the bottle of Excedrin.

Somehow, I made it to the airport. By the time I got there, the Excedrin had kicked in. A sign. Getting out of this fucking country, getting away from *him* was the relief I needed.

I turned my phone on once I was seated on the plane back home, parked on the tarmac, waiting for take-off. And just as I suspected, more missed calls from Sean's cell and that German number, and as many voice mails. I erased them all, each and every one of them, and decided to think about just getting home, back to America, back to my warm and beautiful L.A., back to my warm and beautiful family, the people who loved me, my mother's judgment-free hug, Frankie's shoulder to cry on, my brother Andre's killer barbequed beef ribs and his wife Dee's Cuban rum punch, my fool brother Craig and his wife and their kids, Uncle Mickey, Aunt Till, cousin Laura and her new girlfriend Cheryl.

I dialed Frankie's number. She picked up on the first ring.

"Hey, Doll," I said when she answered.

"Hey, Junie," she swooned, the hunger for sweet gossip bringing her voice to a delectable hush, "so how's it going?"

"I'm on my way home."

"So soon?" Then she panicked. "Oh nooo!"

Chapter Three

"Your son is gay," I overheard one of my father's friends say to him in the middle of their weekly poker games, back when I was in middle school.

"He's also left-handed," my father replied smoothly without ever looking up from his cards. He won the pot with a straight flush.

"Life is too short to be hating somebody because they're different," Dad would always say. He would also always say, "A man is determined by what's in his heart, not what's in his pants." Okay. That's sweet, if not so terribly original.

Dad was a sweet guy. If he were still alive today he would be man enough to cry watching Oprah. I remember how he broke down and cried after he brought Mom and my new little baby sister Frankie home from the hospital, sitting in the corner watching Mom gently rocking Frankie, listening to his wife gently singing "Summertime" to his new baby daughter.

Dad was only sixty-eight when he died; still a young man. If he had a fault, it was that he loved to eat all the wrong things.

Mom spent their whole marriage trying to trick him into eating healthy, but he always managed to get hold of fatty pork ribs, six-cheese macaroni and cheese, chitlins cooked in bacon drippings, cornbread pan-fried in butter, and too-sweet Kool-Aid by any means necessary.

Everybody loved my dad, especially the women he worked with down at the post office on the graveyard shift. Oh, and they all knew he was Mister Strait-Laced, happy with what he had at home. There was no getting into the pants of Jesse Lee Templeton, Jr., no matter how many eyelashes they fluttered or curvy hips they sashayed in front of him, so they decided to get into his stomach.

Now there was no great conspiracy involved here. They truly did appreciate a man who appreciated his wife so much that it seemed she was all he rhapsodized about, her and his kids. In fact, he made them, inadvertently, demand respect from their own men at home. And whenever they showed up at work, they were glad to bring Jesse Lee, Jr. a foil-wrapped plate from their own table, and Jesse Lee, Jr. was always grateful.

Dad had a heart attack running down the stairs of our family home toward the car where Mom was idling the engine for their weekly Denny's senior citizen's discount meal routine. I'm pretty sure he died with visions of chicken-fried steak, mashed potatoes, and banana cream pie dancing in his head. I'm sure he died a happy man.

"Mom, would you ever get married again?" I remember asking her once.

"Who could compare?" she said so matter-of-factly that she stunned me into silence. To have lived with and to have loved that which was the very best for her was her continued joy, now to be cherished through memories. No one could equal Dad in her heart, in her mind. And no one else would fill that place inside of her that was held sacred just for him. She was happy with that. I could see that. We all could.

And that's what I wanted. That's what I foolishly thought I could have had with Sean.

Oh, by the way, I did finally contact him, via text. I could not bear hearing the sound of his voice. I knew he would be in Europe for the next few weeks, doing the film and getting done by Brad Pitt's twin, no doubt, and which was now none of my business, but other business had to be taken care of, therefore necessitating contact.

I called my housekeeper Mrs. Tremaine and asked if she would be willing to come in an extra day and help me pack up all Sean's belongings which I would then deliver to a public storage facility, and then mail the keys and vital information to Sean in care of the Bayerischer Hof hotel in Munich, Germany. Mrs. Tremaine was more than willing. She actually danced a jig.

From the moment I walked into my brother Andre's house that Labor Day Monday, I knew that town crier Frankie had apprised the family of my return to singlehood and the spicy details that prompted it. That they loved me so much was never in doubt, but the group hug they smothered me with, the saddened eyes, the smoochie and piteous puckers, the head pats—yes, head pats—were just a bit much.

"You all right, dude?" my fool brother Craig asked, with a stunned look on his face as if I'd just escaped a burning building.

"Baby, I knew from the moment I set eyes on him," my mother cooed, pinching my cheeks like she did when I was three, "that boy was no good for you." Having never met him, she made that assessment from a fashion layout she saw of him in *Details*.

Uncle Mickey and Aunt Till, bless their hearts, having been forewarned of my unfortunate situation, did not come empty-handed. Fresh from their church choir, they offered up Hector Henderson. Now I love my Uncle Mickey and Aunt Till, but they're just a bit too Pentecostal for my Religious-Science-Agape-Church-going taste. And although Hector seemed like a nice enough guy and was as gay as pink ink (because Lord knows I don't do DL), bad teeth, bad skin, and "more-to-love" are not qualities I seek in a man I'm intending to romance. At least clean under your nails! But since he's a good Christian brotha, or seemed to be, I'm sure the Lord will provide him with a gay Kirk Franklin, or a Kirk Franklin as is.

Having escaped the well-meaning clutches of my caring adult relatives, it was rather nice being bombarded by all my young nieces and nephews who always saw me as the fun uncle, the playful one, the big kid in the family who could really relate to their devil-may-care youthful derring-do. Boy, if they only knew.

Andre's twin girls, Denise and Debrina, were, at nine, two of the most beautiful little brown fairy princesses one could imagine. The only time they ever got ugly was when they openly bickered over which one of them was going to marry me.

And fool brother Craig's brood of five—Kimberly, the ten-year-old gymnast, eight-year-old Herbie, Peewee, the Pop Warner Junior, six-year-old Dempsey, the dude from another planet, four-year-old Miss Cynthia, destined to be a future America's Next Hip-Hop Top Model—was as foolhardy as their daddy. It's a good thing Andre and Dee's property was childproof.

And then there was my beautiful cousin Laura. Laura was the political lightning rod of the family. The first black lesbian to head the gay-straight alliance at her conservative Orange County high school, a prominent organizer of the radical "Snatch Back Your Snatch" campaign, and a major activist in probably half the marriage equality campaigns in the state of California, Laura was always on me about settling down with a good and decent man so that he and I, and she and her partner Cheryl, could be two of the first black couples to walk down the aisle of same-sex marriage in the state, once the state legalized.

In the meantime . . .

The thing I have to realize about my family is that they believe everybody ought to be in love twenty-four/seven. I get it. But after Sean, I was about as in love with love as Dracula was in love with a spike through the heart.

So in spite of my family's Von Trapp–Swiss Family Robinson– Huxtable gaiety, gay me was currently queer for the cynical delights of anything but love. I wanted some of what Brad Pitt's stand-in was getting, the milk without being bothered with the cow.

So it was fortuitous that my phone vibrated in my side pants pocket as I looked over my kith and kin in the throes of the dizzying power of love and family. The music was too loud, the laughter too boisterous, the joy too feverish for me to have heard it ring.

I pulled the phone out of my pocket, hoping that Sean had gotten the message. Perhaps he had. I checked the caller ID. It wasn't Sean, thank God. It was William. William Castle.

"I heard."

"Hey, Will."

"You and Sean."

"There is no me and Sean."

"That's what I heard."

"You heard right."

"You poor thing."

"Please, I'm fine."

"Trash."

"Already on the street for pick-up."

"Good for you, Jesse."

"Thanks."

"You *do* sound fabulous, though."

"Thanks."

"Considering."

"Thanks."

"And it sounds like you're already celebrating."

"A family get-together."

"What you need is a *real* get-together."

"You don't know my family," I laughed.

"You deserve to treat yourself to something naughty."

"Like I said, you don't know my family."

"So what does February look like for you?"

"Why? What's going on? Another all-boy cruise?"

"Better."

Let me tell you about William Castle. Will. Will always smiles, even when you can't see him. There's always a smile in his voice, even on the phone. That's because Will Castle is always happy, always mellow, always satisfied, like a gourmet after a fine meal. It is totally impossible to be down in the doldrums when Will is speaking on the opposite end of the phone.

A bald-headed, mahogany butterball with a salt-and-pepper mustache that is always impeccably coiffed, and the hand flutters of an Italian maestro, Will has done quite well for himself as a travel agent specializing in leisure excursions that are of a particular interest to black gay men and men who love them.

Two years ago I made extra brownie points with my sister Frankie when I took her on Will's Southern Caribbean New Year's Cruise. It wasn't so much the ports of call that had baby sis in such rapture, but spending parts of eight days and seven nights with her favorite author E. Lynn Harris, who had been booked as Will's special celebrity guest, was a dream come true for her. I was even able to get Will to arrange for her and me to be seated at the same dining table as E. Lynn.

Frankie and E. Lynn became more than celebrity and fan. They became friends. The quintessential gay literary luminary had found in Frankie the perfect good-girlfriend fag-hag. She has a wall in her study covered with the dozens of photos I took of her and Lynn horseback riding on the private Bahamian island of Half Moon Cay, sunbathing on the white beaches of Aruba, hiking through the lush landscapes of Curaçao, and dancing the night away in the ship's disco. She didn't even mind that not one of the two-hundred-plus men in our group was sexually available to her. As long as she could laugh and gossip and hang out with E. Lynn, she was more than satisfied. Besides, there were plenty of drop-dead-gorgeous waiters, busboys, barmen, cabin stewards, and fitness instructors from around the world more than willing to take my drop-dead-gorgeous sister down to their rooms in the bowels of the ship and sexually service her in ways she breathlessly described as multilingual.

Although there was definitely debauchery intended on these exotic sojourns orchestrated by the illustrious Mr. Castle (after all, boys will be boys), there was also a great deal of genuine romance permeating the titillating sea air, prompted by the smiling moon in a clear black sky reflected off a gently rumbling sea, pulsating with a swooshing rhythm that seemed to sing of love in four-four time. Not every man on Will Castle's gay cruise client list was looking simply to get laid. A good many of them were looking to get loved.

Same gender-loving couples signed up enthusiastically for Will's dream cruises. Even I had been thinking about surprising Sean with a late honeymoon trip on Will's upcoming Christmas cruise to Costa Rica. Obviously that was scrapped.

Also, there were always a few lesbian couples that joined the party. Will, being the smart cookie that he always has been, made sure he orchestrated specific all-girl events for his female clientele, as well as co-ed, non-sexual events suitable for both genders and the handful of straight friends and relatives who just wanted to be on a cruise with a bunch of fun people, and Lord knows, nobody knows how to have more fun than a bunch of black gay folk.

But what Will had in mind for February was something completely different and right up my newly cleaned-out alley.

"How does a Santo Domingo land excursion sound?"

"The Dominican Republic?" I asked with stupid glee.

"But of course," he cooed.

"I want all the details."

I stepped out onto my brother's front porch, away from my family's festive howling, and listened intently to the naughtiness Will was about to describe.

"Just imagine," he began softly, slowly, conspiratorially, "three weeks of the most incredible sex with some of the most beautiful men to walk the face of the earth, men with erotic skills honed to please your every fantasy. Imagine, dear Jesse, dozens of men to choose from, buff and slim, every shade of chocolate, tops and bottoms, dick for the Gods, ass for the nation, romantic Afro-Caribbean Latinos to coddle you, to kiss you, to suck and to taste every part of your body, offering up every part of their bodies with an erotic generosity and dexterity that will reduce you to panting, a shortness of breath, moans and groans of sheer pleasure and indescribable delight.

"Imagine unimaginable international ecstasy, my friend, the pungent aroma of man-to-man sex floating on a tropical breeze."

If nothing else, Will Castle was the ultimate drama queen. My embarrassing hard-on out here on my little brother's front porch was a salute to his royal gift.

"And all, so very much for so very little."

"Huh?"

"The *bugarrones* await you, my friend."

"The who?"

"The *bugarrones*. The Dominican men who play for pay."

"For pay?"

"But of course, dear Jesse. Do you think all that pleasure comes for free?"

"I don't know, Will. I've never paid for sex before," I said, a little nervous even as pre-cum dripping in my boxers revealed my intrigue. "And I don't know if that's something I want to start doing now."

I know, I know. That's what they all say. But really, I had

never done anything like this. The thought had never crossed my mind. Well, maybe crossed it. But it kept on stepping. Ego and vanity cheerleadered me past those occasional men who pleasured the desperate for pay.

But the way Will described it made it sound, not so desperate, but adventurous, an adventure that costs money like any good adventure, like a cruise or a movie, like a good lap-dance. Or what it was: three weeks in Santo Domingo for the sole purpose of making love, no, having sex with beautiful Dominican men who knew how to make a traveler feel good for a price.

"About a hundred pesos," Will continued, ignoring my weak protest. "A hundred and fifty, if they particularly impress. Twenty dollars. Thirty."

"So who else is going?" I needed to know. Nasty loves company.

"Well, let's see. Oliver Bevins from Atlanta of course."

"Of course."

"And Doctor Mo from our neck of the woods, oh, and Tim Thompson and Henry Anderson from the Oakland Dinner Club, the Hicks twins, and Art Pierce."

"Art Pierce? I thought he was in a relationship."

"He was."

"What happened?"

"Same thing that happened to you. Trust, there will always be a handful of gay divorceés on board. Oh, and of course, you know Father Martin is coming."

"Martin Carl." I smiled to myself. Knowing that he was coming was nearly enough to persuade me. I always liked and admired Martin. I looked up to him, we all did, that's why we often referred to him as Father Martin, the senior member of our traveling group. Nearly sixty, Martin would go anywhere at the drop of a hat. He'd been working for the City of San Francisco for more than thirty years and was sincerely considering early retirement. But he liked his work, almost as much as he liked his play. And as long as he could build up a week here or a week there to hop on a plane, and as long as he could double up and work all the overtime he wanted, he maintained the best of both worlds; that of a working professional and a world traveler. I hadn't seen him in a while. It would be nice hanging out with him again.

But still, I had reservations, a fear of the unknown, a fear of the unknown me. What if I got down there and went buck wild? I'm not that kind of guy. But could I be?

"I don't know, Will," I hedged. "Let me think about it."

"Well, don't think about it too long. I've extended the invitation to only a select few of my traveling clients, you, of course, being one of my favorites."

"I certainly appreciate the consideration."

"There are only twelve slots, you see; twelve private rooms. That's all Casa de Mita can accommodate."

"Who?"

"Casa de Mita. House of John. Where we'll be staying. Where we'll be playing."

"It sounds very romantic."

"It is, if that's what you're looking for, and a whole lot more."

"Right now, I'm looking for the whole lot more."

"Well, a whole lot more awaits you."

What was I thinking? Yes, it was exactly what I needed to totally free myself from the bitterness I was trying to let go of and let God handle, since, deep down inside, I wasn't handling it very well on my own, in spite of my grandiose posturing, my cavalier response to the pain and humiliation of watching my man being dicked down in a German hotel suite, my phony dismissal of all things Sean.

On the one hand, I'm not a total hedonist, and the idea of traveling to a third-world country to sexually exploit the local men folk for my own selfish pleasure without any thought of what effect this may have on them and their thoughts and feelings about the Ugly American has its own stomach-sinking effect.

On the other hand, I'm not going down there to screw a bunch of kids. We're talking about sex with grown, consenting adults here. And politically, I always believed that prostitution should be totally legalized, organized, and recognized for the joy-giving business that it is.

Still.

God is gonna get me for this. What was I thinking? I was thinking about having myself a good-ass time. That's what I was thinking. Sex is a gift from God, and why shouldn't I enjoy my Heavenly Father's gift. "Let me give you my credit card number," I said to Will.

"Don't worry, Jesse," Will's voice smiled, "I have it on file."

Chapter Four

It is no secret in the African American gay community that African American gay men have a distinct affection for Dominican men, gay or not, which explains why Casa de Mita, euphemistically known as Casa de Juan, or House of John, was so popular.

Perched on the corner of a cozy intersection of two small streets, Casa de Mita was, once upon a time, the most intriguing structure in the Colonial Zone of Santo Domingo, the oldest city in the Western hemisphere.

Years ago Casa de Mita had been a high-class, low-profile bordello, so I was told. Legend has it that the women who worked there began to take the kindness and the patronage of the local police for weakness. In time they were soliciting from their windows and the local police, whose own children attended the school just down the street, hastened its demise. It stayed closed for many years and many a *dueña* sold flowers in its locked gilded doorway.

The passage of time did not, however, diminish the ancient charm or enduring legend of Casa de Mita, which, decorated in time's moss and cobwebs, stood as historically elegant as the venerable towers, Catholic cathedrals, stone gardens, and ancient fountains that surrounded it and shadowed it. Shadowed it. Did not overshadow it. Casa de Mita's notorious netherworld beauty was its own small contribution to the Colonial Zone's distinction and mystique.

And so it was no surprise to anyone when Cedric Whitehead, a black American gentleman from Brooklyn, a man whose desire for other men, Dominican men, was as ancient and as familiar as the city he visited more than any other, decided to buy the small, deserted hostel of lore and transform it into the perfect retreat for his American brothers visiting the cobblestone streets of desire in search of young, too-pretty, golden, olive, red-brown men, black-haired and long-lashed, with moist inviting, thick-lipped smiles and sultry Spanish accents, tight round hocks and large uncut penises that hung freely beneath hip-hugging summer shorts, tight-fitting jeans, and slacker, revealing slacks; ass and dick that boasted Negro ancestry, to have Will Castle tell it.

The history of Cedric Whitehead's House of John was as delicious as a gentle kiss in Will's able and romantic telling, and the red-eye flight from Los Angeles to Miami, where we would change planes and take an hour-plus flight across the sea to the tropical Island of Hispaniola, home of Haiti and the Dominican Republic, was not filled with anything less than the romantic ruminations of one truly glowing from thoughts of pleasures past, pleasures present, and pleasures planned with glee in the city of Santo Domingo.

I was more than ready to begin my three weeks of tropical delight and sexual satisfaction on one of the few Caribbean islands I had not yet visited, and one of the few cities that was an erotic haven for men who loved men who loved sex.

Coming in for its landing our plane (and my camera) hovered over thick brush, tropical splendor, and white sand sparkling against the bluest waters I'd ever seen.

The actual landing at Las Americas International Airport was amazing. Like some giant dirigible we floated onto the runway that lay between the sparkling Caribbean Sea and a stunning mountain range where cattle, sheep, and goats grazed lazily. We disembarked and were greeted by the gentle swoosh of a tropical breeze, not to mention the complimentary rum so freely dispensed by smiling hostesses lovely enough to turn the gayest man straight. Well, almost.

Once through customs, the descent into the main terminal was as gleeful as a red-carpet stroll toward a movie premiere. Friends, relatives, cabbies, shuttle drivers, souvenir hawkers, and tourist guides greeted my fellow travelers and me like we were visiting rock stars. The faces and smiles of my Caribbean cousins, tinted and hued by the blood of West African slaves, Spanish conquerors, and indigenous Taino Indians, were astonishing in their beauty, an island version of our own U.S. miscegenation, producing so much physical splendor from so much historical crime.

But I digress.

My wide-eyed, jaw-dropping awe did not escape Will's notice, and so he pulled my sleeve and whispered to me as he casually perused the crowd he knew so well, "It's okay, Jesse. First-timers are always dumbstruck by the vision."

From the crowd emerged a man so handsome that it made me blink and stare. He stretched wide his arms and smiled.

"Will!" the beauty sang as he approached us and gave Will a big brothaman hug.

"¡Carlos! ¡Que paso!"

"Same-o, same-o. Welcome back, my friend."

"Thank you. Carlos, this is Jesse. Jesse Templeton. Jesse, this is Carlos Estrellas. He works at Casa de Mita."

I extended a hand that he refused to take. He wrapped me in his arms instead, and his light cocoa butter scent was deliciously dizzying.

"*¡Hola!*" he said, nearly kissing me, "and welcome to Santo Domingo."

"*Gracias,* Carlos," I answered, enjoying his strong masculine embrace.

"Here," he said, pulling away, "let me take those."

And without giving us a chance to protest, he relieved us of the two carry-on bags Will and I had each traveled with ("Travel light, my friend," Will had instructed me before we left, "swimwear, shorts, jeans, T-shirts, slacks maybe, socks and underwear if you must but purely optional.")

As Carlos led us out of the crowded terminal, I could not help but notice the contour of his beautiful behind as it rolled firmly inside his tight khakis.

"Forget it, Jesse," Will whispered to me, "Carlos is staff. Staff doesn't fraternize with hotel guests."

My disappointment must have shown mightily.

"But don't worry," Will assured me, "Carlos is only the tip of the iceberg."

And Will was so right. Sexy brown and yellow beauty was everywhere. Now don't get me wrong. It's not that I have sex on my mind twenty-four/seven, but there are some hot-ass men in Santo Domingo! I mean, I thought the crowd of hotties that greeted us in the terminal was merely an aberration, but the drive from the airport and through the city boasted every kind of boy candy imaginable. Even in its poverty, and Santo Domingo is indeed a poor city, the citizenry glows with incandescence; a young, shirtless turk in raggedy cut-offs saddled up behind his amigo on a sleek-cruising moped, half-naked golden boys wrestling each other in the shallow waters of the sea, dark buff Adonises strutting down a dirt road bow-legged with the weight of their manhood, and plazas dotted with discerning male hustlers—*bugarrones*—enticing potential customers with lurid eyes, suggestive smiles, and a slow handful of themselves outlining length and girth.

Policías too phine to be legal and bad-boy beauties too good to be true were everywhere we looked.

But even paradise has its thorns and the ugliness of despair was not invisible. Homelessness, little children begging on the streets and eating from trash heaps, pockets of squalor, stray dogs roaming through ancient palaces was the sad and sinful irony. In the city of Santo Domingo beauty and the beast co-existed as easily as lions and sheep in Jehovah's Eden.

While Will and Carlos laughed and caught up in the front seat of the tiny shuttle bus, I kept my camera busy recording images too rich and profound to trust to mere human memory.

And then finally we came upon the Zona Colonial. The Colonial Zone. It was as much a world wonder as anything I had experienced in all my world travels.

Tiny brick dwellings with winding staircases leading to second-story trellised courtyards dating back to Columbus's brutal oc-cupation delicately lined the narrow cobblestone streets, while fortress-like churches loomed magnificently in the background against a sky whose blue was deepened by the piercing bright-ness of a high-noon sun. And all the while beautiful locals— men, women, children, and seniors—went on about their daily way almost oblivious to the rugged paradise that surrounded them and, I suspected, barely impressed with the commonness of their ravishing appearances.

Carlos finally pulled the shuttle bus up to the main entrance of Casa de Mita, and it seemed everything, if not more, that Will had described. A storybook cottage, a tropical hideaway right out in the open that, at first glance, hinted at all the clan-destine pleasure that it promised.

Proprietor Cedric Phineas Whitehead, like an ebony version of Mr. Roarke from *Fantasy Island*, appeared vision-like in the gated doorway of his establishment.

"Welcome, my friends, to House of John," he swooned. A wide smile revealed deep dimples, and his inviting arms stretched high with hands opened wide as if the world he was bouncing like Atlas on his Brooklyn-bred shoulders was beach-ball light. I could not determine whether he was high on drugs or high on the setting, but his mellowness was something I immediately and lovingly envied.

Carlos unloaded our bags and followed us in past his boss, who described the amenities available to his guests: Internet service, cable TV, air conditioning, Casablanca fans, breakfast and dinner, city and beach tours at modest prices, pre-screened *bugarrones* ("always negotiate up-front"), his assistant Emilio at our beck and call, and plenty of condoms and lube available at the front desk, gratis. I could hardly wait.

Though exhausted from the sleepless red-eye flight, I was energized by the prospects, but once led upstairs to my lovely balconied room, my body, seduced by the soothing shower and lullabied by the easy sounds of street bustle and indigenous music, succumbed. I laid my nude body across the bed and fell into a deep sleep that I did not wake from until after the sun had set and there was a gentle knock on the door.

"*Hola.*" I recognized the voice. It was Carlos.

"Hey, Carlos," I said sleepily, "come on in."

He entered and without as much as a glance at my sprawling nudity, informed me that dinner would be served in a half an hour, and that the others from America had arrived and were having cocktails in the foyer. When he left, I still could not resist a gander at his beautiful ass despite his unavailability.

I got up and showered again, dressed, and descended the staircase into the jovial buzz of my giddy American comrades, most of whom I was familiar with from Will's cruises; my San Francisco buddy Martin Carl, Tim Thompson and Henry Anderson from Oakland, Jarvis McCready from Chicago, gay twins Myron and Byron Hicks from Philadelphia, Art Pierce and Oliver Bevins from Atlanta, Sylvester Winfrey, who claimed to be a distant cousin of Oprah, and Doctor Moses Franklin, a dentist affectionately known as the L.A. Tooth Fairy.

We greeted each other festively, toasted each other with Brugal, the Dominican Republic's national rum, then sat down at the huge round candlelit table on the terrace and feasted on crab, lobster, brown rice, sweet potatoes, plantains, gossip, and sexual fantasies.

And not long after dinner, having retired to the parlor for more Brugal and heightened expectations, fantasy became reality.

Chapter Five

The first chime of the doorbell reduced us to a sudden hush and caused all of our hearts to skip a beat. Well, all of our hearts except Cedric's and Will's, whose exchange of knowing glances and delicious smiles let it be known that what we had come for was just a foyer away.

"Excuse me, gentlemen," Cedric begged pleasingly as he got up and left the parlor. We all leaned toward his exit and watched our rotund host click across the tiled foyer with Giselle-like grace, open wide the front door entrance, and unlock the wrought-iron gate that guarded it.

"This is it," Will whispered with assurance, as we strained to hear Cedric exchange words with sexy male voices in slow and gentle Spanish.

When we heard them step in and the clang of the wrought-iron gate being locked behind them, we quickly resumed our positions as nonchalant gentlemen of leisure, even as our hearts beat in time with the sound of their footsteps crossing the tile, drawing nearer and nearer.

First in the doorway was Cedric, blocking it for maximum

dramatic effect, a smiling father figure with an impresario's élan, enjoying our disguised hunger, as we subtly tried to look around his near three-hundred pounds.

"Gentlemen," he announced with a widening smile, "I'd like you to meet some friends of mine."

Only then did he step aside, and with an elegant gesture of the hand ushered in a trio of young men as different as they were tempting.

"This is Rodrigo," he said proudly, introducing the tallest of the three. At six-two, Rodrigo's Latin and African roots made for a delicious medley. His dark bedroom eyes, short thick black hair, luscious lips, and full and gorgeous nose perfectly accented the yellow complexion beneath a healthy tropical tan. And although he was as lean as he was tall, his sinewy physique hinted that he liked to work out, either at the gym, on the beach, or in the bed.

Efraín, an olive-complexioned mystery, was introduced next. His smile was not as eager as Rodrigo's, but his eyes spoke of new and unexpected pleasures.

For the truly adventurous of our group, Efraín seemed the perfect imperfect match; the devilishly angelic face, the open shirt down to his navel, the school-boy chest, the nipple ring, the virgin and the freak, the pose that said that anything goes, take me and be taken.

"And Tomás," Cedric declared with knowing pride. Tomás was the shortest of the three. Stocky and muscular, a thick battering ram, what we would call in the States rough trade. And with the unnatural bulge between his legs, Tomás was indeed the perfect delight for our more submissive colleagues.

All throughout the night the doorbell chimed, the wrought-iron gate unlocked and locked and unlocked, and stunning young Dominican men of all shapes, sizes, and colors were paraded in like models on a runway. And though precious few spoke even a little English, the international language of sex and desire hummed throughout the parlor. Twelve horny American tourists exchanged flirtations and negotiations with, and escorted to their rooms, locals who had little else to offer but their gorgeous Afro-Caribbean bodies in exchange for American dollars much needed for rent, food, and general subsistence.

I was immediately drawn to Davide, a brown-skinned, boyishly handsome young man who seemed to be in his mid-twenties, and was about as suited to this night's work as a cherub to ditch digging. Clean-cut, clean-shaven, and small-framed, he lacked much of the overt machismo of most of the other *bugarrones*. I noticed him through the crowd, seated against the wall on the other side of the room. Our eyes met. I smiled at him. He returned the smile, shyly, nervously.

My shaky confidence bolstered by his shyness, I moved slowly through the crowd and approached him. He stood, almost stumbling, to face me.

"*Hola,*" I said.

"*Hola,*" he said.

"*¿Cómo está usted?*"

"*¿Muy bien, gracias, y usted?*"

"*Muy bien.*" Hey, you can't live in L.A. without knowing *some* Spanish. "*¿Cómo se llama?*"

"*Me llamo Davide. ¿Y el suyo?*"

"Jesse," I answered, extending my hand, which he shook gently.

It seemed to me that Davide was as new to this as I was. Although I was the more aggressive, both our demeanors contributed to the awkwardness of our situation, which was certainly not aided by the little Spanish that I knew and the few words of English Davide had at his disposal.

Still, we managed some small talk and eventually got around to the business at hand. Per Cedric's instructions, a price was negotiated up front—twenty U.S. dollars—and we awkwardly discussed the anticipated activities.

I led him to the stairs and escorted him up ahead of me, admiring the tight frame of his body, neatly fitted into his white jean shorts and skimpy tank top; the tiny waist, the small bubble-butt, the lean calves, the slightly hairy legs and arms, the silk-like hair along the back of his neck. His body was, quite frankly, pretty, as pretty as his baby face.

When he reached the second-floor landing he turned and looked down to me for further instructions. I joined him, then led him down the hall to my room, opened the door, and gestured him in.

I don't know why, but for some strange reason I had created an atmosphere of total romance in what was essentially a bordello flop room. Candles flickered softly; burning incense scented the air that was gently waltzed about the space by the lazy rotation of the Casablanca fan. I even had soft jazz oozing from my Bang & Olufsen iPod and mini-speakers.

"*¿Puedo yo?*" he asked, pointing toward the bathroom. I suddenly remembered Cedric telling us that no matter how clean the *bugarrones* were, he, Cedric, always insisted that they showered again before entertaining a client.

"Please," I insisted, leading him into the bathroom, providing him with soap and towels, and shutting the door gently behind him. My God, you would have thought I was on my honeymoon.

I then stripped down to my boxers and sat on the edge of the bed, trying to control my hard-on as the sound of the water running in the shower sent my imagination soaring with visions of water streaming down his lithesome body, and him luxuriating in the baptism, soaping then rinsing the soft hairs of his underarms, arms, chest, legs, ass rim, and pubes.

And the thought of his dick sent me throbbing; him soaping the wrinkled balls and veiny shaft, pulling the delicate loose foreskin back, a sensation that infant circumcision deprived me of, soaping the lovely dick head, the rim, the stretched-back foreskin, the thick shaft, rinsing himself, all of himself, preparing himself for me.

The fantasies had enslaved me. My boxers were now around my ankles and my rock-hard manhood dripped with pre-cum. I grabbed hold of it, trying my best to calm the beast that throbbed in my hand with a mind of its own.

Then suddenly the shower stopped. I waited with a shortness of breath, waited for my prize to appear, a wait that seemed a lifetime.

Finally, the bathroom door opened, slowly. Davide stepped into the candlelit room, still the shy vision, a towel wrapped round his tiny waist. He was a delicate vision; modest pecs, midnight nipples, whisper chest hairs, the perfectly indented navel, the angel face looking almost too young to be legal. He eased toward me with the awkwardness of the schoolboy he seemed to be. I sat up and subtly kicked off my boxers, unashamed of the throbbing salute my dick was offering. He stood between my legs and slowly undid the towel and allowed it to drop to the floor.

Pretty. There was no other word to describe it. Pretty. As pretty as his face, his feet, his legs, his chest, his tiny little smile. His dick was as pretty as I had imagined it. In its flaccid state, with only a hint of the head visible beneath the wrinkled opening of his foreskin, it was a thing of beauty.

I kissed it. It pulsed like a newborn. I gently cupped his balls in one hand and cradled his lovely piece of meat in the other. I looked up into his beautiful dark eyes and felt him growing in the warmth of my delicate grasp.

I slowly released his dick and his balls and wrapped my hands around the small bubble-butt of an ass. And as my fingers discovered the soft hairs that lined his crack, his dick reached out to me, throbbing.

I kissed it again, over and over and over again, like a long-lost lover, and then I held it again and slowly retracted the foreskin and beheld the beauty of the sparkling, naked head.

I could not hold back any longer. I wrapped my lips around it, filled my mouth with it, all of it, and gave it slow and gentle suckling.

The taste of him was a humbling delight and I wondered what had I done to reap such pleasure. I stayed there forever and yet not long enough, feasting between his legs, filling my hands with his small hips, slowly jamming him into my hungry face.

His moans became halting whimpers, and I knew he was close. He knew he was close, and with a shiver he pulled himself out of my mouth. I felt like a baby deprived its bottle.

His dick bobbed up and down, having been brought so close and still not completely there. Not yet.

He then knelt down between my legs. His small hands found the firmness of my calves and his mouth found my stiffened dick, and slowly took it in, all eight inches of it. I gasped, and some strange sound of unimaginable pleasure escaped from me. He sucked with a rhythm that fired up near intolerable ecstasy, and everything within me begged for it and begged it off.

I held his bobbing head, ran my fingers through his midnight locks while I strained to hold on to my sanity in the face of maddening pleasure.

I could not take it any longer. I was too close to exploding. I pulled his face back, his mouth back, his tongue back, away from my crazed penis, slapping itself against my stomach, begging for the mouth I now deprived it.

Davide looked up at me slightly embarrassed, yet modestly pleased at giving me such oral pleasure. I looked down at him, smiling, shaking my head in amazement. My approval put a smile on his face.

I took both his hands and lifted him up from between my knees. I stood, facing him, our hardened dicks met and mingled as we held each other. I kissed him on the lips. He kissed me back; our tongues found warmth in each other's mouths. The crazy thought of falling in love with Davide flashed in my crazy mind, but practicality and reality did, alas, prevail.

I then guided him onto the bed; laid him there face down. I stared down at him. His body was perfect, his slightly hairy ass, so beautiful. I touched it, then gently ran my fingers over the soft hairs on each lovely mound, then between them, where my shivering fingers found the hairy crack and savored the moisture. I knelt down between his slightly spread legs and kissed the moistened crack, then kissed the balls and dick stretched stiffly down his leg beneath him.

The desire was overwhelming. Never before had I anticipated entering anyone more. I wanted desperately to be inside of him, to be inside that beautiful ass of his, to feel his walls consuming me, swallowing me.

I reached for one of the condoms on the nightstand, tore open the packet with my teeth, removed it with dexterous fingers, and rolled it down my stiff shaft.

He lay there in submissive stillness as I moistened the tiny pucker of his ass with lube. Only when my jelled finger penetrated the pucker, ever so slightly, did he flinch.

There was no doubt about it. He was very tight, perhaps even a virgin. I would have to take my time; be very gentle. And so as I crawled up behind him, applied an extra glob of lube on my latex-covered member, I approached his beautiful hole like the precious jewel that it was.

My dick gently touched his tight opening. Slowly, very slowly, I proceeded to enter him with the very tip of my dick head, hoping that the slow delicateness would cajole his tight ass into giving a little, allowing the muscles to relax. Instead, he stiffened in pain. Though barely in, I pulled out immediately.

I massaged his throbbing pucker, and it seemed to bring some small relief.

Again, I tried to enter him, even slower than before, and managed to bury half of my head inside of him, but this did not come without a price. His agonized squeal frightened me, and the head of my dick felt unpleasantly choked by the severe tightness that had no physical way to accommodate my desire. Still, I tried once again, and the involuntary pain I inflicted on this poor child without as much of an inch of penetration was sheer torture for us both.

"*Por favor,*" he cried, pushing my body away from his agony. "*Por favor, señor.*"

I was not some savage sex fiend, tearing into some poor boy's booty-hole just to get my nut without thoughts of and/or consideration for him. Or was I?

Besides, I'm only eight inches. Not a mere morsel for sure, but certainly no one's prize-winning county fair cucumber.

Suddenly, Sean's asshole flashed into my memory. Sean loved getting fucked by me, and obviously loved getting fucked by Brad Pitt's stand-in.

Davide did not love, did not even like, getting fucked. And as much as he tried, I could get no satisfaction in bringing him so much pain.

"Davide," I said as he continued to whimper, unable to look at me. "Davide."

I crawled up beside him, lying so innocently violated, and took his face into my hand. I wiped away his tears, and looked him in the eye.

"*¿Ninguna problema, bueno?*" He could not answer, and tried to look away again, but I would not let him. "*¿Bueno?*" I said again. "Understand?"

Sniffling, he finally nodded his head. He then got up and went into the bathroom. The shower water ran again, not as long this time, or perhaps longer than I thought, as I was anxious to rush the miserable thoughts out of my head, and hoped that he, Davide, would somehow realize that maybe this is not the job for him.

When he finally came out of the bathroom, he was fully dressed. Without looking up at me, he started toward the door.

"Davide," I called after him, "wait." He turned back to me, still shackled by a shame he did not need to feel.

I grabbed my pants and reached inside the pocket. I retrieved a twenty-dollar bill. I tried to hand it to him. He held his hand up in protest.

"*No, señor,*" he begged, "I do nothing."

"No, Davide," I said. "I want you to have this."

"Please, *señor,*" he insisted.

"Here," *I* insisted, and stuffed it in his pocket.

He lowered his head and almost started to cry again. Then he slowly looked up and once again our eyes met.

"*Gracias, señor,*" he said. "*Esto será bueno para mi mujer y mi bebé.*"

Good for his wife and his baby? It hit me so hard that I barely noticed him leaving. I quietly closed the door behind him.

Wow. What the hell was I doing? Granted, my dick is my dick but my dick has a conscience. Or maybe I'm really just that dork in Francesca's phone photo taken at the family get-together.

"So how was he?" Cedric asked when I finally reappeared in the parlor, newly showered, emotionally sober.

"Very nice," I said, "Very nice indeed."

"And how was the sex? Did you get everything that you asked for?"

"That and more," I lied. But did I? No, I didn't lie. When Davide said *Thank you. It will be good for my wife and baby*, I felt human again. What more could one ask?

"Good," Cedric said, interrupting my thoughts. "Davide is one of my newest. You are his first here at House of John. What a little angel he is. I hoped that his performance would be as pleasing as his appearance. I am so glad that it was."

"Totally, Cedric. Totally."

I truly believed that Davide would never be back at House of John again.

Chapter Six

It was two o'clock in the morning. I lay wide-awake in my bed staring up at that damn lazy Casablanca fan thinking about my first night in Santo Domingo and House of John, still thinking about my encounter with Davide. What a helluva way to start off a vacation.

Just a few hours ago, House of John was brimming with beautiful men for me to choose from, and here I was lying up in this strange bed, in this rented room, whacking off like a pimpled teenager. I don't know. I guess the thought of trying to cram my dick up Davide's unrelenting ass temporarily took me out of the mood, but now that my horniness had returned full throttle, all the *bugarrones* were either gone for the night or hooked-up with somebody else.

I finally fell asleep on my cum-stained towel around three. Six hours later I was awakened by Carlos's knock on the door and the announcement of breakfast in a half hour on the dining terrace.

I showered and dressed quickly; anxious to be tortured by my fellow travelers' tales of sexual exploits, enviously sure they all fared better than I.

When I stepped out onto the palm-shaded terrace, they were all there, and then some. By the bright salutations, varied grins, dreamy eyes, hearty appetites, and extra guests, it appeared they had all fared *very* well, dammit. I tried to put on my best game face, headed for the buffet table and filled my plate with enough salted cod fish, scrambled eggs with cilantro, topped with sautéed onions, something called mangu, mashed plantains, boiled cassava, and deep-fried Dominican cheese to hopefully make them think that my previous night's activities were invigorating enough to make me famished, too. I then swaggered over to the empty seat next to Sylvester Winfrey, hoping that the swagger wasn't overkill. When I sat, he gave me the high-five.

"All right, dude," he said admiringly.

"What can I say?" I smirked, sucking on an imaginary toothpick. I set my plate down in front of me and attacked it with cool elegance. On my right sat a stunning local who, by the under-the-table foot play I casually peeped, was Jarvis McCready's sleepover trade.

Doctor Mo, facing me, had obviously found Tomás, seated next to him and chowing down like an athlete in training, to his liking. How could any of us forget Tomás, the thick battering ram rough trade with the unnatural bulge between his legs, one of the first three we were introduced to last night? It was no secret that the good doctor was a devout bottom. In fact, his strictly dickly status was legendary. I suspected that Doctor Bottom and the big dick battering ram made the perfect match.

As breakfast progressed, kiss-and-tell stories abounded. Most of my colleagues had turned a trick or two, others like Art and the Hicks twins had gotten worn out after a single encounter, while Doctor Mo, Henry Anderson, and Oliver Bevins were so impressed with their *bugarrones* that they became full-fledge sponsoring johns, offering lavish fees for full night, multiple day and/or full three-week exclusivity; vacation boyfriends, if you will.

Doctor Mo became the envy of hungry bottoms like Tim Thompson, Art Pierce, and Martin Carl, who had waited in line for a piece of the Tomás action, only to be informed that the show was now sold out.

Talk of what the coming night might hold was as delicious as the food laid out before us.

"Will Efraín be back tonight?" Myron Hicks asked. "I really liked him. I wouldn't mind some of that again."

"He *is* quite nice, isn't he?" Cedric said, smiling with sweet memories of his own. "And Rodrigo will be back too."

"Oh hot!" Sylvester squealed. "I had my eye on that, but Father Martin got to him first."

"Age before beauty, chile," Martin crooned.

"You mean bucks for the fuck," Sylvester snapped good-naturedly.

"Money do talk," Martin snapped back.

"And I bet you talked big time, didn't you?"

"You saw what that boy looked like. I paid him what he was worth. And then after he sexed me down, I tipped his phine ass double."

"So the sex is as good as it looks?"

"Is a Bentley as good as it cost?"

Everybody fell out in a howling laughter, except for the *bugarrones*, unable to understand much English.

"Well now if it's that good, maybe I should try some of that," Byron Hicks chimed in.

"Wait yo' turn, bitch!" Sylvester declared, standing with both hands on his hips, sending the table into convulsions.

"Now, now, gentlemen. No need to fret," Will refereed with ease. "If you thought last night was something, wait until to-night. Trust me, Cedric has promised plenty of lovelies to go around, all with exceptional skills."

You would have thought Will had just announced recess to a bunch of fourth graders.

I must confess I was just as excited about the prospects of the coming night, even though when Will said "all with exceptional skills" I couldn't help but think of Davide.

Think positive, I said to myself. I needed to realize that, vacation-wise, this was just the beginning, not the end. All I had to do was look around the table at all the smiling, laughing faces and satisfied customers, and realize that the best was yet to come. I vowed to begin Jesse Lee Templeton III's sexual odyssey in earnest that very night. Equipped with my modest but eager eight inches, I was now fully prepared to indulge in the recreation I had wet-dreamed about. Three weeks of seriously fucking my brains out!

Chapter Seven

The next night couldn't come fast enough. And I was not about to make the same mistake I had made the night before. I realized that something inside of me had chosen Davide for his romantic qualities more than his blatant sexual appeal. Well, I wasn't down here for romance. I was down here for sex. And that's exactly what I was going to go for.

I ditched the candles, rejected the idea of smooth background jazz, and kept the doors leading out to my balcony open all day to fumigate the scented sissy shit that still lingered.

That night, I descended the staircase into the foyer with a new determination and a bit of the swagger I had tried out at breakfast. I made an entrance into the buzzing parlor, surveyed it, spotted my target and made my approach. In no time at all I made a thirty-dollar connection with Rafael, whose body, and the language he spoke with it, promised great sexual satisfaction, and it was not a promise unfulfilled. We had the kind of knock-down-drag-out sex that one usually sees between porno professionals. Well, that's exactly what was going on. He was a professional *bugarrón* and I was a professional john, and what we did to each other was nothing less than pornographic. We fucked like yard dogs and sweated like pigs. By the time we had both cum, simultaneously I might add, we were huffing and puffing like boxers after eight rounds.

But it didn't stop us from having one more go at it. Again we fucked, sucked, ate, and spanked each other against the wall, on the floor, in the shower, over the sink, out on the balcony, and straddled in the doorway of the closet, which was draped by a curtain of multi-colored fiesta beads. Feet strained for the ceiling as we took turns banging each other on the bed, sending the springs of the mattress wailing in rhythm. We both gave as good as we got sideways, doggy-style, harness-style, every style.

When we finished, I paid Rafael double. We saluted each other as equal champs, and promised to get together a few more times before my vacation was up.

Now I had the hang of it, and I was ready to use those lusty skills re-awakened by Rafael on some of his hot Dominican brothers.

Each night after that I brought a different, phiner piece of island trade to my room and did not finish with him until he gave me at least what Rafael had, in spades.

But every once in a while, in between pumping or getting pumped by some beautiful young local, sixty-nining with greed, imitating Brad Pitt's stand-in fucking my ex on a damask-covered settee, snapping pictures of one gifted *bugarrón* flexible and hung enough to give himself a blow job, Davide would cross my mind, and what he had subjected himself to in order to feed his family.

But was he any different from any of the others? Was he any different from Rafael, or Hector, or Miguel, or Hermes? Like Oprah said, everybody has a story. And like I always say, we all do what we have to do to get what we have to get. In that sense I suppose we're all whores in one way or another.

All I knew was I was getting mine, and a week into my Caribbean sexcapades, I was enjoying the hell out of every minute of it.

Or was I?

Chapter Eight

Okay, I had determined that I was going to fuck, suck, and pluck Sean right out of my mind, and Lord knows I tried my best. But you know something? That's a lot of work. Not that I had any lingering feelings for Sean outside of contempt, but that's exactly the point. There's really not a lot of satisfaction in revenge sex, only symbolic vindication.

Yes, the beautiful young men that lingered leisurely, seductively, invitingly, in the foyer and parlor areas of Casa de Mita like so many Tennessee Williams boy toys, were choice indeed, as beautiful as a—picture, and Cedric's supply of lube and condoms was nearly depleted by us twelve disciples of carnal indulgences.

Yes, I did spend my first week in the DR taking beauty after beauty up the stairs to my room, and paying them for all kinds of sexual favors, and, yes, it was a total turn-on.

And to be perfectly fair, we dirty dozen did occasionally come up for air. During the day we often headed over to the Condistre, the Colonial Zone's main pedestrian walkway, a cobblestoned street lined on either side by a kaleidoscope of chic sidewalk cafés, fifteenth-century fountains, electronic stores, Internet call

278 / Stanley Bennett Clay

centers, souvenir shops, even a Pizza Hut, and peopled with tourists, street peddlers, and aggressive little boys selling shoe shines and, yes, alluring bigger boys selling themselves.

Yes, we would head over there, not always in a pack, and people-watch, take pictures, have a drink, and soak in the local atmosphere. Sometimes at night we would head over to the gay clubs and dance and flirt and be flirted with, or hang out on the dining patio and play dominoes and Uno, which Carlos taught us all to play.

But for me, after a week of primarily all-night fucking, I was feeling . . . numb. Sean had slowly become a nonentity. I was becoming one, too.

I stood on the balcony of my room and breathed in the moist air of the city, hoping to clear my mind, hoping to re-assess my hopes, dreams, desires, and purpose; hoping to re-assess myself and make some sense of me. I thought I knew what I wanted in life, but then, as a thirty-eight-year-old black gay man paying men for sex, I wondered if that dream was possible in a world where legal commitment was denied those who loved, liked, and lusted like me. I wanted what my parents had, what my little brother Andre had with his wife Dee. I wanted what Uncle Mickey and Aunt Till had, what my fool brother Craig had with his wife Rebecca. At the very least, I wanted the dream that my lesbian cousin Laura shared with her partner Cheryl.

But as second-class-citizen as that was, I didn't even have that, and I can't blame that on legal marriage restrictions. I have to blame my own callousness, my impatience with the cultivation process that allowed my parents' love to grow and flourish over time.

I wanted to fall in love with some man's heart and soul and being, not the hole he shits out of. But that doesn't happen overnight, and it's foolish of me to think that some flying fairy godfather with a sparkly wand was going to zap me, and the love of my life would suddenly appear in a cloud of pastel stardust.

Instant gratification is easy, that I know. But according to those who truly know best, love is hard. It only looks easy.

Carlos had earlier knocked on my door and in charisma-ese let it be known that an Uno game was starting on the dining terrace and all American suckers needed to apply, especially considering that some of the daytime *bugarrones* were at the table, booking customers.

The announcement did little for me, well, except for maybe the game of Uno, which I had gotten quite good at. But sex with the *bugarrones* had become too steady a diet of candy and cookies.

Here I was, standing on this balcony, overlooking this beautiful city full of beautiful people and history, and most of my time was spent locked in a room having sex with a stranger. Wouldn't it be nice to make love to someone I knew?

I showered and dressed in my white linen shirt, my long, loose-fitting khaki shorts, and a pair of sandals. I strapped my camera on my shoulder and checked my camera bag to make sure I had plenty of batteries, and walked out of my room.

As I walked down the stairs I was gleefully struck by the ruckus that poured from the dining terrace outside. A game of Uno was indeed in full swing. Cedric was parked at his computer behind the front desk. He looked up, saw me, and smiled.

"Hola," he said in his usual friendly tone.

"Hola," I returned, staring out toward the terrace where my American friends and their Dominican guests competed and partied and drank Cuba Libres and Presidentes.

"You're not going to join them?" Cedric asked with allure.

"Nah," I answered, "I'll check them out later."

"So where are you off to?"

"I'm going to go and check out your beautiful city."

"Well, just be careful out there."

"I will."

"And don't get lost."

"Don't worry, Cedric. I think I can find my way back."

Chapter Nine

"So where have you been?" Sylvester asked when I entered the foyer at sunset, just in time for dinner. The young man he was ushering out of the building was obviously worth every dime he had paid him, if lingering looks had a say in it.

"Sightseeing," I beamed, as Sylvester waved at the boy who, crossing the street, waved back with a devilish smile. "Just out being a typical tourist."

"Did you meet anyone interesting?" Sylvester sighed, watching the boy disappear down the street.

"Actually, yeah."

"Hmmm," he purred, still watching the boy. "You better be careful. Will said the *bugarrones* who come here have all been pre-screened and Cedric has copies of all their IDs. I wouldn't venture too far off the reservation, if I were you. I hear street trade can be dangerous."

"Oh no," I said quickly. "It wasn't anything like that, Sylvester. I met this wonderful older lady. Her name is Señora Lupe Hilario." As I continued my story I scrolled up the photos I'd taken of her. "She's a walking history of the city."

"My God, she's ancient," he said, finally looking my way and checking out the photos. "How the hell old is she?"

"Come on, Syl, I'm a gentleman. I wasn't about to ask her her age."

"So what else did you do?"

"Oh, man. I got some great shots of the Catedral de Santa Maria," I said, scrolling them up.

"The what?"

"The Cathedral of Santa Maria," I said, showing him, "the oldest cathedral in all the Americas. It was completed like in 1544. Isn't it magnificent?"

"Fabulous. How'd you find it?"

"Señora Hilario took me."

"Took you?"

"Yeah, on her moped," I said.

"Really?"

"And then she took me to this ancient fort, Fort Ozama, built in 1507, and it has this staircase that goes all the way to the roof of the tower. And, man, you can see the whole city from up there. And then it has this side building, which has the most beautiful statue of the Virgin Mary inside," I gushed on, flipping through picture after picture. "I mean, check this out. Can you believe it?"

"Fascinating."

"You really need to check out the city, dude."

"Well, I'm not really the touristy type. I came down here to lay up, relax, and get laid."

"You don't know what you're missing."

"I ain't missin' shit," he laughed. I laughed right along with him. "Speaking of which," he continued, "you made it back just in time."

"What?"

"After dinner, there's somebody I want you to meet, the crème de la crème, baby. His name is Edgar; hot as hell and right up your alley, or can be, if the price is right. I had him last night, and he's coming back this evening. I highly recommend him."

"Thanks, man, but I think I'm gonna turn in early tonight. Roaming all over the city kinda wore me out."

"Really."

"Yeah. Oh wait. Check this out," I said, scrolling down to the shots of the House of Gargoyles.

"So you really *were* out there being the tourist."

"Yeah, man."

"Damn, Jess. All this good-ass boy-pussy down here and you runnin' around taking picture of monasteries?"

At dinner I shared the photos I'd taken with the other guys in our group. Will was particularly elated and used the opportunity to remind us of our trip to Boca Chica Beach the next day and the city sightseeing tour on Saturday.

As I lay in my bed that night, I felt comforted by all that I had experienced that day, particularly my enchanting encounter with Señora Hilario, even though she stiffened a bit when I told her where I was staying. I had no idea that Casa de Mita had such a notorious reputation. "There is much more to us than you think, young man," she had said to me knowingly.

I also remember trying to give her money for her time and kindness, but she absolutely refused to take anything. "You are a guest in our country," she said with a sweet sternness. "Our hospitality is not for sale."

After I thanked her and we said our good-byes, I found my way to the Malecón, the picturesque boardwalk that lay between the bustling city's touristy commerce district, which included a Hilton Hotel and Casino on one side, and the ancient mocking sea on the other. It was, quite surprisingly, within walking distance of the Casa de Mita.

The next day I rose early and, armed with my trusty camera,

headed back to the Malecón, had breakfast at the little outdoor café that jetted out over a rocky ledge above the water, and took pictures of the beautifully diverse locals as they started their day; opening their shops and businesses, setting out their wares, hawking fruit and vegetables from horse-drawn carts, push-carts, and bicycle baskets. Uniformed children skipped along the Malecón headed off to school, while gray-haired men loaded fishing gear onto fishing boats and headed out to sea.

So many smiling faces and interesting-looking people in-dulged me as they passed my way, glad to let me take their pic-tures. Some would even stop and pose, and school kids gave me the victory sign.

As the traffic began to thin out and the people reached their destinations, I decided to head back to the hotel, which was only four or five blocks away.

But the sound of a church bell ringing mysteriously drew me in. Was it the fresh tropical morning air upon which rode the tolling bell? Was it the memory of the smiling, sun wor-shipping citizens, young and old, along the Malecón, in their school uniforms and sundresses and work jeans and fishing togs? Was the bell calling out to me as it had called out to them; had been calling out to them all their Catholic lives, lulled into the security of their spiritual devotion and the romance of their simple and complex existence? Was it the tolling bell marking time every hour on the hour that hypnotized them into a calming humbleness that freed them to move along their island paradise as easily as the palm trees swayed and rustled in the gentle breeze?

I was hypnotized by it, helpless in my resistance, yet lucid enough to still fancy its magical hold on things. I followed the sound without realizing I was moving toward it. It rang ten times. I turned the corner and saw the ancient dome just as the ringing stopped. The haunting echo hung in the air.

I gasped. The beauty of the castle-like cathedral took my breath away. Its sand-white façade lured and frightened me.

The detailed carvings round the base of its roof were so perfect and caring that decades of artisans' sacrifice and devotion was its own reward. Giant statues of saints and Madonnas of all sizes posed on pedastels carved into the walls. I was transfixed by it, unable to lift my camera, unable to do much else but let my eyes slowly take in the structure that was older than my country.

A large marble plaza lay out before it, and a wide four-step staircase made from some kind of alabaster granite with tiny flecks of gold led up to the grand and holy entrance.

All I could do was stand there and stare. The splendor was almost too much for my eyes to bear, the plaza too beautiful to cross.

I finally aimed my camera, and captured the cathedral's beauty at every angle.

I then crossed the plaza, and stopped in front of the massive sacred structure, aware of how small I was as I looked up and tried to take in all its towering glory. I then slowly walked up the stairs to the wide open doors and entered its sanctuary.

Inside, a woman, her bowed head covered in white lace, was kneeling at the altar. Candles flickered gently in front of her, flanked her. She finally stood, crossed herself, and walked past me, her brown face glowing. She was at such peace that I was compelled to turn and follow her with my eyes; I watched her leave the dark calm of the sanctuary and enter the bright morning sunlight of the outside world.

I looked around at the beauty: the gilded walls and ceiling, the stained-glass windows, the cloisters and the ancient monastery garden visible through a side entrance near what seemed to be confessionals. I fingered my camera, but could not bring myself to commit what somehow seemed like blasphemy.

I took pictures in my mind, and left the sanctuary in its stillness, undisturbed. I do believe from the bottom of my heart that that one moment of restraint, that tiny regard for sacredness was being rewarded because when I stepped out into the sunshine, I saw the perfect picture.

Chapter Ten

I don't know what it was that made me notice him, providence perhaps, but there he was, across the plaza, for one brief moment. He stepped out of the little shop called Bodega Colonial, placed a stack of newspapers in the stand, looked up at the sky, and stepped back in. But in that brief moment everything about him registered. The picture of him in my mind was as indelible as my mind's picture of the beautiful cathedral, and seemed just as sacred. I had never seen a face so striking in my life. I had to take his picture.

I crossed the plaza and headed toward the little shop he had reentered. I got to the doorway, and stared in. He was standing behind the counter, placing bottles of Coca-Cola in one of those old-fashioned coolers. He looked up and saw me standing there. He smiled, and I thought I would faint, but somehow held on to my cool. Up close he was more beautiful than one man had a right to be; the baby face, the midnight eyes, the sparkling jet-black hair and goatee, the sweeping lashes, the perfectly plump and soft-looking lips, the beautifully pronounced nose, the smooth smoky-gold complexion, the small scar across his left cheekbone, the modest muscles peeking out from under rolled-up sleeves, the stomach flat against his tucked-in shirt, the small waistline.

"*Hola,*" he said.

"*Hola,*" I said, transfixed by him. He returned to stocking the sodas and I finally pulled myself out of my trance, and walked over to him at the counter.

"*Perdóname,*" I said, running my fingers through my dreads. When he straightened up from the cooler I could see that we were the same height. We definitely weren't the same age. He couldn't have been any more than twenty, twenty-two at the most.

"*¿Sí?*" he asked with a merchant's smile.

"*¿Puedo tomar yo algunas fotografías de usted, por favor?*" I struggled through my limited Spanish, and pointed at my camera hanging around my neck.

He chuckled a bit. "*Sí, como no,*" he then said.

"*Gracias,*" I said anxiously as I fumbled to adjust my camera.

I then stepped back and focused the lens. He stood there smiling. My camera was instantly attracted to him. I took four shots and stopped. I didn't want to push my luck.

"*Muchas gracias,*" I said.

"*De nada,*" he answered, looking at my dreads with curious admiration. "*¿Usted es jamaicano?*"

Jamaicano. Jamaicano. I ran through the Spanish-to-English dictionary in my head. Aha! Am I Jamaican!

"No. American."

"Ahhh." He smiled again. "I speak some English. Not good, but some."

"Ahhh," I said, inadvertently mimicking his inflection, and wanting to kick myself. "What is your name?" I asked.

"Étienne," he said, extending his hand. "Étienne Saldano. Étie."

"Jesse Templeton," I said, taking his hand and shaking it. "You have a very interesting look, Étie."

"Oh?"

"Yes." I reached in my pocket and pulled out my business card. "See? I take pictures. That is my profession."

"Oh."

"I would like to take more pictures of you, all around the city, especially here in the Colonial Zone, maybe some in front of the cathedral across the plaza."

"It sounds okay."

"And I'll pay you."

"Oh?"

"Yes."

"¿*Cuánto?*"

"How much?"

"*Sí.*"

"How about . . . twenty U.S. dollars an hour?"

"Each hour?"

"Yes. For about five hours."

"That is good."

"Great."

"*Pero* only on el sábado."

"Saturday?"

"*Sí*. Saturday. *Mañana*. The day I no work."

"Okay. *Mañana*. Is eleven o'clock in the morning good? I wanna make sure we have very good sunlight."

"Yes. Eleven o'clock is good time."

"Do you have a white shirt, like one you would maybe wear to church?"

"A white shirt? Yes."

"Good. Wear that. And the jeans and shoes you have on now will be just fine. By the way, how old are you?"

"¿*Qué?*"

"¿*Cuántos años tiene?*"

"*Veinticinco.*"

"Twenty-five?" I was astonished. "My God, you look like a baby."

"Is good, no?"

"Is *very* good. Your skin. It's astonishing!"

"Astonishing?"

"*Muy excelente.*"

He smiled that smile again.

"Let's meet in front of the church across the plaza. We'll start there."

"Okay."

"And may I say something else to you?"

"*¿Sí?*"

"*Usted es muy hermoso.*"

"*Muchas gracias.*" He blushed, although I could not imagine him not used to being called "very beautiful."

"*Hasta mañana*, Étie."

"*Hasta mañana, mi amigo.*"

I started to leave, but I had to turn around and take one more look at him. "Are you sure you're twenty-five?"

"*Sí.*"

"My God, Étie, you . . . you look so young."

"My soul is very old."

"Are you fucking him?" Sylvester asked when I showed him the four shots I had taken of Étie. We were the first in the parlor, waiting for our shuttle bus excursion to Boca Chica Beach.

"No, I'm not fucking him."

"Well as phine as he is, you should be."

"It's business, Syl. Strictly business."

"Down here, dude, fucking *is* strictly business."

"Jesse?" Will entered with mild concern and a new young companion trailing behind him.

"Hey, Will."

"What's this I hear you're not going on the tour with us tomorrow?"

"He's got a photo shoot," Sylvester cut in, just as the Hicks twins made their entrance.

"A photo shoot?" they asked in unison.

"Man, you're not supposed to be down here working," Myron Hicks fussed. "You're supposed to be on vacation."

"Now, now, Myron," Will defended. "If Jesse wants to spend his vacation taking pictures, then let him. We are going to miss you tomorrow, Jess. We have a fabulous itinerary lined up."

"You should see what Jess has lined up," Sylvester snickered.

"What?"

"Show 'em, Jesse."

"It's no big deal, guys."

"What y'all talkin' about?" Father Martin joined us, yawning, and plopped down at the table.

"Jesse found himself a hot model."

"He's not a model. He's just a guy I met with an interesting look that I'm taking some pictures of."

"Are you fucking him?" Father Martin asked.

"Damn, guys, why I have to be fuckin' him?"

"Because that's what you down here for, dude."

"Well, one thing for sho'," Sylvester said, "the boy is definitely fuck material."

"He's a nice kid."

"Well, can we see?"

With a sigh, I passed around my camera. Eyes popped, teeth got sucked, and grown men purred like children eating candy.

"Goddayamn!!!"

"Now that's what I call hot!"

"Not for me." Doctor Moses, with vacation boyfriend Tomás in tow, grimaced. "A little too pretty for my taste."

"He kinda looks like a dark-skinned Sal Mineo," Father Martin said, as he thoughtfully analyzed the pictures.

"Who?" Jarvis, Art, and Henry asked in a dumbfounded chorus.

"Forget it, children. You way too young to even know what I'm talkin' about," Martin laughed, slapping Dr. Mo's outstretched hand.

"Jesse, you sure you ain't fuckin' that?" Oliver Bevins asked, staring at the camera picture with hunger.

"I am not fucking the boy, okay?" I said, snatching the camera back and getting a little pissed.

Suddenly I was having some real misgivings about letting this gang of hounds even know about Étie. Yes, I know. I can be as sex crazy as any one of them, but Étie was a special project that had nothing to do with sex or them. Suddenly I began to feel very protective of him.

"Listen, guys," Will said, gauging the tension building in the air, "what do you say we leave Jesse to his working vacation, and think about all the lovely gentlemen dropping in to see us tonight?"

To further ease the tension, Carlos appeared and announced that we were ready to go. We all gathered up our beach gear, piled into the hotel's shuttle bus, and headed for Boca Chica.

An hour later we arrived at the beach adjacent to the small resort town of Boca Chica, a reef-protected lagoon of tranquil blue water and powder white sand. The still waters, only waist-deep a hundred yards out, were in great contrast to the beach activity, Will had earlier explained to us. In addition to the friendly Dominican and Haitian vendors that offered such goodies as silver and turquoise jewelry, beautiful indigenous artwork and paintings, hair-braiding and corn-row masters, massages, and some of the best fresh-out-of-the-water broiled fish dishes in the Caribbean, Boca Chica Beach was also known (to those in the know) as the quiet domain of a different kind of *bugarrón;* the beachcomber breed, topless young men with rock hard pecs, impossibly perfect abs and obliques, wearing only thin tight swim briefs that barely contained their manhood, packages made profanely revealing by routine dips in the sea.

And Will was totally correct. From our beach chairs and under our beach umbrellas, these beautiful men were experts in the art of beach seduction, and more than a few from our group indulged, being taken off to secluded cabanas and returned with smiles on their face.

Under other circumstances perhaps I would have indulged. After all, I had not had sex in quite a few days, but all I could think about was Étienne and our photo shoot the next day. Perhaps he could direct me to some desolate beach area to include in our shoot. For as beautiful as Boca Chica was, its bustling commerce did not seem quite the setting for Étie's tranquil, nature boy quality.

Étie. Étienne.

I could barely wait for tomorrow.

Chapter Eleven

The next morning I woke with the rising sun. I had a million ideas for the shoot. Some of them came to me in my dreams; some were inspired by the places Señora Hilario had taken me, while others were spiritually motivated. The beautiful façade of the cathedral that faced Étie's job would provide a moving and contrasting tableau of ancient art and Étie's youthful beauty.

I sat at the little table in my room and made notes.

I could hear moans and groans from the room next door. I smiled and shook my head. It sounded like Sylvester was getting his early morning groove on.

By nine, I had my list complete and organized. I even made a note to ask Étie if he knew of a secluded beach where we could shoot. Dammit, I should have gotten his telephone number. I needed to ask him to bring swimming trunks. I rummaged through my bag and found two pairs of mine. I was a thirty-three waist. Étie could not have been any more than a thirty. The bagginess just might work. If not, I would resort to the old safety-pins-out-of-the-shot routine. I stuffed the trunks and a pack of pins in my smaller carry-on, along with towels, my groom kit, and my small contractible reflector.

I opened my camera case and checked my camera, the three lens attachments, my light meter, and my battery supply. Everything was fine and well stocked.

I shaved and showered, then dressed in a khaki shirt and shorts, and tennis shoes.

I stepped out on the balcony into the bright morning sun. It was exactly 10 A.M. In the distance I began to hear the tolling of church bells, and I knew. It was a sign. Those were the same church bells that drew me to that beautiful cathedral, the same church bells that drew me to Étie.

Cedric was at his computer behind the front desk when I came down the stairs, camera case and carry-on strapped and crisscrossed over my shoulders. The smell of fresh brewed Dominican coffee drew me to the coffee maker on the service table.

"You look like you're going on safari," Cedric said as I poured myself a cup.

"Well I'm definitely going to be doing some shooting," I joked.

I got to the cathedral early and surveyed every angle of its façade through each of my lenses. The mid-morning sunlight silhouetted it perfectly and I just prayed that it would hold until at least eleven-thirty.

It seemed the plaza wore a different face on Saturdays. The monastery calm I had experienced two days earlier had taken on a festive tone. Children off from school and parents off from work skipped and strolled across the sacred marble as casually as a skip across a schoolyard, a stroll across a park. Merengue music pulsed from passing cars. A young boy played his mini-sax from the stone ledge that separated the plaza from the tree-shaded grassy knoll where locals chilled on leisure benches.

The cathedral itself had its own traffic, as every now and then worshippers and tourists and sinners and saints entered and exited the sanctuary with reverence.

And through all of this I saw him, appearing as if out of nowhere, approaching me, waving lightly, smiling broadly, his teeth as white as his crisp white dress shirt. The slight breeze danced a jet-black curl down his face as he bounced eagerly toward me. He was picture perfect.

"*Hola,*" he said, extending his hand.

"*Hola,*" I said, shaking it. "You're early."

"Yes."

"Good. The light behind the cathedral is perfect. Come on. Let's get started."

I posed him humbled at the feet of sculptured saints sentried on pedestals near the sanctuary's entrance. I captured his wonder as a flurry of pigeons ascended from the plaza to the sky, his laughter with children who beat him in a race across the plaza.

I zoomed in on his dark pensive profile, the scar across his left cheek, while blurring children playing in the background. The contrast was magical; a sweet saddened angel, wounded and estranged from the fiesta of celestial glory.

I still could not bring myself to take pictures inside the cathedral, so I captured him praying in the Gethsemane-like monastery garden.

We then bused and taxied all around the Colonial Zone where I captured his classic look against romantic ruins, his quiet walks through quaint and colorful colonial streets, his youthful glee in crowded marketplaces where he draped necklaces encrusted with native amber around ascended fingers and offered them to the sun. My camera had fallen in love with him.

Our final location was not a beach, but a small, secluded, black-rock cove hidden beneath the Malecón, not far from where we started. So near and yet so far away from the bustling thoroughfare, Étie told me that this small patch of land, dotted with gothic-looking trees, had been one of his favorite play spots as a child.

"My escape," he said quietly.

"Escape from what?" I asked.

He stared out over the water, lost in some strange thought. I took the picture. The click of the camera brought him to. He turned to me and smiled.

"You show me the swim things?" he asked with a sudden brightness.

"Okay," I said as I rummaged through the carry-on and pulled out the trunks and the towels. I handed him the yellow boxer-style ones, the color I felt most suited his skin tone.

"I go put on."

"Okay." I had to smile as he took the trunks and a towel and went to change behind a tree. His modesty was endearing.

While he changed I checked the battery on my camera then measured the shaded light with my meter. I then looked out over the sea where the sun sparkled brightly upon its water, which silhouetted the shore much like the morning sun had silhouetted the cathedral. It was a hauntingly beautiful setting.

"I am ready."

I turned to him. As thin as he was I didn't expect his body to be so perfectly sculpted. Yes, the trunks did indeed hang loosely from his small waist, but from the slightly hairy, well-defined chest and arms, the modest six-pack and flat stomach to the perfectly formed calves and beautiful feet, he was a work of art.

"Yeah, we're gonna have to do something about those trunks," I finally said.

"¿Perdóname?"

I went to my bag and pulled out the pack of pins. "Come, please," I said, sitting on a rock. He did, and stood directly in front of me. I turned him around. Thank God for his nicely formed behind. It did hold the trunks up a bit, even though the hairy top of his crack peeped over. I pulled the trunks up a bit, gathered it at the waistband, and carefully pinned the gather. I took another pin, tightened the play between his cheeks, and pinned it with a tailor's neatness.

"Okay, kiddo, turn around. Let's see what we have here."

A bit confused, he did manage to turn around, then waited for further instructions.

"Now step back a bit," I gently commanded, throwing in a pushback hand gesture for good measure. He backed up a few steps. I stood and surveyed the fit. I smiled and gave him the thumbs up. He smiled and returned the thumbs up.

This final leg of the shoot was the best in a series of greats. We had come to understand each other's language, had created a shorthand, and he was definitely in his element, playing in and around the water. It was easy to see why his body was in such great shape. He was an excellent swimmer and boasted that he had been swimming almost every week since before he could walk.

We laughed and joked and got downright silly out on that cove. Confessing that his favorite foreign television show was *America's Top Model,* he vogued along the shore with abandonment.

"Look! I am supermodel!" he declared, striking a pose that completely reduced me to convulsing hysteria. I don't know if I really thought about whether he was gay or not, but watching him camp it up truly gave me pause. But whatever it was, he expressed a special freedom out there that I had not witnessed before. It truly was his escape. From what? I did not know.

The shoot ended at around four o'clock. Étie was truly wonderful, so natural in front of the camera and so photogenic that the pictures took themselves. He had more than earned the one hundred dollars I paid him.

"You were fabulous, kiddo, you know that?"

"Really?"

"Totally."

"Thank you, Jesse."

"In fact, what are you doing tonight?"

"*Nada mas,* why?"

"I wanna take you to dinner," I said, "to show my gratitude."

"But you already pay me."

"Well, consider dinner a tip."

"Tip?"

"Extra. A gratuity."

"Dinner."

"Yes. I would be so honored, Étie."

"Okay," he finally said. "Where?"

"Hmmm. Let me think. The Hilton, over by the Malecón?"

"Oh yes. It is not far from here."

"Let's say we meet in the lobby at eight o'clock."

"Yes."

"Yes."

We stood there, staring at each other for a long time. We both blushed. And then he extended his hand.

"I go home now," he said.

"Okay," I said, shaking his hand, holding it maybe a bit longer than I should have. "See you tonight."

I watched him as he walked away. He knew I was watching him. I could tell by the look on his face, the smile on his face, when he turned around and waved at me. I waved back.

Before returning to Casa de Mita, I stopped off at the Hilton and made dinner reservations.

It was a little after five when I got back to Casa de Mita. It was pretty desolate, save for Cedric at his post behind the front desk and in front of his computer. The guys had not gotten back yet from their city tour, and actually, I was rather glad. I wasn't really ready for the Spanish Inquisition.

Cedric and I greeted each other as I rushed past him and up the stairs to my room. I couldn't wait to download the pictures on my laptop. Once done, I put them on slide show.

"Damn, I'm good," I had to confess to myself as I watched shot after shot of Étienne in complement and contrast to his country's beautiful setting.

I let the slide show continue as I picked up the phone and dialed my baby sister's number. I hadn't talked to her since leaving Los Angeles. I know part of it was because I had not told her my real reason for coming down here. Not that I thought Frankie would be bothered that I was coming down here to pay for sex, but it was just a little embarrassing. Now that I had this great photo shoot, I had something else to talk to her about.

"Junie!" she screamed gleefully after picking up on the first ring.

"Hey, Doll."

"Now why the hell are you just now calling me?"

"Sorry, sis. Been having too much fun checking out the sights, getting drunk, and partying my ass off."

"You always did know how to vacation."

"And besides, that works two ways. You ain't called me either."

"Well yeah, you right," she confessed.

"So what's his name?"

"Huh?"

"Whenever you go MIA, sis, means you got a new man in your life."

"Okay, okay, okay," she laughed. "You got me. His name's Burt, and it's just a temporary thing. He's a bit too needy for my taste but the sex is off the hook."

"You just never change, do you, baby girl?"

"And why should I?"

"So what are you up to? What's going on there?"

"Well actually, I'm working."

"What? Good for you."

"I booked a guest-starring spot on *How I Met Your Mother.* I'm playing Neil Patrick Harris's piece of the week."

"Well all right!"

"I'm at the studio now. We're on lunch break. Now, enough about me. How's it going with you down there? Are you enjoying yourself?"

"Loving it! It is so beautiful down here, and the people are so friendly. I've taken a lot of pictures."

"Cool, can't wait to see them."

"And Frankie, I met this guy—"

"Really?"

"A Dominican who is *sooo* drop-dead gorgeous—"

"Okay."

"I just finish doing a whole photo session on him. I mean this guy could really be a great model. There's just something really magical about him; in his eyes, in the way he smiles, the way he moves. It's almost unearthly."

There was a long pause.

"Junie," Frankie finally said.

"Yeah?"

"Not another model type."

"What?"

"Didn't you learn your lesson with Sean?"

"Oh, no, no, no, no, no, Frankie. It's not like that. It's strictly business. Nothin' going on between us."

"Then how come I'm hearing what I'm hearing in your voice?"

"What?"

"I been your sister a long time, Jesse."

"And your point is?"

"Okay now."

"And besides, he's not really a model. He's a kid that works in a bodega. It's just that he has this . . . this . . . quality."

"Uh-huh."

"Look, I'm gonna e-mail you some pictures of him. You tell me."

"All right," she said, not very convinced. "Hey look, baby, lunch break is over and I gotta get back on set."

"Okay, sweetie. Tell the family I said hi."

"I will. Love you."

"Love you too."

"And take care of yourself."

"I will."

"And take care of your heart."

"Good-bye, Frankie."

I hung up.

Okay, what was that about? There was nothing in my voice. Étie's a nice kid and, yes, the feelings I had for him were strong, but I wouldn't necessarily call them romantic. Besides, I didn't even know if he was gay, even though I had to wonder about a guy whose favorite show was *America's Top Model.*

Nonsense. I'm old enough to be his . . . big brother. I wondered now if I should even e-mail pictures of him to her, confirming something that didn't really exist. Sure, I was a hopeless romantic and Frankie knew it. And Étie was just the kind of guy hopeless romantics fall in love with: soft, vulnerable, angelic, thoughtful, funny, sweet, kind of spirit, generous of heart. Thank God I didn't tell her I was having dinner with him.

Forget about Frankie, even though, Lord knows, she means well.

It was almost six o'clock. It was time for me to get ready for my date . . . my *meeting* with Étie.

At seven fifteen I stepped out of the shower, fussed a bit in the mirror, then slipped on my yellow Talsa Elba pima cotton polo shirt, my chestnut-colored Perry Ellis slacks, and slipped my bare feet into a pair of Italian loafers. I then sprayed on a hint of Annuci. I looked and smelled fine.

When I left my room and walked down the hallway toward the stairs, I ran into Sylvester, who was headed toward his room.

"Wow, aren't we all dolled up," he said. "Who's the lucky piece?"

"Nah, I'm just taking myself out to dinner."

"You're not dining with us tonight?"

"Not tonight. I just don't feel like being cooped up here in the hotel all evening."

"You will be back in time for the boys, won't you?"

"I . . . I'm not sure."

"Edgar'll be here tonight. He really wants to give you some, Jesse. He thinks you're hot."

"We'll see," I said as I skipped down the staircase, with a wave.

"Headed back out for safari?" Cedric asked slyly, eyeing my attire and the light whiff of cologne as I passed by the desk and headed for the door.

"Something like that," I said, noticing some of the fellas sipping on cocktails and peeking out at me knowingly from the parlor while Carlos and Emilio prepared the table out on the dining terrace.

"So how was the photo shoot?" Will asked quietly as he walked me to the main entrance of the hotel.

"It went really well," I answered.

"Good, good," Will continued, "I'm just glad you're having a good time."

"I am, Will. Thanks. See you later."

I walked through the front door and the wrought-iron gate, listening to them both lock behind me. The night air was humid, but pleasant. I checked my watch. Seven forty-six. The Hilton was an easy ten-minute walk away. I didn't want to rush. With the moisture in the air, I didn't want to work up a sweat.

I started down the street and noticed the handsome young man walking toward me. He looked familiar. I looked familiar to him.

"*Hola,*" he said with a smile, stopping.

"*Hola,*" I said, but kept walking. I didn't want to be late meeting Étienne. I felt the young man watching me. In my mind I remembered the face. But of course. He was one of the *bugarrones* who had visited House of John on more than a few evenings. Without stopping, I looked back at him, over my shoulder.

"*Me llamo Edgar,*" he said, eyeing me seductively.

I nodded, still without stopping. "*Hola,*" I said, then turned to look straight ahead of me. Ahhh. Edgar. The guy Sylvester wanted me to meet. I kept on walking. A smile of confidence and relief decorated my face. I could hear the doorbell of House of John ringing behind me. I could hear the clang of the door unlocking, the wrought-iron gate unlocking. I glanced back once more, just in time to see him disappear inside, and I was happy. I was on my way to have dinner with Étienne Saldano.

Chapter Twelve

I arrived at the Hilton at eight minutes to eight. I guess I rushed after all, in spite of myself. I entered the lobby and anxiously looked around. He wasn't there yet. I took a seat. A smiling cocktail waitress approached me and asked if I wanted a drink. "*No, gracias,*" I said. She nodded and walked away.

I checked my watch again. Five of eight. When I looked up, there he was, all twenty-five years of him, as neat as a prep school boy, as handsome as a prince. He wore a simple white shirt, white pants, and white bucks, a complementary ensemble against his beautiful brown skin and black hair.

I watched him as he scanned the room. Then he saw me. He smiled that smile of his as he approached me. I smiled as I stood.

"*Hola,*" he said, extending his hand.

"*Hola,*" I said, shaking it. "Shall we?"

I escorted him to the elevator, which took us to the fifth floor. We rode in smiling silence before the doors opened onto the beautiful dining room of the Sol y Sombra restaurant. I was as stunned by its beauty as Étie was.

The maitre d' promptly found the reservation I had made earlier and led us to an intimate candlelit table that overlooked the sea beyond the glass wall.

Again I raved on and on about how great he was during the photo shoot.

"You really could be a professional model, Étie."

"Do you think?"

"I know."

The waiter came over and took our drink orders. Étie ordered a Presidente beer. I ordered a glass of Chardonnay. As we studied our dinner menus, the photographer in me could not help but notice how the candlelight played upon his face, giving it a sort of Rembrandt sheen. He caught me staring; studying his face.

"*Qué?*"

"Oh it's nothing," I said, snapping out of it. "Yeah, kiddo, you really could have a great future as a model."

He blushed and smiled.

The waiter came and took our dinner orders. I had a taste for Dominican cuisine so I ordered one of the house specialties, a crayfish medley with brown beans and rice and a frog legs appetizer. Étie ordered steak and fries.

The food was as nourishing as our conversation. I learned a lot about Étie that night, and I revealed much about me. I no longer had to guess whether he was gay or not, not that it mattered. He was very forthcoming about it, in fact rather cavalier. Somehow we had gotten on the subject of relationships. That we had both recently gone through breakups based on our ex's infidelity was something we had in common. Neither one of us wanted to spoil the evening by going into sordid details, but when he said "my boyfriend was total asshole," he wanted to make sure that I knew it wasn't a woman he was talking about.

"I am proud gay man," he declared with a sweet arrogance.

"Me too," I said.

"I know."

"You did?" I asked, not remembering if I had identified my ex as male or female, not that it mattered to me either.

"*Sí.*"

"How did you know?"

"How you say? Gaydar?"

"Very good gaydar," I laughed.

"*Sí, muy bueno gaydar,*" he laughed too.

He told me so much about his life. His mother died delivering him. His father raised him with an iron fist.

"He hate my softness," he said without pity. "Call me señorita, sissy, faggala. He say why I no die with *mi madre.*

"He try beat gay out of me. That is scar on my face. From beat me. That is why I go to my escape. Swim all day when not in school. Stay from home, stay from beating.

"Maybe it was good he put me out when I was, how you say? Fifteen. Living in street better than living with him. Hungry many nights, but hunger better than beatings.

"Get jobs, shine shoes, wash car windows at stoplights, make jewelry and sell to tourist. Men try to buy my sex, but I say no. Never me be *bugarrón.* Never!

"Now I have good job at bodega. *No mucho dinero,* but boss good man. Kind, like *padre* I never had."

I sat there for a while in silence, not knowing what to say. I saw a side of Étie that I could not have known existed. Behind the child-like innocence, the gentle smile, the fragile beauty, was a strength of character, a survival instinct anchored in dignity and self-respect. Behind the delicate demeanor was a man.

"You no worry, Jesse," he said, gently touching my hand. "You no have to say anything."

"Let me get a taxi to take you home."

"Oh no, I no live far from here. And it is beautiful night to walk."

306 / *Stanley Bennett Clay*

"Well then at least let me walk you home."

"No, *gracias,* Jesse. You be so nice to me already."

"Then you be so nice to me and let me walk you home."

How could he refuse?

We walked along the brightly lit Malecón into a sleepy neighborhood lit by gas-fueled streetlights straight out of an old black and white movie. Colonial houses, their brick and stone façades peeking through brightly colored stucco finishes, lined the winding narrow cobblestone street. I expected a horse-drawn carriage to come clickity-clacking by any moment, but no. There was just the silence of the night and the echo of our quiet conversation.

"This is where I live," Étie said. We had stopped in front of a lovely place with a gated and canopied archway that opened onto what seemed to be a tropical patio dotted with lush mango trees. Beyond the patio was the house. A single lantern light, il-luminated, hung over the large wooden door. "I have room here."

"Nice," I said admiring it, then admiring him. "Étie?"

"Yes, Jesse?"

"I'm really glad I met you."

"Me too."

"I'll be here for ten more days. Maybe we can hang out some more?"

"Hang out?"

"Be together. Go places."

"Oh . . . I would like."

"Good. I will call you."

"Okay."

"Except *yo no tengo su número de teléfono.*"

"Oh!" he realized with wide eyes. He reached in his pocket and pulled out a small note pad and a pen. "I write down." He did, and handed it to me with a small giggle.

"Thank you."

"You are welcome, Jesse . . . And Jesse?"

"Yes?"

"Thank you for tonight, for everything."

"*De nada*, kiddo."

"Jesse?"

"*Sí?*"

"What is 'kiddo'?"

"Hmmm. Let's see. It's kind of like 'amigo.' "

"Ahhh. Amigo."

"But not totally."

"I no understand."

"Okay. It's more like what an older amigo like me would say to a younger amigo like you."

"But you are not 'older.' "

"I'm a lot older than you, Étie."

"Oh? How old?"

"Thirty-eight."

"*Qué?*"

"*Treinta y ocho.*"

"*¿Treinta y ocho?*"

"*Sí.*"

"But that is not so older."

"I'm afraid it is."

"But look at you. Remember what you call me? You said *'Es muy hermoso.' Usted es muy hermoso también.*"

"You think I am very beautiful, too?" I asked in quiet amazement.

"Yes," he said softly, his eyes never leaving mine. "From moment I first saw you."

And then it happened. Slowly, he drew closer to me, our eyes still unwavering, closing only as our lips touched, softly, ever so gently. We parted slowly, but held in the embrace neither one of us realized we had been in. We stared in each other's eyes. We smiled.

308 / *Stanley Bennett Clay*

"I will go in now," he whispered.

"Okay," I whispered back, finding myself gently pushing back the curl that had fallen over his eye, touching his face, the scar on his cheek, caressing his earlobe, allowing my fingers to scan a picture of his beautiful face, before letting him go.

"You will call me, no?"

"I will call you, yes."

He then entered the gate. The gentle clang as it closed brought me out of my daze. I looked after him as he walked through the patio, past the mango trees, to the big wooden door where the illuminated lantern hung overhead. I watched him wave to me, and I waved back. And as I watched him open that big wooden door and disappear behind it, I had to finally admit what my heart had been telling me. Not only had my camera fallen in love with Étienne Saldano, so had I.

Chapter Thirteen

I nearly danced my way back to Casa de Mita, wondering if I had dreamed it all, *afraid* I had dreamed it all.

As Casa de Mita came into view, I had to decide what I was going to do. There was no way I could disguise the glow that lit up my face, quiet the joy that filled my heart. Did I dare tell the others what just happened? But then, what was there to tell? I had fallen in love with the most wonderful guy in the world. I could hardly explain it to myself, so how could I possibly make them understand? Or did I even want to?

And I certainly did not want to spoil getting to know Étienne with the specter of sex hovering like a dark cloud. If I told them about him, my feelings about him, they would be right back on the sex thing again. How was he in bed? And even if something intimate were to happen between Étie and me, that would be the last thing I would discuss with them. I didn't know why I was feeling that way. Correction. I knew exactly why I was feeling that way. I was in love.

Although it was late, I entered Casa de Mita to raucous laughter and loud music. The fellas were in a festive mood, having obviously had their physical needs satisfied. Except for Tomás, Dr. Mo's vacation boyfriend, and a couple of over-nighters, most of the *bugarrones* were gone for the night, but that did not stop my American friends from celebrating, excited by Cedric's announcement that a new crop of fresh young men would be making their appearances over the next few nights.

"Of course some of the old standbys will be back," Cedric assured them.

"Including Edgar," Sylvester updated me with a whisper and a wink. "Edgar said that he saw you tonight, and that the two of you made eye contact."

"Oh yeah," I said. "Seems like a nice enough guy."

"Nice enough guy? The motherfucker is phine as fuck. And he's got the hots for you, dude."

"You mean he's got the hots for my dollars."

"Nah, Jesse, seriously."

I gave him a look.

"Okay, okay, okay," he demurred, "Yeah, he wants to get paid, what's wrong with that? But dude ain't just gay for pay. He's gay for real. And you saw what he looks like."

"Yeah."

"Good-lookin' dude, man."

"So what's up, Syl? You dude's pimp or something?" I joked.

"Just tryin' to share the wealth, baby. Just tryin' to share the wealth." We knocked knuckles and shared a laugh and a brothaman hug. As I headed toward the stairs, Will stopped me.

"Is everything okay?" he asked, looking at me like a doctor looks into the eyes of a patient in denial.

"I'm fine," I assured him with more enthusiasm than I wanted to display.

"You've been so quiet, sort of off to yourself," he continued. "Are you having a good time?"

"I'm having the most incredible time of my life, William," I said, barely able to contain myself. In fact I wanted to find a mountaintop and sing from it, sing that old Rodgers and Hammerstein song, "I'm In Love With a Wonderful Guy," but I was trying to play it cool. I grabbed Will, gave him a big hug, and kissed him on his big fat cheek, then skipped up the stairs.

I entered my room and plopped on my bed. I didn't even undress. I just lay there, hands folded behind my head, and stared up at the ceiling, at the wonderfully stupid ceiling fan, my face aching with a silly grin I couldn't erase from my face. Sleep? Tonight? Hardly. But somehow I did fall asleep, and what a wonderful sleep it was. All I did was dream of Étie.

The next morning I woke at eight and hoped that it was not too early to call Étie. I knew he had to be at work at ten, so I was hoping that we could have breakfast together first.

He picked up the phone on the second ring. The mellow sleepiness in his voice portended a nocturnal solace as sweet and as satisfactory as mine. I could hear him smiling that smile.

"That would be nice," he said when I asked if we could meet at the little café on the Malecón. We agreed to meet at nine, which was not soon enough for me. I showered quickly and rushed to our rendezvous early. I sat there sipping the delicious Dominican coffee the lovely copper-toned waitress had brought me. Something in her smile let me know that she knew what I knew. Love cannot keep itself secret. And when she came to re-fill my cup, she looked up before I did; saw him before I did. And she knew. He was the one I'd been waiting for all morning, maybe all my life. She sat him at the chair across from me, and without asking, brought another cup and filled it to the brim.

"*Hola*," he said, extending his hand.

"*Hola*," I said slow and melodiously.

"I so glad to see you," he whispered.

"Me too, Étie." Our eyes met with memories of last night's kiss.

We picked over our egg, bread, and sausage breakfast and cursed the clock that would soon part us.

I walked him to his job, sharing glances and smiles and silly conversation so common in the early stages of courtship.

Courtship.

My God, that's what was happening. We were actually courting each other. I certainly knew what I was feeling inside about him, and I could tell that he was feeling much the same way about me. Though neither one of us uttered the L word, our eyes, and our smiles, said it all.

"May I see you later, Étie?" I asked as I watched him unlock the door to the bodega.

"Yes. When?"

"When you get off work?"

"That be nice."

"We'll get something to eat."

"Okay."

"Now you know your country better than I, so why don't you pick a place."

"Hmmm." He thought long and hard. "How about Pizza Hut?" he finally said.

"Pizza Hut?"

"You like pizza, no?"

"Yes, yes."

"I like pizza too."

"Well then, Pizza Hut it is," I said. "So I'll be back here at four. Then we'll go to Pizza Hut!"

"*Bueno,*" he said, lingering in the doorway of the bodega. "See you later, my beautiful man." He touched my face. I kissed his hand, watched him go inside. The cathedral across the plaza struck ten. I turned to it and smiled.

Chapter Fourteen

At exactly three forty-five I arrived at Bodega Colonial. It was my first time being there so late in the day, and I was surprised by the afternoon festiveness. Inside, customers milled, swayed to the merengue music playing from the radio, or just plain lingered. Some had gathered round the mounted TV set where a baseball game was being played. Others sat at the little tables outside and sipped rum and Presidente beer.

Étie was busy and happy as he served up cold drinks, packaged goods, cold sandwiches, and warm laughter. When he saw me, his eyes lit up. He said something in rapid Spanish to the older man behind the counter, who waved at me and smiled, then beckoned me inside.

"Jesse, this my boss, Señor Trujillo," Étie said. "*Señor Trujillo, esto es mi amigo norteamericano. Su nombre es Jesse.*"

"*¡Hola, Jesse! Hola!*" Señor Trujillo bellowed, pumping my hand with gusto.

"*Hola, señor.*"

He then turned to Étie. "Go, go," he urged him.

"*¿No problema?*" Étie asked sheepishly.

"No, no," Señor Trujillo continued. "You go. Have good time."

"*Muchas gracias, señor.*"

"*De nada*, Étie." He continued ushering us out the store like children stuck too long in the house.

"Señor Trujillo seems like a nice guy," I said as we walked down Calle Jose Gabriel Garcia toward the Condistre. The late afternoon sun reflected against a pink melon sky.

"He is very nice," Étie said softly, admiring the sky. "I tell him all about you."

"Really?"

"*Sí.*"

"So what did you tell him?"

"I tell him how nice you are."

"So, you think I am nice, huh?"

"I think you are very nice, Jesse."

At Pizza Hut we shared Cokes and a sausage and pepperoni pizza that Étie would not let me pay for. "I big model now," he bragged, throwing his head back and sticking out his chest. "I make one hundred U.S. dollars in just one day."

I felt like I was in high school again, hanging out after the big game. The corny jokes we exchanged in that rear booth were not lost to language differences, and our raucous laughter made the restaurant manager look up more than once.

Afterward, we toured the shops along the Condistre, bought toffee, and then went to the little park a half a block away. We sat on the warm grass. The sun had set and the lights from the Condistre illuminated the sky above us, filtering through the trees that surrounded us, painting a lovely, moody picture around us.

I learned so much more about Étie as we sat there in the park.

A self-confessed geek, he was always very smart and creative in school and, much to the consternation of his father, showed little interest in sports and outdoor activities, except swimming in the sea. Teachers took note of Étie's intellectual and artistic abilities and started teaching him English as a second language in primary school, as well as computer literacy, which he took to very well, and encouraged him to join the school choir, which his father made him quit after coming home and finding him draped in sheets and tablecloths in front of the television singing along with videos of Madonna and Cher.

"I guess *mi padre* was right," he said a matter of fact, "I was sissy boy. But there is sissy part in all. How you say? Effeminacy? Science book say that. I know. I read. And no beating can destroy what The Father in heaven make. It is like being left-handed, white skin, black. You may no like, but all are in Heavenly Father's garden. All His flowers, beautiful and good. My gay, beautiful and good. Your gay, beautiful and good. Our gay beautiful and good."

When his father put him out of the house and stopped paying for his schooling, Étie would roam the streets at night and sleep in the bathroom stalls of museums and libraries during part of the day. But when he would come out of the stalls, out of the bathrooms, he found himself fascinated with the artifacts of his country, and other countries. And the books in the library always held his attention. There were always many English books in the library, and he managed to match the spelling of English words with their phonetic sounds. He continued his education on his own.

Though fifteen when his father put him out, Étie looked twelve. His youthful appearance made only menial jobs—shining shoes and sweeping out shops—available to him. Señor Trujillo would often see the scrawny little boy hanging outside his shop. Feeling sorry for him, he gave Étie food to eat, and Coca-Colas to drink. Eventually, Señor Trujillo started paying Étie to come and sweep out the shop.

Étie never let on to Señor Trujillo that he was living on the streets, sleeping in toilet stalls, and bathing in the sea.

On Saturdays and Sundays, the busiest days, Señor Trujillo's wife would come and help out at the shop. Señora Trujillo and Étie got along very well, and Étie slowly began to open up to the older woman, though he did not let on that he was homeless.

The Trujillos recognized what a hard worker Étie was, and how bright he was. Soon they hired him to stock the shelves and sell behind the counter. He had been working there ever since, was even able to save enough money to find a room to rent.

"Then I meet boy. I twenty-two. He three years older. We fall in love. Live together. Have good life together for two years. Then I find out about him. What he do. So I leave. Move into new place. Get new room."

"What did he do, Étie?"

"*No importa,*" he said coldly. "Only *importante* I leave him to his ways."

I could tell by his steely silence that the pain had not totally gone away. But I knew, knowing what kind of person he was, knowing his strength, that the lingering pain would not prevent him from moving on to a sweeter future. I knew that we could have something wonderful together; in spite of the pain we had both suffered.

We saw each other every day that week, when he got off work. The next evening he took me to a mall in the city's business district where we pigged out on ice cream and hamburgers. We went to the movies afterward and held hands in the dark of the cinema.

I would not be able to see him until very late the next night because he had to do data entry for a weekly newspaper he worked part time for.

We promised to meet at the little outdoor café he pointed out to me in the Condistre when he got off work. We met at ten, just in time to order before the restaurant closed. There were few customers, and we were the only patrons sitting out at one of the sidewalk tables. The Condistre itself was unusually quiet, as most of the businesses were closed, proprietors were gone, and save for a few adventurous tourists who strolled the cobblestone street hand in hand, the Condistre was empty of people but filled with romance.

The setting was not lost on us as we dined under the moonlight.

That Saturday, Étie's day off, we decided to spend the afternoon at his escape. He brought his own swimming trunks this time, wore them under his pants. Carlos had given me a blanket and towels and I met Étie at Bodega Colonial. Señora Trujillo prepared a small basket of sandwiches, mangos, sodas, and candies for us.

The water was warm and still. The setting was so quiet despite the rustling traffic on the Malecón high above us. It was as if we were on some remote enchanted island, a little bit of Eden created just for us. We played in the water and basked in the sun, had our picnic underneath the shade of a coconut tree. We stretched out on the blanket and napped for a while. It was so peaceful and relaxing that when I opened my eyes, I had no idea where I was, nor did I care. I slowly turned to see Étie staring down at me, wearing that beautiful smile of his. I smiled up to him. He leaned down and kissed me.

"I love you, Jesse," he then said, laying his head on my chest. I went weak. From what? I don't know. Was it the scent of his hair, the touch of his softness so small in my arms, or the words that he said for the very first time?

I love you, Jesse.

I knew it, I felt it, I prayed for it. But hearing him say it was a new kind of feeling. It humbled me to a heaving. Tears swelled inside. I took the hand he had gently and slowly brushed against my cheek, and kissed it. It made him smile, and he looked up at me. I looked into his eyes. They, like mine, sparkled with tears.

"I love you too, Étie," I somehow managed to say. "I love you so . . . so much."

He turned to fully face me, to totally wrap himself in my arms; him looking up, me looking down, staring at each other with tear-filled eyes. He then snuggled into my chest, and I held him. I then said a silent prayer, thanking God and all His lucky stars. It was as if Étie heard me, heard my silent prayer.

"Baby?" he asked.

"Yes, sweetheart?"

"Will you go church with me tomorrow?"

"Of course."

"I want to thank Heavenly Father for giving you to me."

Chapter Fifteen

"Cedric, I'm in love!" I declared, rushing through the door of House of John, huffing, damp shirt open and flailing, swim trunks spilling out over my low-hanging shorts, my carry-on bag stuffed with wet towels, oily sun block, and gritty sand.

"But of course you are," Cedric mused with a philosophical ease acquired only by those who understand the marriage of tropical sun and white beaches lounged up against the Caribbean sea; what the vision, the aroma, the attended breezes conjure in mere mortal man.

"No, Cedric, I mean, *really* in love," I insisted. He looked up from his computer screen, assessed the dumb look on my face, my newly acquired tan, and then sighed. "What do you mean '*really* in love,' Jesse?" he asked carefully.

"I met someone."

"A local?"

"Yes."

"Hmmm," he hummed.

"What?"

"Your dick and your ass are in love."

"No," I protested. "I've known him for over a week and we haven't even had sex yet."

"You will before your trip is over."

"This is the real thing, Cedric."

"How can it be the real thing in just one week, Jesse?"

"I know what I'm feeling, Cedric. I know how I feel. And he feels the same way about me."

"He loves you."

"Yes!"

"Be careful, Jesse. Don't fall in love with a *bugarrón*. He only loves your dollars."

"No!"

"He only does what he does for the dollars."

"He's not a *bugarrón*, Cedric. He works at a bodega. In fact, he has two jobs."

"They all have two jobs, Jesse. They all work at a bodega, or selling trinkets in the Condistre, or as *policías*, taxi drivers, even husbands. But they're struggling in a poor country, so they make ends meet working with the best they have to offer, their beautiful faces, their beautiful bodies, their beautiful sex."

"He's not like that." I looked Cedric squarely in his eyes. "Trust me. He's not."

He could tell that I was dead serious, even if he thought I was dead wrong. He went back to his computer. I slowly started up the stairs, my head lowered, pissed off that anyone could think that about my Étie.

I almost collided with Dr. Mo and his vacation boyfriend Tomás, who were coming down the stairs.

"Well, if it isn't the prodigal son." Dr. Mo smiled. "Haven't seen much of you lately."

"I've been busy, Moses."

"So we hear." He smiled slyly.

"Hear what?" Sylvester asked, entering through the foyer from outside, followed by William, Martin, and Oliver Bevins.

"Hey, Jesse, where you been?" Oliver asked.

"Missin' all the good action," Sylvester snickered.

"Not from what I hear," Jarvis offered, coming in from the terrace.

"Who? What?" The Hicks twins peeked in from the parlor where they were getting their asses kicked in a game of Uno with Carlos and a couple of locals.

"Jesse's got a boyfriend," Jarvis sing-songed.

"We *all* got a boyfriend," Myron Hicks laughed.

"Why you think we down here?" his brother Byron added.

"No, I mean a *real* boyfriend."

"What do you mean, a real boyfriend?"

"As in a steady piece."

"Well, hell, I got that," Dr. Mo said, allowing big buff Tomás to squeeze his bony ass.

"Naw, I mean like in lover."

"Okay, guys, look. None of you know what's going on with me."

"That little model is what's going on with you, isn't it?"

"Well, I ain't mad atcha. I'd be tappin' that ass too, phine as he is."

"It's not like that."

"Then what's it like, Jesse?"

I felt like they were all piling up on me; the laughter, the coos, the snappage and the reads, the trivializations and wrong assumptions, making it something that it totally was not.

"Hey, chill, y'all!" Father Martin yelled out, bringing everyone to silence. "Leave the brotha alone."

"Look, old man, *you* chill," Sylvester laughed, breaking the silence. "You just worry about buying you up some dick so you won't be alone."

"You know what?" I finally said. "Let me talk to y'all later." I bolted my way up the stairs, stormed down the hall, entered my room, and slammed the door shut behind me. I couldn't believe how angry I was, especially after having such a beautiful day.

And then I thought about it. Did I really have any reason to be angry with any of them? We all came down here looking for the same thing. I just happened to find something different. I just happened to find something I had been looking for all my life and didn't even know it. I shouldn't be angry with them for not understanding. I should be happy that I understood. But still.

There was a knock at my door.

"Yeah?" I called out, trying to hide the frustration in my voice.

"Jesse, it's me. Will."

"Yeah."

"May I come in?"

I hesitated for a moment. Then I gave in. "Yeah, man. Come on in."

"So, Cedric says you're in love."

"Yeah."

"Well, if love makes you look like that, I don't know if I want any parts of it," he joked.

I looked at him. I had to chuckle a bit. "Have a seat, man."

"Thanks." He did.

We sat there in silence for a few moments. I could feel him looking at me, but wasn't sure if I was ready to meet his eyes.

"So what's his name?" he asked.

I hesitated again. "Étienne," I finally answered, softly, suddenly soothed by the image of Étie in my mine.

"Étienne," Will repeated slowly, as if reciting a poem. "What a beautiful name."

"Yeah."

"You know the guys are just messin' with you."

"Yeah, I know."

"Not too often one of the guys on one of these excursions falls in love."

"It wasn't my intention, Will. Trust me. It just happened."

"I understand."

"Do you?"

"What? You don't think I've been in love before?"

"No, man, I'm sure you have."

"Yes, I have. Not often, maybe a couple of times. But one thing's for sure. Love is never a plan."

"You got that right."

"And another thing."

"What?"

"You can never be too sure."

"I'm sure, Will."

"Are you?"

"Yes!"

"Were you sure about Sean?"

It was like a blow to my heart. I simply could not answer.

"All I'm saying, Jesse, is that if it is what it is, then it is. If it's not, then that's okay, too."

"Huh?"

"You're on vacation. Do whatever you want to do. And afterward, you'll go home."

I didn't feel like dining with the fellas that night so I strolled over to the Condistre and bought a couple of chicken burritos from a vending cart. Afterward I visited some of the shops that Étie and I had gone to three nights earlier. I made it a particular point to return to the jewelry shop we had gone to. When I first saw the beautiful gold crucifix and chain in the display case three nights ago, it caught my eye, but I didn't know why. Now I did. I purchased it and had it gift-wrapped. I couldn't wait to give it to him tomorrow before church.

It should not have surprised me that he attended service at the beautiful cathedral across the plaza from Bodega Colonial. It was the perfect setting for my little angel. Because he had to work, we would attend the first mass at eight o'clock. I couldn't wait.

I stepped out of the air-conditioned jewelry shop and back into the warm night breeze, back into the pedestrian traffic of locals and tourists. I noticed a pair of lovers. I tried not to stare, but I couldn't help myself. I stared and I smiled. I didn't even notice the guy walking toward me, not until he spoke.

"*Hola,*" he said.

"*Hola,*" I answered, continuing my walk.

"*Americano?*"

"*Sí.*"

"You like?" he asked with quiet seduction, touching the bulge in his pants.

"*No, gracias,*" I answered with a polite smile, and kept on walking.

I returned to House of John around nine-thirty, just as the parlor was filling up with *bugarrones*. That guy named Edgar saw me as I headed up the stairs to my room. He rushed out of the parlor and called after me just as I reached the second-floor landing.

"*Hola,*" he said.

"*Hola.*"

He started up the stairs toward me.

"*Yo tengo una pinga grande,*" he said when he reached the second-floor landing. I almost laughed, but contained myself. I knew enough dirty Spanish to know "I have a big dick" when I hear it. I respectfully declined and headed toward my room.

I was anxious to turn in early, anxious to meet Étie at church tomorrow, and anxious to give him his present. Despite the music in the parlor downstairs and the sounds of sex in adjacent rooms, I fell asleep quickly. I was anxious to dream.

Chapter Sixteen

I rose early Sunday morning, grateful that I ignored Will's packing advice and brought along a suit and tie, something an old travel veteran like me does automatically, no matter how casual the trip. After all, you never know. Back in Los Angeles, nice casual was what most of my fellow parishioners at Agape Church donned on Sunday morning, but I had never been to a Catholic service before, and I didn't want to take a disrespectful chance.

The light gray suit hung nicely on me and the matching tie was humble enough for a church service of any denomination.

I arrived at the plaza outside the cathedral at seven-thirty. I was amazed at how what I saw so mirrored the picture in my mind. So many beautiful people—seniors, children, families, and couples—greeted each other in the plaza, ascended the four steps of the cathedral, and entered the sanctuary. It was a sea of raven-haired Dominicans of every shade of brown, dressed mostly in white; white dresses and veils, white shirts and slacks, white patent leather shoes and bucks.

"*Hola,* my gorgeous man," he said, easing up behind me. I

smiled as I slowly turned to him, took in his innocent beauty, dressed in his white shirt and white pants, a silk beige tie neatly knotted at his neck. My Étie was a vision.

"Hi, baby," I said, doing everything I could to keep from kissing him. "You look beautiful."

"*Gracias.*" He blushed. "You too."

"*Muchas gracias.*" I reached in my pocket and pulled out the small gift-wrapped box. "This is for you."

"Oh?" His eyes widened as I placed it in his hand.

"Open it."

"Okay."

It was amazing how delicately he opened the gift-wrap, so careful not to tear it. He then neatly folded it and put it in his pocket. He looked at the small felt box that was inside, curiously. He slowly opened it. Then he gasped. A ray of sun tapped the gold crucifix and chain and the reflection bounced onto his awe-struck face.

"Oh baby . . ." He could barely get the words out. I eased the jewelry from the case and draped the chain around his neck. I stepped back proudly. The gold crucifix sparkled brightly against his silk beige tie. He looked into my eyes. The cathedral bells sent out their call. He moved in close to me. I felt his arms go around me. I felt him lean into me. I felt him kiss me on the cheek.

"I love you, baby," he whispered in my ear. "I love you so much." I had just been given my present, too.

It is hard to put into words the beauty of a Catholic Mass. I have seen many ceremonies related to the Catholic faith in movies and documentaries. I remember being glued to the television during Pope John Paul II's funeral, and being mesmerized by the sheer beauty of the pageantry.

But being in the middle of it, even in its modesty compared to the papal funeral, was quite another kind of humbling experience. The heavenly sound of the boys choir, the lighting of the candles, the priest in his finely detailed robe, kneeling at the altar, an altar boy kneeling on either side.

And the people in the pews, their heads bowed, their devotion deep, their prayers, though silent, trumpeted manifestations of faith in and love for a Higher Power I completely understood and felt devoted to as well.

I cannot describe the feeling of kneeling with, praying with Étie. I suddenly realized the spiritual power of our love and, like him, I found myself thanking our Heavenly Father for giving us to each other.

I opened my eyes and looked around this holy place again. I imagined Étie and I one day being married in such a romantically spiritual place as this. I closed my eyes and began to pray anew. I asked the Lord to please, please make it so.

After the service, I walked Étie across the plaza to Bodega Colonial, which the Trujillos had already opened. We greeted each other like family, and I had to compliment them on how lovely they looked in their Sunday finery. They looked like parents of a bride on their way to the wedding.

It turned out that they would be attending the second Mass at the cathedral while Étie minded the store. It was a wonderful arrangement that allowed them all to receive their spiritual nourishment.

Étie and I waved good-bye to the Trujillos as they left and started across the plaza. I then turned to Étie, and kissed him gently on the lips.

"See you after work?" I whispered.

"You better," he joked, kissing me back.

I left, so full that I thought I would burst. There were so many things running through my mind, things that I had to figure out. The one thing I didn't have to figure out, the one thing

I was sure of, was that I wanted to spend the rest of my life with Étie. And I knew he felt the same. Would he come to America? Would I move here? There was so much we had to talk about, to think about. When he got off work, I would suggest that we go to our little sidewalk café in the Malecón, and discuss our future.

I headed back to the hotel. I needed to get on my computer and research immigration procedures. I picked up my pace as I walked the short distance. I greeted Carlos, who was washing the shuttle bus out front, as I entered House of John.

The foyer and parlor were rather sparse when I got there. Cedric was at his usual spot behind the front desk and Emilio was coming down the stairs with bags of dirty linen and towels. They both greeted me with warm smiles and *holas* as I returned their greetings, bounced past Emilio, and headed toward my room.

I got on my computer and was directed to the U.S. Department of Homeland Security, which began overseeing the Immigration Department after 9/11.

The information was voluminous, complicated, and discouraging. Although it would be very easy for me to emigrate here, it would take forever for Étie, a single young man in a poor Caribbean country, with no real family ties, to immigrate to the United States.

The surest way would be for him to become a sponsored relative of an American citizen, a spouse. Unfortunately, U.S. federal law did not recognize same-sex marriages, and so the chances of bringing him home were slim. If only all America could be like Massachusetts.

I spent hours on the research, until my eyes blurred. There had to be a way.

There was a knock on my door. I got up and answered it.

"Martin. Hey."

"Hey, Jesse. How you doin'?"

"I'm good."

"Really?"

"Yeah . . . yeah."

"Just don't pay any attention to those fools."

"The guys? They all right. They don't mean anything."

"And they don't *know* anything. All they thinking about is today. They don't have a clue about tomorrow."

"Okay."

"Come walk with me. Let's go have a drink."

"Well, I'm kinda in the middle of something right now, Martin."

He noticed the computer open on the table, and the screen full of immigration data.

"Boy, close that thing down and come have a drink with me."

I smiled. I did need a break, and I hadn't spent as much time with Martin as I wanted to. "Okay, Father," I said.

We ended up at the La Capella restaurant over on the Malecón and sat at the bar, which offered beautiful views of the beach and sea below.

"You know I turned sixty last June," he sighed into his third Cuba Libre.

"Really?" I said. I was still nursing my first drink. I knew I would be meeting Étie later on and I wanted to be alert for the discussion of our future. "Congratulations."

"Please." Martin threw up a hand in protest. "No back pats. I'm not sure I'm all together with it just yet."

"Sixty is fine, Martin."

"How would you know?"

"Well, I don't," I conceded, "but I'm sure when I get there I'll be fine with it. I mean, sixty is not that old."

"Spoken like a true—how old are you?"

"Thirty-eight."

"—Thirty-eight-year-old." Then he chuckled, as if to some private joke to which only he got the punch line. Down on the small beach below us, three young boys, in ragged, cut-off pants, their makeshift swimwear, bony torsos, blackened and bronzed by too many carefree days in sun and sand and tumbling sea, played as only young boys could. I watched Martin watch them, admiringly, envious, a vintage memory made melancholy by the clarity of the recollection.

"My God, was I ever that young?" he quietly asked himself, letting the question linger in the air. "You know in the movies, sixty-year-old guys still get the girl," he finally continued, "but in *our* world, sixty-year-old guys don't always have the same kinda luck. Well, now of course, unless you're free with the cash. But I'm old-fashioned. I still want them to like me for me."

"So why are you down here?" I dared to ask.

"Because I like sex a lot more than sex likes me."

"Okay."

"I'm old, Jesse. Older. Way older than I was at thirty. I'm sixty. And sixty's not what's moving in the marketplace. As real as love is supposed to be, it still needs something sweet and young and fresh to look at; something muscled and hard and firm to the touch. Look at this."

"What?"

He grabbed a handful of his backside. "When did this happen? When did my ass get so soft? You know, there comes a time in every gay man's life when the physical can no longer compete with the wit and the wisdom. Wit and wisdom get pushed up to the front lines when looks go on life support. When cute can't make no money no more, you better have wit and wisdom. For the old queens, that combination is always a cash cow. When you get old, if you don't have love, you better damn well have cash, and the wit and wisdom to make it. Aging. All the gym time in the world can't stop it.

"Don't ever disrespect love, my young friend. Get it now. Cherish it. Take care of it. 'Cause when you get old, you don't wanna make a fool of yourself, running down here, paying a bunch of pretty young things who don't give a shit about you to stick some dick up your flabby ass.

"See, you may get too old to attract something young and cute, you may get too old to get it up. Hell, you may get too old to just sit up. But you'll never get too old to be in love.

"If you love that boy, then good for you. If he loves you, even better. No matter what happens to the two of you over the years, it'll be all right if it's really love. 'Cause love's a keeper."

I know a lot of what Father Martin was saying was ramblings from his cups, but I think I understood what he was trying to say to me.

When I told him I had to go and meet Étie, he shooed me away with his blessings.

I arrived at Bodega Colonial at four o'clock on the dot. Étie was waiting for me with smiles and kisses.

We went to our little café in the Condistre and were seated at our favorite outdoor table.

You know that feeling that you have when you realize you're sitting across from the best thing to ever happen in your life? That's where I was. That's where I was floating.

"You know how much I love you, Étie?"

"*Sí*, like I love you."

"*Sí*. I want us, you and me, to be together forever."

"That be nice, baby."

"I've been checking on the computer . . ."

"Jesse?" I knew the voice without ever having to look up. I was too busy staring into my baby's eyes.

"Hey, Syl, what's up?"

"*No mucho,*" he crooned in sloppy Spanish. I finally looked up at him, watched him lock on to my baby.

"My God, the pictures don't do you justice," he said to Étie. "I can certainly understand Jesse keeping you hidden away from us." This time Étie did not blush.

"Étie, this is Sylvester," I began the introduction, "Sylvester, Étie."

"Hello," Sylvester said with too much suggestion in his voice. He extended his hand.

"*Hola*," Étie answered, shaking Sylvester's hand.

"Oh, and you remember Edgar, Jessie."

I hadn't seen Edgar come out of the little shop next door to the restaurant until he joined Sylvester.

"Yes," I said. "*Hola.*"

But Edgar was staring at Étie. Étie was staring at him.

"And this is Jesse's amigo. Étie."

"*Yo le conozco*," Edgar said coolly. "*Él es mi ex-novio.*"

"Huh?" Sylvester asked. "What did he say, Jesse?"

I could barely get the words out. "He said Étie is his ex-boyfriend."

"Oh," Sylvester crooned, "well, isn't this a small world?"

I could see that Étie was steaming silently. He finally got up without ever looking at Edgar again. "We go, Jesse," he said to me.

I got up and put some money on the table.

"Étie, you should have Jesse bring you by our hotel so you can meet the rest of our American friends," Sylvester said slyly, then he turned to me. "You will bring him by Casa de Mita, won't you, Jesse?"

"Let me talk to you later, Sylvester," I said. "Come on, Étie, let's go."

But Étie had already hit the pavement of the Condistre. I had to hasten my pace to catch up with him. "Étie!" I called, "Étie!" But he wouldn't stop.

I finally caught up with him, and took his hand. He snatched it from me, and kept walking away.

"Baby?" I pleaded, trying my best to keep up with him. Finally he stopped, turned around, and faced me.

"You lie to me!" he screamed at me, vicious tears slinging from his eyes.

"What are you talking about, Étie?"

"You lie!"

"About what?"

"You no live at Hilton!"

"Huh?"

"You no live at Hilton."

"I never said I was staying at the Hilton."

"You live at House of John! You live at House of Whore!" He started rushing away from me again.

"Wait a second, Étie," I said desperately, chasing after him. I caught up with him, held my pace with him, but he kept on moving. "Let me explain," I pleaded.

"That is place you *americanos* come to exploit our people, to be with *bugarrones*. That is all you think we good for. Well, I am NOT *bugarrón*! If that is what you look for, then go back to your whore hotel, pull down your pants, and pull out your wallet for somebody else!"

He began running, running away from me. I couldn't keep up. I stopped in my tracks. I was the plague. And now I was crying, too.

Chapter Seventeen

I returned to Casa de Mita and went directly to my room. I didn't want to talk to anyone or see anyone, only Étie. I stood out on the balcony. The sun was setting behind the mountains. I hated myself for being the center of Étie's pain, for feeling the pain that I was feeling, for possibly dissolving the one great dream of my life. When the pulse of your heart runs away from you, you're just a fucking dead man walking. And that's what I was.

I stood out on the balcony feeling sorry for myself. And then the cathedral bells rang out in the distance, the same bells that had brought me to Étienne Saldano. I smiled even as tears streamed down my face.

Suddenly I began to wipe the tears away, defiantly, as the bells tolled on, telling me, giving me the determination to fight the self-pity, fight the surrender, to fight for my man. In three days I would be leaving Santo Domingo, and I was not about to leave without a fight.

I grabbed my phone and pulled the phone directory from the nightstand drawer. I looked up *Hoteles.* There it was, the

Santo Domingo Hilton. I called; made my reservations, then packed up all my things.

Carlos was preparing dinner in the kitchen and Tomás was putting on a show for Dr. Mo and the Hicks twins in the parlor. In the foyer Cedric and Martin were reminiscing about the early days of the gay revolution and the drag queen riots of Stonewall, when I came down the stairs with my bags.

"Well, what have we here?" Cedric smiled with surprise.

"Listen, Cedric, it's been great, but there are some things I need to do, that I can't do here at Casa de Mita."

"Oh?"

"I know I have three more nights here, and they're already paid for, so don't worry about it."

"You also paid for shuttle service back to the airport on Wednesday. Where will you be staying? I'll have Carlos pick you up."

"Thanks, Cedric. I'll be staying at the Hilton over on the Malecón."

"Is that where you're headed now?"

"Yes."

"And how will you get there?"

"A taxi. It's not that far."

"Nonsense, Jesse. Casa de Mita has not forgotten about hospitality. Carlos is preparing dinner now but I'll have Emilio drop you off."

"Thanks, Cedric."

"Is it your young man?"

"Yes."

"So, it really *is* love."

"Yes."

Father Martin had been standing by quietly, but the smile that decorated his face and the sparkling moisture in his eyes said everything to me. He reached over, took me in his arms, and gave me a warm long hug. That's why we call him "father."

I didn't want to stick around to say good-bye to the rest of the fellas. I figured I'd call them later, once I was settled in at the Hilton and after I had put into motion what I had to do to get Étie back.

Cedric called Emilio and instructed him to drop me off at the Hilton. I said my good-byes to Cedric and Martin and followed Emilio out the front door, just as Sylvester and Edgar were coming in.

"So where the hell are you headed?" Sylvester asked, seeing me with my bags.

"I'm going to get my man!" I said proudly. I then climbed inside the idling shuttle bus and nodded to Emilio, letting him know I was all set to go. We pulled away from House of John, and I never looked back.

I checked into the Hilton, dropped my things off in my room, and walked down the Malecón to the entrance of the colonial neighborhood where Étie lived. I went to the house where he had a room. The lantern above the big wooden door was illuminated. I rang the bell on the outer gate. The door opened and a beautiful silver-haired woman emerged from the big door and came to the gate. She looked at me curiously, taking a fascinated look at my dread locks.

"¿Hola?" she said, curious.

"Buenos tardes, señora. Mi nombre es Jesse Templeton. Yo soy un amigo de Étie Saldano. ¿Está en casa?"

"¿Étienne?"

"Sí."

"Oh, lo siento, señor, pero Étienne no está aquí."

"Bueno, está bien, muchas gracias."

"De nada."

I then doubled back and headed for Bodega Colonial. Even though I knew he wasn't working, he might be there with the Trujillos. They were like family to him. Being upset, he may have turned to them for comfort.

I rushed toward the cathedral, and crossed the plaza where the lights were burning brightly inside Bodega Colonial. Merengue music poured from the tiny speakers of the radio while customers drank Presidentes, shopped, danced, and milled about. The Trujillos were joyously holding down the fort, but there was no sign of Étie.

"*¡Hola!*" Señor Trujillo called out to me when he saw me looking around from the doorway.

"*Hola, señor,*" I called back, huffing. "Have you seen Étie?"

"No. He go with you."

"Thank you," I said. "*¡Gracias!*"

I stood in the middle of the plaza, lost as a child in the woods, turning to all four corners of the world, and not knowing which way to go.

I had to calm down and think. I had to chill, put my thoughts in order, and get some clarity through solitude.

I plopped down on one of the plaza benches. I bowed my head into my hands, and allowed the warm Caribbean breeze to soothe me.

I don't know why I didn't notice it before, but the gentle sound of music, ancient music, sacred music, echoed from the cathedral. I looked up slowly. I could see inside the sanctuary. Amber candlelight seemed to flicker in rhythm with the sacred songs. I stood up from the bench. I slowly walked toward the light, toward the music, toward the sanctuary. I knew it was time to pray. I knew it was time to pray for Étie's forgiveness. I knew it was time to let go and let God.

I entered the sanctuary quietly. It was evening Mass. I took a seat on one of the middle pews and immediately went to my knees and bowed my head.

"Dear Father God. How do I begin to ask for what I may not deserve? But I call upon Your good mercy to grant me this. I love Étienne Saldano. He is the gift that You have given me. I know how precious gifts are, and how much they must be appreciated and cherished. I ask, Heavenly Father, that You give me another opportunity to let him know how deep my love is for him. I ask, Heavenly Father, that You forgive me, and that he forgives me. I ask You for my future happiness. In the name of Your Son, Jesus Christ. Amen."

I lifted my head, opened my eyes, but stayed on my knees. The beautifully painted ceiling of the cathedral smiled down on me.

Let go and let God.

I stood, stepped into the aisle, and crossed myself. I lowered my head and walked toward the exit of the sanctuary, leaving my love in God's hands.

And that's when I saw him, seated on the back pew. How could I have missed him? Was I so deep into my grief that I did not see him? Or did my Lord and Saviour miraculously place him before me?

He looked up into my eyes. Tears streamed down both our faces. He stood up and looked away from me, then dashed outside. I followed desperately.

I found him on the bench in the plaza. I sat next to him, afraid that he would bolt again. He did not.

I didn't know how to begin. I simply opened my mouth and let the words fall out.

"Étie, I am so sorry. You were so right. I did come down here to just have my way with your people. Whether that was right or wrong, I don't know. All I know is that when I met you, all changed for me."

"Stop," he said through tumbling tears. "I pray to Heavenly Father that He no let me love you, that He kill this feeling I have for you. I pray to Heavenly Father to make me not think of you day in and day out, that He make me not want to spend all my days with you. I pray Him turn back clock and change course, so I no meet you, so I no be in love with you, so I no ache for you, for your smile, your laugh, your dread hair, your kisses, your touch. I pray to Heavenly Father for ignorance of you. But Heavenly Father no answer my prayers. I cannot help me. I love you, Jesse. I cannot help me. I love you."

He reached up to me and gently pulled me down to him. He kissed me. Our tears mingled. And the cathedral bells tolled.

Epilogue

I am sitting up in our bed, have been sitting up all night, as long glances alternate between the stars that sparkle in the moonless sky and my beautiful man, my partner, my lover, my life mate, my friend, my rhyme and my reason, my husband. Étienne. I am watching him next to me, lost inside a deep sleep, filled no doubt with sweet dreams. It is the dream I am awake to enjoy. His baby whimpers through an unconscious smile make me smile. They always make me smile.

Every once in a while I think about House of John and William and Cedric, Martin, who passed away last year, Sylvester, the Hicks twins, and all the fellas still running down there every year to get their groove on. And, you know, I'm so glad I *did* go down there with the guys that one time almost thirteen years ago. I met the man of my dreams in Santo Domingo.

I just turned fifty-two and I feel fabulous. And, yes, my ass is a little flabbier. But that's okay. It's called gravity. All I know is that Étie still calls me "sexy papi." He's thirty-eight now and last week we celebrated his one-year anniversary as a full-fledged American citizen, and he is so proud. He now works as a bilingual voice-over actor in film and television, a hook-up made a few years back by my wild and wonderful sister Frankie, who, by the way, finally landed a TV series. She's playing a novice opposite Jennifer Lewis's Mother Superior in an update of *The Flying Nun*. Go figure. She's not completely over E. Lynn's death; probably will never be, but she's hanging in there.

He's stirring now. Étie, that is. His eyes open slowly and he catches me smiling at him in the dark of the moonless sky.

"Hey, sexy papi," he says in a soft sleepy voice. I slowly bend down to kiss him. His smiling lips are soft against mine. His tongue is warm and sweet inside my mouth. He then kisses me softly on the tip of my nose. He then nibbles gently on my ear, and whispers to me, "I needed that." He tucks himself back under the covers. His back is to me. He reaches back and pulls me close to him. He snuggles his body into mine. He wraps my arms around him. I hold him. He is warm and gentle. In a moment he is baby-whimpering in my arms and we lay spooned as one; still; peaceful. A tear runs down the side of my face to the corner of my smile. And I hear myself saying it, and saying it again. *Thank you, GOD. Thank you.*